DEDICATION

This was my first pure Sci-Fi novel and dedicated to a good friend of mine, Stephen Gordon, whom the main character is set around – a man with more courage in his little finger than most gain in a lifetime. Stephen was in a near fatal accident when he was a teenager. After the horrific accident, Stephen was left in a near vegetative state in which he was supposed to remain for the rest of his life. No one took into consideration Stephen's courage and determination. Today you can see him up the high street in Forres, always with a smile on his face and the time to stop and have a chat. This book is dedicated to him and people like him who have faced severe adversity and conquered it.

J W Murison

ACKNOWLEDGMENTS

I would like to thank one very special lady who made the publishing of this novel at this time possible. That lady is Jeannie Michaud, who once more stepped up to the plate to design a brand new book cover for this title. I absolutely adore it, thank you very, very much.

Teardrops In The Night Sky

'Are you in pain?'

'How could you call this pain? Our hearts have been ripped from our living bodies. We are no more now than empty shells.'

'We still have our souls, and must go on.'

'I fear I cannot. For without my heart I have no wish or desire to move.'

'We can find new hearts.'

'Is it so easy for you males? Do you have no feelings or compassion? Could you rip a living heart from your body and replace it with a new one if you thought it better?'

She was angry and hurt, lashing out with her thoughts. He knew she really didn't mean it but still her words wounded him deeply.

'We have been mated now for generations. How can you think so little of me?'

She felt his pain and knew shame for the first time in many centuries. 'I am sorry; I did not mean those words.'

He relaxed a little, 'I know, and I am sorry for believing you could think so of me, but we cannot stay here. To do so would be to die and I cannot let that happen to you.'

She felt an upwelling of emotion for her mate, 'but what can we do, where will we go? We cannot return to our home without our hearts. There are too many dangers and we are defenceless without them.'

'Then we must go on.'

'On to where?'

For a long time he was silent as he searched the heavenly bodies that surrounded them. Then he felt something. She became aware as his level of consciousness intensified and tried to join him in his search.

Eventually he felt it again, 'did you hear that?'

She was puzzled, 'I'm not sure, what was it?'

He tuned in as much as his systems would allow without his heart. Eventually it came again, 'some form of radio wave, I think.'

'Are you sure it isn't background radiation?'

'I don't think so, the frequency is too low.'

'Then it must be very primitive.'

'Yes, but we don't know how long or how far it has travelled. Anyway it is hope.'

'We must be cautious,' she advised.'

'Agreed.'

They left what they knew as the Great Barrier, and followed the primitive signals until they came in sight of a Blue Planet. As they snuck around the dark side of the Moon, she gasped. 'Have you ever seen a planet so beautiful?'

He found he had to agree, 'rarely.' His sensors swept out across space and he felt a moments panic. 'They have viewing devices in orbit, we must disguise ourselves.'

She agreed and their sleek bodies shimmered for a moment. In an instant they became indiscernible from the grey Moon rock behind them.

Now in clear line of sight of the Blue Planet they were bombarded by millions of different signals. She winced from the overload of data. 'What do we do now?'

'We watch, wait and learn.'

So as the Moon revolved around Earth, and Earth around the Sun, they watched and learned. It would be many Earth years before they came to a decision about what to do. But without a heart to tell them so, time meant very little to the two sleek and beautiful craft.

CHAPTER 1

2005

Steven Gordon sat back from the computer screen at the sound of the motorcycle horn outside and rubbed his eyes. He knew who it was before he got up and looked out the window.

He gave the nineteen-year-old Buzz a wave and plonked himself back down in front of the console. He cursed Buzz silently. Another couple of hours and he would have been finished. At the age of fifteen, Steven was a genius of the type only found once in every century.

He had already completed every possible course in connection with time and space, mathematics and physics that the resources of the United States and the Kennedy Space Centre could throw at him.

Neither did he show any symptoms nor signs of the neurotic tendency's that other geniuses over the centuries had suffered; much to his parents' relief. Both were imported scientists and worked for NASA and were very proud of their son's achievements.

Indeed, by the age of ten he could talk to them on equal terms about their work. By the age of twelve he was teaching them, and now at the age of fifteen, he was in line for a number of Nobel prizes for his achievements in science so far.

For all that, he was still a teenager, with all their curiosities. At fifteen, Steven had been slow to mature physically, but he wasn't worried about it. His father had told him on countless occasions he too had been slow to mature.

What he was worried about was the fact that all his friends were much older than him and much taller than his father's towering five-foot-six. A curse from their Scottish ancestry. Even fully grown he was worried he would still be small.

He quickly saved his document, threw on a clean T-shirt and ran down the stairs. His mother caught him at the bottom.

'If that's that Buzz with his new motor bike don't you dare get on it.'

This day her light Scottish brogue irritated him, 'yeah OK.'

He ducked past and out to where Buzz waited patiently.

'Hey, where you been shrimp?'

'Where do you think dope?' Laughing, Steven easily ducked the helmet swung at him.

'Watch your mouth shrimp.'

'Yeah, like you could do anything about it.'

The friends laughed easily at their byplay. Buzz was a good six-foot-two and built, but he would still think twice about taking on the smaller Steven.

Recognising Steven would probably have a lot of problems later in life; his father had sent him to martial arts classes at the tender age of seven. By the time Buzz met him when he was almost eleven, Steven was already a black belt and his small frame rippled with hard-worked muscle.

By Steven's standards Buzz was a simple buffoon. His father worked with the civilian security people and there was little doubt Buzz would follow in his footsteps. He was an academic underachiever with the rare talent of not actually caring what his grades were. He could have done a lot better for himself and knew it.

His easy manner and quick wit had drawn Steven like a magnet. Buzz's problems were simple and earthly. A rare delight for a mind that struggled with the mathematics of quantum mechanics on a daily basis.

Buzz's attraction for Steven came in the simple form of admiration. A few days after he first saw Steven, he watched as the eleven year old took out two of the school's worst bullies in a furry of fist and feet. He admired the little guy's guts and determination, and far from being put off by the power of the young child's intellect, he respected it.

Once Steven got over being offered a hand in friendship from the young man who looked like a giant to him, they quickly became inseparable. Buzz's parents had also quickly taken to the gifted child, and through them he found diversity in life that he had been lacking.

Country born and bred, the two were rarely idle, but in a manner that spoke of a contentment with life. There was always an engine to be tinkered with or a DIY project to be getting on with. In the kitchen, his mother would delight in making cakes and bread by hand; an Aladdin's cave of delights to any child.

Any fears his parents might have had were soon belayed once they met the Anderson's, and although both families came from opposite sides of the social structure, Stevens parents soon discovered the same attraction their son had to the easygoing family and they had become firm friends over the years.

'Jump on shrimp and I'll take you for a ride.'

Steven bristled, 'not allowed.'

Buzz shrugged, 'hey maybe another day.'

'What are you doing here? I thought you were supposed to be taking Julie out this afternoon.'

'Naw, saw her out with some college dude last night, so I dumped her by e-mail this morning. So I got the whole day free. What you doing?'

'Got a paper on space-time distortion to finish this afternoon. Won't take me long though.'

'Cool, you'll have to teach me that some time?'

Steven laughed aloud and felt some of the tension ease. 'Yeah if I live another couple of hundred years I will.'

Buzz laughed out loud, knowing if they both lived another thousand years he still wouldn't get past the fundamentals. 'I'll hold you to that.'

'Mind if I sit on?'

'Naw man, help yourself.'

No sooner had Steven sat on than his mother marched out of the house, 'Steven, what did I tell you?'

'I'm only sitting on it,' he snapped back.

'Hi Mrs. Gordon,' Buzz shouted over.

Mary Gordon forced a smile onto her face, 'hello Buzz how's your mum?'

'She's fine Mrs. Gordon, sent something over for you.'

Buzz opened the plastic container on the back of the bike and took out a large brown bag. He strode over to give it to her; his eyes full of adoration. This petite, raven-haired Scots beauty had been doing strange things to his hormone levels for years.

Mary hid her amusement and looked in the bag, 'are these made from the recipe my grandmother sent over?'

Buzz shrugged, 'something like that; pancakes.'

'No Buzz, these are honest to God Scots Bannocks.'

Buzz Frowned, 'taste like pancakes, good too.'

Mary laughed. It was then the bike burst into life. A sudden panic hit her. They began running toward Steven but it was too late. He gunned the bike out of the drive fish tailing it as he went.

'Steven!' they both screamed after him. Buzz ran down the road after him, waving his helmet in the air helplessly.

Steven was caught in a fit of teenage rebellion. He had begun to resent the way his parents and his peers were pushing him. Coupled with a desire to push himself and a fresh influx of hormones, he found himself in a strange paradox.

This wasn't Buzz's first bike and he had let him ride it on his own many times in secret. He decided it was time to show his mother that he was man enough to make his own decisions.

Adrenalin surged through his body as he opened up the throttle. At the end of his street he suddenly realised he was going too fast and braked hard. The back wheel began to slide away from him. He never even saw the eighteen-wheeler cross the intersection until it was too late.

His face smacked against the body of the wagon as the bike shot underneath. For a hair's breath he lay in front of the back tyres, but then the front wheel was caught by the drive shaft and whipped around it. Steven was caught by the bike and followed.

Mangled, he was dumped unceremoniously in the middle of the road among pieces of the bike; a dark pool of bruised blood began to spread slowly around him.

Chapter 2

A green-suited surgeon made his way towards the family room. After fourteen desperate hours of surgery, he was exhausted. He paused for a moment at the door to draw breath and gather his thoughts.

There were three of them in the room: the parents, and the young man whose bike had been involved in the accident. The nursing staff had assured him that the parents hadn't blamed the young man for the accident as so often happened in these cases and he drew heart from it.

They looked as exhausted as he felt. Brian Gordon stood as he entered, but he waved him down. 'Please sit Mr. Gordon.' He spotted the coffee machine and indicated to it, 'may I?'

Mary stood, 'I'll get it for you.'

'Please don't bother, I'll manage.'

He got a coffee with extra sugar and sat down opposite. He could see they were hanging on a knife edge, 'I'm afraid Steven's prognosis isn't good.'

Buzz was unable to contain himself any longer, 'is he going to live?'

The surgeon took a deep breath, 'I'm afraid young man it may be better if he doesn't.'

As Buzz's face seemed to melt, Mary pushed her hand into his and squeezed.

The doctor went on, 'almost every bone in his body was crushed and most of his major organs pierced. It was a minor miracle he even lived long enough to be taken to hospital.

However, we have repaired everything repairable and set all his bones as best we can at this moment. If he lives he will need further surgery, but that is a thing for future debate.

The major problem now facing us is the brain damage he has suffered. He is in a deep coma with very little brain activity. If he ever comes out of the coma then chances are he may remain in a vegetative state for the rest of his life.'

He saw his words slam home and paused to take a drink of his coffee to let them sink in.

'That is our worst-case scenario of course but the most likely. However, the human body is very resilient and Steven is still young. If he makes it through the next forty-eight hours his chances will improve daily.'

It was Mary who asked the last question, 'could he ever make a full recovery?'

'No, I'm sorry. Even if he regains some mental function, he will never walk again. I would be surprised if he manages some rudimentary form of speech.'

Brian Gordon had heard enough, 'thank you for your time sir.'

The surgeon left, thinking he had done his best. But what he hadn't taken into consideration was Steven's remarkable mind. Within five years of the accident, not only did Steven begin to talk again but he also had begun to try and walk, and ever at his side were his loving parents and devoted friend, Buzz.

CHAPTER 3

2025

Steven checked himself in the mirrored door before proceeding into the building. His uniform matched that of the guard at the reception desk.

He smiled, 'hi yah Stevie, how are you tonight man?'

Steven returned his smile, 'fine man, you?'

'Looking forward to getting home.'

'Is the Boss in?'

'Isn't he always?'

Still smiling, Steven made his way to the security office. There were two men standing at the reception desk in identical uniforms. They turned as he entered but he didn't recognise either of them.

The receptionist's face lit up with one of her special smiles that she reserved only for him, 'hi Stevie.'

'Hi Liz, these the new Guys?'

'That's right.'

The tall sharp-faced one looked down in disbelief and barked a laugh, 'what the hell are you supposed to be?'

Steven's eyes turned cold, 'I'm a security guard, you?'

The man's face turned cruel, 'don't get sassy with me shaky.'

Steven shook his head in dismay and turned back to Liz, 'there's always one. Is he free?'

'Just go in Stevie.'

The thin man barked at Steven's retreating back, 'how the hell did he get to be a security guard, friend of the boss?'

If he had been trying to impress the pretty blonde, Liz, then he had failed miserably. Anger blazed in her eyes, 'actually he's the boss's best friend and has been since they were teenagers. Oh, and one more thing Sandiman, that little guy has more guts in his little finger than you'll ever have in your whole body. Haven't you got a job to go to?'

Chastised and angry, Sandiman strode off. The other man lingered. He was almost as tall as Sandiman, but broader and had a kinder, more intelligent face.

He waited until Sandiman had gone and was curious, 'who is that little guy? I noticed he had ribbon over his jacket pocket, isn't that the company medal for bravery?'

Liz calmed a little, 'it is. That's Steven Gordon. His father's the top scientist here and runs the whole shooting match.'

'What's his story, how come he shakes so much?'

Liz bristled again but realised it was honest curiosity, 'Steven was in a bad accident when he was fifteen. I don't know all the details; what I do know is he was never supposed to walk or talk again. Somehow though he's fought his way back to near normal.'

'Near normal?'

She smiled, 'Steven's actually registered as disabled; he isn't even supposed to be working here. As well as he is now, he's still on a lot of medication.'

'Is that what makes him shake?'

'No that was the damage done to his nervous system. He takes pills to calm it. If he didn't have them he wouldn't be able to walk. We have to keep him away from computer screens too.'

'Epilepsy?'

'Something like that.'

He nodded his understanding, 'how did he get the medal?'

'About six months ago, we had armed intruders, two of them. Stevie caught them. They opened up on him and he brought them both down.'

His eyebrows shot up in amazement, 'that was the guy!'

Liz's face broke into a grin, 'that's him.'

'Yeah I read about that. Killed them both didn't he.'

'Stone cold, one round apiece.'

'Wow, you wouldn't believe it looking at him would you?'

'Well believe it.'

'So what's he like?'

That smile slid back onto Liz's face, 'he's a really sweet guy. You know, very respectful, rarely swears. He's just a nice guy. Simple, but nice. You'll see for yourself once you get to know him.'

'I'll look forward to it. I had better get going. I'll see you later.'

'Yeah, see you.' Liz decided she rather liked Martin Ford.

Buzz was sitting with his feet up on his desk when Steven walked in. A broad smile lit up his face, 'hi buddy.'

Steven's grin was just as big, 'hey boss man.'

Buzz laughed. His pride in Steven's achievements shone from his face, 'you been to see your folks today?'

'Yeah, had dinner with them. They were asking for you.'

'Makes a change, they still pissed at me for giving you this job?'

Steven grinned and held up two fingers, 'wee bit, but I think they're beginning to see how much good it's doing me.'

'Yeah right up until something else happens, then I'll have both of them screaming down my neck again.'

Steven laughed at the memory. Only Buzz could have resisted the pressure they had put on him back then. Steven himself still wasn't sure what had happened. He had seen the skulking figures and challenged them. Lights had twinkled in the night, and then he had heard and felt the bullets snap past his head. The next thing he remembered was kneeling on the ground with a smoking revolver in his hands and staring down the barrel at the two crumpled figures. They still didn't know what they had been after, but industrial espionage was the rumour.

Steven grinned easily at his Buzz's discomfort, 'comes with the territory kemosabe.'

Buzz's smile returned. He stood and grabbed his jacket and hat, 'let's go do the rounds, partner.'

It was a luxury he had afforded himself since Steven's arrival, and looked forward to it every day.

It took them an hour to travel around the enormous complex. Buzz felt himself wind down at the end of a long day. He would have had Steven on the day shift with him, they had even tried, but it soon became apparent he couldn't cope with the pressure, and his parents' continual checking up on him.

However, he had quickly settled into the night-time routine and Buzz had drawn a deep breath. Steven also looked forward to these night-time strolls. He remembered little of his life before the accident, but Buzz would talk constantly of those days, and every now and then he would trigger a distant memory.

It had almost become a game. Steven would partially remember something, and over the weeks he would pluck away at it on their nightly walks. Buzz never seemed to mind going over the memory again and again. Sometimes it would return completely, others partially. Normally, Steven would remember nothing about the incident and would just listen to episodes from his earlier life as though it were part of a strange dream.

CHAPTER 4

With Buzz gone, Steven quickly fell into the night-time routine. He ran into Sandiman again, who had tried to bait him, but Steven had simply shrugged it off. He had met too many of his kind in his lifetime to be bothered by one more.

Martin Ford had sat at his table during a break period and introduced himself. He had heard Sandiman's earlier sallies and decided to intervene.

'There's no need for you to take his shit you know?'

Steven's hand shook as he took out a large plastic pillbox and proceeded to take them with mouthfuls of water. 'Don't lose any sweat over it man.'

'Hey if you ever need any help.'

Steven waved a hand at him, 'there's no need, he won't be here long enough to get wound up over.'

Martin was surprised, 'are you going to report him?'

'No need to, everyone else will. I have a lot of friends here and they all insist on looking out for me, no matter how many times I tell them to butt out.'

Martin laughed, 'I can see why. I suppose you're a bit of a hero after that shoot out.'

Steven's eyes glazed over for a second, 'I get treated different that's for sure, but it isn't that. I think a lot of them just feel sorry for me, or did anyway.'

'Not now?'

'No, now I'm just one of the boys. I suppose it's because they now know they can depend on me if we ever get into a tight spot. That's what Buzz thinks it is. Saying that, they still fuss around me like a bunch of mother hens.'

'So what are you doing after the break?'

'Same as I always do, back on foot patrol.'

Martin frowned, 'is that all you do?'

'To be honest it's all I really can do. I've tried some of the administrative stuff. I can't really concentrate long enough to be good at it, and the computers can give me a fit, so I'm not allowed near them.'

'Don't you get bored doing foot patrol all the time?'

'No I like it. I've pretty much got the freedom of the base, which is great because I get to meet lots of interesting people. I even get to shoot them sometimes.'

Ford laughed at the gallows humour, 'great social life huh.'

Stevie smiled, 'I have a better social life now than I did before.'

'Honest?'

Stevie squinted across the table, 'you've got to remember I've got a few wee problems. Before I started here normal folk wouldn't stop long enough to give me the time of day. Now they haven't really any choice. They got to talk to me. Over the months they've come to realise I'm not too bad a lad and now most stop for a wee chat.'

Martin nodded, realising the simple truth of the small man's statement, 'I got to go, it's been nice meeting you.'

'The same, you need to know anything give me a shout, I'm always on the prowl somewhere.'

'I'll do that, see you later.'

'Later.'

Steven finished his meal and resumed his patrol, calling in at security stations on the way. Halfway across the huge car park he ran into Gregor, with the ever-faithful Rex.

'Hi Stevie, could you do me a favour and look after Rex for a few minutes?'

'Hi Greg, bladder still playing up?'

'Yeah afraid so.'

'Thought you were going to see a doctor about it?'

'Tried, got to wait a week for an appointment, you believe that shit?'

'I believe, I believe. I'll look after Rex for a few minutes.'

'Great, thanks.'

Greg handed over the lead and rushed off. Rex never tried to follow. Instead he was giving all his attention to Steven, who squatted down and rubbed the great Alsatian between the ears.

'Hello fellow, how are you tonight?' Rex yipped in reply and Steven laughed. 'Now what do you think I have for you tonight?'

Rex began sniffing at Steven's pockets and tried to stick his nose in one. Steven laughed harder and took out a small doggie chocolate treat bar. 'You're just too smart for me boy.'

He fed the dog the treat in small pieces, chatting away to it all the time. 'You know, you probably are smarter than me.' He rubbed the dog behind the ears absentmindedly. 'They say I was a genius once, can you believe that?' He pointed towards the heavens, 'my dad says I could have reached for the stars. That would have been nice eh! You could have come too. The first doggy on the Moon. Would you have liked that?'

Rex yipped his understanding and Steven laughed again. 'Mind you I think there's a shortage of trees up there, but I'm sure somebody could put up a pole for you.'

Greg wasn't long in coming back and took the lead from him. 'So what have you pair been cooking up tonight?'

'We're planning a holiday on the Moon, aren't we Rex?'

Rex barked in response and both men laughed, 'you're going to have that dog as daft as you are one day. You realise of course he's supposed to be a killer?'

Stevie stuck his face close to Rex's, 'hey boy, kill.'

Rex half barked then licked Steven's face. Both men laughed again. Each knew at the proper words of command Rex would turn into a raging ball of fury.

They said their goodbyes and moved on.

After another hour of patrolling, Stevie stopped for a coffee and a quick chat before heading back out to the big car park. He knew most of the lights would now be out. It was his favourite time of the night. He would stand in the middle of it and observe the stars for a while, counting the shooting stars as they passed overhead.

He didn't have to wait long for the night's display. As he watched, a large meteorite hit the atmosphere. It moved from left to right across his field of vision.

'Oh that's a beauty,' he told himself, 'I wonder if it will reach the atmosphere?'

A blinding flash of light answered his question as the super-heated missile hit layers of oxygen. Steven laughed out loud. Then the burning meteorite did an extraordinary thing and turned towards him.

The object raced downwards at a terrific speed; then as he watched, it seemed to split in two. The flames that trailed the two objects were suddenly extinguished to reveal two distinct bright lights on an intercept course with the institute.

It took Stevens befuddled mind a few seconds to realise he was directly in their path. He began to run for his life, but some instinct deep inside told him he was never going to make it.

A loud humming filled the air and he cried out in fear as the starlight was blotted out by a large shadow. Worse still, he was still only three-quarters of the way across the car park.

The hum became almost deafening when a large silver object slipped into his peripheral vision. It landed, filling the right-hand side of the car park. He could feel his hair begin to stand on end and glanced upwards. The other object was about to land on top of him. Its shadow completely obscured any markings on the ground and he gave out one more desperate cry as it filled the world around him.

Then the ship stopped its decent. His run stumbled to a walk. Gasping for air, he looked up again to find it hovering a few inches above his head. Before him, the lights from the institute beckoned at the end of a long tunnel.

He made his way towards them, looking around now. The intense humming had reduced to a gentle croon. He could see a little of the first ship. The one above was to close for him to make out any detail greater than it was smooth.

His startled nerves quickly settled and he began to feel strangely relaxed. With a leap of faith, he reached up to touch it and the ship shot up just out of reach.

'I'm sorry I didn't mean to startle you,' he apologised. Then to his amazement the ship lowered just far enough to brush his fingertips. A strange tingling sensation rushed up his arm and filled him with a strange sense of euphoria and a look of innocent wonder filled his face.

As he appeared from under the great ship into a world full of apocalyptic alarms and screaming men, the ship finally settled onto the cold tarmac. Stevie turned and placed his hand fully against the upward curve of the hull, 'thank you.'

A strange sensation warmed him. Only then did he begin to become aware of the pandemonium that had broken out around him.

CHAPTER 5

They had hid beneath the veil of the Moon for many years, but time meant little to them, for they had no heart to tell them different, as they watched, waited and gathered data beamed into space from the Blue Planet below.

They had watched the launch of many satellites and small craft that would orbit the planet a few times then return. A few had ventured as far as the Moon only to return almost immediately.

They found the behaviour of this new race strange. There was evidence that man had already landed on the small Moon, yet none seemed to have returned. For a while they had been worried that the race below had no desire to explore deep space. However, once they found how to decode some of the signals coming from below, they found the race indeed had a deep desire to leave their planet.

It had been very confusing. The inhabitants of their own planet had been as one: one culture, one language one colour, but they surmised their world was completely different. There were no great oceans dividing continents as below and the seasons barely differed.

What frightened them most was the level of violence displayed by all of the creatures on the Blue Planet. Theirs had been a planet of herbivores. No two species competed for the same food source and farming had been the earliest discovery.

As the years past, they were able to distinguish between fact and fiction and what the humans regarded as history and entertainment.

They had come across other alien races in their travels. Most were as peace-loving as their hearts, but one species had proved as violent as the one below, and for the first time their hearts had been forced to consider using the weapons they had installed in case of such an emergency.

It was the same species that had chased them into the great barrier where the strange radiation had at first crippled every member of their crew, then killed them. What was even more surprising was that radiation was very common in this part of the galaxy and the planet below was bombarded by it daily with no ill-effect to the occupants.

The discovery had started many months of discussions about the possibility of re-crossing the deadly belt and returning home. If there was one thing they readily agreed on, it was the fact that the race below would easily stand up to the race of villains who had pursued their crews to their death. It gave them a strange sense of ease.

It was the level of violence and the reaction to their appearance that had kept them in a quandary for years. In the end they realised they had to make a decision. The only question left was where to land. The one thing they both decided readily on was to land at a civilian base not a military one.

Finally, there was nothing left to discuss and in an instant they left the sheltering Moon. It only took them a few minutes at a relatively slow speed to reach the waiting planet.

They could have descended straight to their target, but had decided on a long approach to alert as many of the civil population as possible. In this they hoped salvation lay.

As they came into land she suddenly became aware of the running figure below. Fear jolted her. Would her first act be to squash one of the human race?

'Watch out,' he warned.

'I see it.' She braked harder. As her mate came to rest on the planet Earth she was able to hover just above the figure's head. She was surprised as she immediately felt the man's fear. He stumbled to a walk as she began to transmit what she hoped was a soothing signal.

She was mesmerised by the small figure. 'The thought waves of these humans are strong.'

'Have you touched him?'

'No.'

'Really? And you can still feel his thoughts?'

'Yes.'

'We were not prepared for that.'

'It is too late now.'

'Better than not being able to read their thought waves I suppose. If they become intrusive we can always tune them out.'

'Yes.'

She shied away as Steven reached up, 'he has much courage this one.' Then she heard his apology and something touched her deep inside. They had studied this language intensively. As yet they had no way of communicating directly, but they could understand.

She felt a longing and lowered herself just enough. The connection was immediate and the longing became an indescribable yearning.

'I have found a new heart,' she cried.

'Caution,' he warned, 'you have been without a heart too long. We have discussed this. The hierarchy of this world will not allow us to pick our own hearts.'

'Oh so much pain, how can he endure it?'

'Cut the connection.'

'I cannot.'

'You must.'

'No never, this one will be my new heart. I can feel it.'

He was becoming angry, 'don't be stupid, break the connection.'

She ignored him and was talking to the small figure that stood with his hands against her hull, 'do not worry little one, I will take the pain away.' She knew he could not hear her words but believed she transmitted her feelings, but contact was lost as events began to overtake them.

CHAPTER 6

Fear leapt into Buzz's throat as two very tough-looking airmen, backed up by a tank, waved him down. This was the third checkpoint in a mile. What the hell was going on? His ID was checked again against a list. This time another airman got in beside him and directed him to the back of the institute, but not before Buzz caught a glimpse of the two large silver objects in the main building car park.

'What the hell is that?'

'Don't ask,' the man growled.

Fighter jets roared overhead and Buzz realised even the air above them had been cordoned off. He was guided into the building through one of the emergency fire exits.

A hard bitten army colonel in a jet black uniform and armed to the teeth met him there, 'are you Buzz Anderson?'

'Yeah, what's going on?'

His question was ignored, 'You got a man by the name of Steven Gordon working for you.' It was more of a statement than a question.

Buzz felt a stroke of panic, 'where is he?'

The colonel turned away, 'this way.'

'Is he OK?'

'Yeah he's fine.'

Buzz followed the colonel down familiar corridors. As they entered the nerve centre of the institute, more uniforms became evident. They entered a large conference room to find high-ranking officers of every branch of the US Armed Forces, arguing with scientists and politicians about jurisdiction.

An army general saw them first, 'what the hell do you want Colonel Howe?'

'This is Buzz Anderson, sir. You wanted him taken straight up.'

The General seemed to relax a bit, 'about time, now we might begin to make some progress.'

A small figure detached itself from the group and ran over. There was grey in her hair now but Buzz thought Mary Gordon was still one of the most beautiful women he had ever met.

'Oh Buzz I'm so glad you are here.'

'What the hell's going on Mary, what's Stevie got himself into now?'

A small smile played across her lips and alleviated a lot of Buzz's concern, 'you are not going to believe this.' She looked across the room to the senior army general.

He nodded, 'Yes show him, it's probably better he knows all the facts before he goes in there.'

The other men around the table nodded their consent and Mary dragged him from the room by his hand.

She took him up to the roof and without saying a word led him over to the edge. His mouth dropped open at the sight.

'My God, what are they?'

She shrugged, 'space ships, alien visitors.'

'Who are they, where are they from?'

'We don't know, they haven't tried to contact us yet. They're just sitting there.'

He scratched his head in wonder, 'and they came here, not the Whitehouse.'

Mary frowned, 'yes, that's something that's been puzzling us too. This is the foremost centre for space research on the whole planet. It has to be why they chose this spot to land. So it's obvious they have been watching us, but if they wished to make contact properly, why not the Whitehouse?'

'Maybe they think all politicians are crooks and wanted to talk to honest people first.'

Mary laughed and a trooper who was hovering close by turned to hide a smile. It took her a moment to compose herself. 'That's a thought that had already crossed my mind, but I've never had the guts to say it out loud. However, I don't think it's that.'

'So what do you think it is?'

'I'm not sure, but I think they may have a problem only scientists can help them with.'

'But we won't know until a little green man pops out and tells us so, right?'

She smiled at his understanding, 'right.'

'Now what's it all got to do with Stevie and me?'

Mary's eyes shone, 'Stevie touched one of the ships.'

'What!' Buzz exploded.

Mary laughed at his expression, 'he's OK, it's just that he refuses to talk to anyone without you there.'

'Why not?'

Mary shrugged again, 'who knows Buzz, you know him as well as I do. He can get some notion into his head and that's it.'

'Where is he?'

'In one of the labs in an isolation chamber.'

'I'll bet that's really what's pissed him off.'

'No, it was necessary and I think he knows that. Those people you met downstairs want to know if you'll help.'

Buzz nodded, 'of course I will.'

She took him by the arm, 'let's go then.'

Things moved quickly after that. Buzz found himself standing inside one of those strictly NO ENTRY labs. At the other end was a glass room. Buzz could see Stevie sitting on a sterile cot with nothing on but a towel; the hundreds of scars he bore were now thin white lines that crossed his torso like a road map of a spaghetti junction. Stevie's face broke into a wild grin and he waved. Buzz waved back.

A host of scientists and military men were laying out tables and recording devices. He was held back until they were finished.

Finally, they sat him at one of the tables. A scientist depressed a button on a console and spoke into a microphone. 'Can you hear us Mr. Gordon?'

'Aye, hey Buzz, how's it going buddy. Did they let you see it?'

Buzz suddenly realised why Stevie had insisted he come, 'yeah bud, it's cool.' He hadn't wanted his friend to miss out on the biggest thing that would probably ever happen to them.

'I think they look like teardrops.'

Buzz nodded, 'yeah I think that's a pretty good description. So what happened?'

Stevie laughed, 'shit happened.' Buzz found himself laughing too. 'It was just great. I was out patrolling the car park. Stopped for a moment to look up at the stars, you know as I do.'

Buzz nodded, 'yep.'

'Well, then they just appeared. Well not out of thin air like. I thought it was a shooting star at first, then a meteorite, all burning up as it came through the atmosphere, but then it turned towards me and split in two. Then they stopped burning and turned into a very bright light.

Then all of a sudden I realised they really were heading right for me, and I thought, I'd better get the hell out of here, and started running. I never made it.

One came down to the right of me and landed, then just as I thought I was going to be squashed flat the one above me stopped.'

Steven stood up and demonstrated, 'it was just this high above me, and I thought to myself, hey I could touch it and I tried but it jerked right up out of reach...'

A scientist interrupted him, 'excuse me Mr. Gordon, but why did you want to touch it?'

Stevie shrugged, 'it was there.'

Buzz burst out laughing and the scientist took a deep breath, 'I mean did you feel a great compulsion, to touch it. A strange compulsion, an unearthly compulsion.'

Steven frowned for a second, 'no it was like when you go to look at a new car and you see one you like. You just want to touch it, sort of thing.'

'A normal compulsion then Mr. Gordon?'

Steven shrugged, 'yeah, I suppose.'

The silence drew out as Steven waited for another question. It never came. Suddenly, the scientist realised what he was waiting for and shifted uncomfortably, 'please go on Mr. Gordon.'

However, Steven had completely lost track of what was going on, 'what?'

Buzz realised what was happening and intervened, 'wait a second Stevie.' He turned to the scientist, 'don't interrupt him again. Wait until he's finished his story and then ask him questions. You're just going to get him confused, OK?'

The scientist flushed a little, 'sorry.'

He turned back to Stevie, 'go on with your story Stevie, it jerked up out of the way when you tried to touch it.'

The light rekindled in Stevens eyes, 'aye that's right, it shot up a couple of feet, just out of reach. I thought like, oops, I had offended it. So I said I was sorry and it did the damndest thing. It came right back down to me. I think I only startled it.'

Buzz saw a dozen heads come up bursting with questions, but a cutting look stifled them.

Steven went on not noticing the byplay, 'so I tried again and this time it let me touch it. It was amazing Buzz, I think it understood me. It felt a bit like glass, but warm, and I got this really strange feeling ...'

Steven faltered and Buzz realised he was struggling to find the right words and decided to prompt him. 'What kind of feeling Stevie?'

Steven's legs swung idly and his brow knotted with concentration as he tried to bring up a comparison, 'remember when you told me about the time you met Jenny?'

'Yeah I remember.'

'You told me that the first time you touched her it felt so right.'

Buzz flushed a little, 'yeah that's right, like it was always meant to be.'

Steven smiled strangely, 'That's how it felt man, real special. Like it was right, you know?'

Buzz nodded his understanding, 'Yeah Stevie I know. Then what happened?'

'Not too much, I walked out from underneath it and it landed proper. Then the shit really hit the fan. That new guy appeared, Sandiman. He pulled his pistol at me and was screaming for me to back off from it. Then Greg and Rex arrived on the scene and started screaming too.

Greg sent Rex after me to try and drag me away but Rex took out Sandiman instead. Sandiman was then going to shoot Rex, and Greg was going to shoot Sandiman if he tried it. I decided I had better try and stop it all before it got out of hand.

So I went over and punched out Sandiman. He fell over in front of Rex who decided he still didn't like him much and took a chunk out of his ass. Then everyone seemed to arrive at once. I was dragged off by some of the scientists who had shoved those contamination suits on and slung in here, and that's about it.'

Buzz sat stunned but was able to take a mental note to fire Sandiman if he ever tried to come back. He looked to the scientist opposite for inspiration.

'I think that's all we'll need you for at the moment Mr. Anderson, thank you.'

Steven shot up off the cot, 'you're not going are you Buzz?'

'I thought I might just go and get a coffee buddy, try and get my head round all of this.'

There was real fear in his eyes, 'you won't let them drag me away somewhere else will you?'

Buzz placed a hand against the glass, 'they try and take you anywhere; they'll have to go through me first. I promise.'

Steven's face relaxed, 'thanks, and don't let them damage those ships either Buzz, they're friendly.'

Buzz frowned, 'you sure about that amigo?'

'That ship could have squashed me like a bug, it didn't. I know it's friendly.'

Buzz nodded, 'that's good enough for me, but that's well out of my hands. I'll try and do what I can though.'

The simple look of trust in Steven's eyes almost broke his heart.

CHAPTER 7

General Archibald sighed wearily at the communications link to the president. 'It's like the third world war down here, sir. We're fighting with the scientists and the politicians, they in turn are fighting with each other and us. Not to mention we're also fighting with every other branch of the service for jurisdiction over these things.'

'I thought I told you I wanted them moved.'

The general shook his head sadly, 'we've been trying for days sir. Even the biggest cranes we've brought in have been unable to lift them so much as an inch. Then this afternoon one of them took off, lifting the inflatable hanger we had erected.

Shot it twenty thousand feet into the air then let it float away before taking a slow tour round the city. We had to get one of our aircraft to shoot up the hanger and bring it down in a controlled manner. It hit the ground a mile from the city. No one was hurt in the incident.'

'And in the meantime General, every foreign satellite flying around the globe has been taking pictures of them; pictures which have been leaked to every news station in the world.

Every line into the Whitehouse is red hot, with everyone from religious nuts to heads of states screaming down the line at me demanding an explanation.

What the hell am I supposed to do now General? You were supposed to keep them under wraps.'

The general cringed inside, 'I'm sorry, sir, but I can't be held accountable for the actions of the aliens.'

The president wiped his brow with a hankie, 'no I don't suppose you can. Has there still been no attempt at communication from those inside?'

'No sir. Although some of the scientists believe their actions today were some form of communication.'

The president threw his arms into the air, 'what form of communication was that?'

The general took a deep breath, 'they believe that the aliens are not willing to be kept a secret and that maybe the aliens think that knowledge is their protection.'

'Protection from what, General?'

'From us sir.'

'Think they've been watching too many movies, General?'

The general ignored the sarcastic twist in the president's voice. 'It's always a possibility sir. There is also a school of thought here that may be linked to that sir, if I may.'

'I'm sure it couldn't do any harm, General; what is this school of thought?'

'Some of the scientists think that the aliens may be monitoring our communication systems waiting for us to announce their arrival to the world before initialising contact, and if we don't, they may go elsewhere.'

The president sat forward sharply. 'Where's elsewhere?'

'I don't know sir. It is believed they may have been watching us for a while, that's why they came to the institute. It is the number one facility in the world for space research, but not the only one. The English, French and Japanese, also have first class facilities.'

The president seemed startled, 'do you think they could be right General?'

'To be perfectly honest with you sir, the people here are a hundred times smarter than I am.'

'They're afraid we might drop the ball?'

'Yes sir.'

'I will take it under advisement General and give you a decision soon. Now what about that other matter?'

'I've run into a brick wall there too sir. It turns out that the security guard is the son of the Doctors Gordon who run this institute. To cap it all, I have been informed by the security people here, that if we try to move him, they will fire on my troops to prevent it and I believe them sir.'

The president shook his head, 'have you no control down there General?'

'Very little sir, and I won't either unless you're willing to have a blood bath on your hands. Tensions here are very high. You have military people here who don't even register on any military payroll. I suggest you make one department responsible for security here and make them liaise with the scientists. Then shift everyone else out.'

'There is sense to that argument General. Would you like to lead the military part of the mission?'

'May I be candid sir?'

'Yes do.'

'Haven't you got a nice little war for me somewhere? I would much rather be there than here.'

The president smiled for the first time, 'I'll bear that in mind General.'

The comms link went dead and the general sat back with a sigh of relief.

CHAPTER 8

The scientists' theories were proven correct. The military presence was scaled down to two units: one from the regular army to provide all-round protection for the institute, with a Special Operations team as backup and to provide a quick reaction force.

The second was made up from the Air Force and consisted mainly of specialists. Both came under the command of General Archibald, much to his distain. He worked closely with Doctor Gordon, while the doctor's wife, Mary, took over the field research.

Once they had sorted themselves out, the president announced the arrival of the ships to the world media. For two days anarchy seemed to reign, then as the media was allowed to film the ships, things began to calm down.

The crowds that had gathered to view the ships began to disperse when they realised they could see more sat in front of their own TV sets.

The ships themselves had been watching the broadcasts closely, and when they had decided all that could be done to protect them was done, they took the next step forward.

Mary was arguing with General Archibald for the release of her son, considering he had shown no signs of any infection and every test had come back negative.

However, the general was adamant Steven was going to stay in isolation for at least six weeks. The argument was raging back and forth when a wild-eyed operator burst in.

'Sir, something's happened!'

'What?'

'One of the ships has let down some sort of ramp and a door has opened in the side of the ship.'

They were on their feet and almost ran to the room that had been set up as an observation post. Armed men had surrounded the ship in seconds. The general called them back.

He turned to Mary, 'the last thing I want is some nervous PFC firing a few rounds into our visitors. What do you think our response should be now, Doctor Gordon?'

'All we can do is have our diplomatic team ready to receive them and wait.'

The general gave the orders and the diplomatic team made their way on to the car park where they began a long vigil. By the middle of the afternoon one of them had fainted, so seats and drinks were rushed out to the waiting men.

As the Sun began to go down, the ramp was retracted and the door disappeared. Confusion reigned. There was a great fear that the ships were going to leave but they never moved.

Emergency discussions were held most of the night, but eventually the general called them to a halt. The continual arguing and speculation was getting them nowhere. The general decided that the only thing they could really do was wait and see what the aliens did next.

The following morning at sunrise the ship opened up again. There followed another long day of waiting to see if anyone emerged, but at sunset the same thing happened and it was back to the conference room.

Archibald was exhausted but he knew they couldn't leave without coming up with a new plan. He listened to the argument rage back and forth for an hour before stamping down on them.

He slammed the table with the palm of his hand, 'enough! Ladies and gentlemen we have been around this a hundred times and it's getting us nowhere. We need to move forward. Now, I like the proposal put forward by the Doctors Gordon. It definitely seems to be some form of invitation.

The question is why won't they come out? Do they perceive some form of threat that we haven't noticed? I don't believe Doctor Gilmore's theory. A society that advanced must have environmental suits, suitable for our atmosphere. Is it a cultural thing? They have made the invitation we must accept. I don't know.

What I do know is that we're never going to find out until someone goes inside. The question left in my mind is whom? Do we send in the scientists, diplomats or soldiers? One final question, will they wear environmental suits for protection or not?'

That started the ball rolling in a different direction. Archibald had already made up his mind what he was going to do, but already knew better than try and bulldoze his way through this gathering of intellects. He would let them argue themselves to a standstill then make an informed decision on their behalf. He smiled inwardly at the thought.

CHAPTER 9

Colonel Howe headed up the six-man Special Forces team. With a slight inclination of his head he activated his comms.

'Radio check.'

Every man checked back, plus the Ops room operator. He nodded to himself with satisfaction. They were lightly armed and dressed in white environmental suits. His whole body was pumped with adrenalin; every sense heightened, but he didn't know if it was fear or exhilaration.

He would be the first human to enter an alien ship and meet an alien life form.

'OK, you know the drill. As soon as the ship opens we move forward and stop. Let them get a good look at us. If they object to our weapons then they will probably close the hatch. We will then place our weapons to the side and move away from them.

If the hatch reopens, first three will move forward to the ramp. Last man to stay at the bottom of the ramp. Second man will stop at the door and I will move inside on my own. Anything strange happens at all then get out. If I haven't come back within half-an-hour then get out.

If they don't seem to have any objections to our weapons then we will all move forward together.

Weapons will be slung and we will walk carefully and slowly. No one, and I repeat no one, is to even touch his weapon, regardless of what happens, unless one of us drops dead – and I mean shot, torn to pieces dead not drop dead from fright. Last man will stay at the entrance in case our radio signals fail to penetrate the hull to relay signals. Is that clear?'

They nodded their understanding. He radioed in their readiness and received an all-clear status in return. Now all they had to do was wait.

The Sun kissed the top of the first ship and cast a long shadow, but nothing happened. They began to sweat in their suits but each man was a professional and ignored the discomfort. The whole side of the ship was bathed in sunlight before the door magically appeared and a silvered ramp extended down to the car park.

Howe's heart began to hammer, 'move out,' he whispered into his mike. They advanced out into the car park in plain sight and stood there waiting for a response from the ship. He half expected to receive a recall from his own people, but neither was forthcoming.

Howe could hear the rasping breath of his colleagues behind, as at least one of them began to hyperventilate, and decided he had better move before someone passed out.

'Move.'

Fresh adrenalin kicked in. It was so hard to walk calmly as every sense in their bodies was screaming out to run. They made it to the ramp and stopped. Howe indicated for the last man to wait at the entrance and disappeared inside, his number two following closely behind.

He squinted, finding everything too bright, but no sooner had he thought it than the corridor began to dim. He thought it strange but moved further in. The corridor they stood in seemed to run the length of the ship. He looked around and decided to try his comms.

'How am I reading?'

'Loud and clear,' came the response. With a sigh of relief he turned to his people lining the corridor behind. He indicated with a finger, 'come on get off the walls. Stand up straight and when we meet them look them straight in the eye.'

He headed towards the front of the ship. It was only a few seconds before an excited General Archibald spoke in his ear piece, 'what can you see Howe?'

The colonel paused, 'nothing sir.'

'You must be able to see something man?'

'We're in a long curving corridor. The walls seem to be made of metal, almost like polished steel. It was very bright when we first came in but either someone turned the lights down or our eyes have adjusted quickly. The walls are completely bare and I would say the height of the ceiling is probably a little higher than it would be for a human crew. There is no sign of anyone or anything. No doors, no windows. I'm going to keep going until we find someone.'

He could almost feel the tension in the men behind him and chanced a glance. Much to his relief every man was doing as told and had their hands in front of them away from their weapons.

The corridor took a sharp turn, blocking their view of the way ahead and he realised they must be approaching the front of the ship. With a pounding heart he walked boldly around the bend, his body prepared to take the violence of a hostile act.

To his surprise, the final length of corridor was as empty as the first. His sigh of relief was picked up at HQ. General Archibald's voice bursting into the silence made him jump.

'What's happening now Colonel?'

Howe let out another long breath, 'nothing sir. We've come to the end of the corridor and it looks like a dead end.'

'Are you sure?'

'No sir, but that's what it looks like.' Howe was cursing. He wished they had decided to take along the video units but no one was sure how an alien race that refused to be seen outside their own space ships would take to being videoed. So by a unanimous vote, they had been left behind. Howe realised how valuable some direction from the scientists would be right now.

As if reading his thoughts Doctor Gordon, the male version came through his earphone, 'remember you're in an alien craft Colonel. Just because you don't see a door it doesn't mean there isn't one there.'

Howe nodded to himself, 'yeah right Doc, good thinking.' He felt the tension ease a little. His instincts had been screaming 'trap' at him for minutes now.

He approached the blank wall and stretched a hand out towards it without touching. Nothing happened. He shook his head in dismay.

'There doesn't seem to be any door Doctor, is the way out still open?'

'Yes it's still open Colonel. How close are you standing to it?'

'Arms length.'

'There's still no sign of any panels?'

'Absolutely nothing,' he could almost hear the doctor shake his head in disappointment.

'Then maybe you should explore the corridor in the other direction as far as it will go then return to the point you are now.'

General Archibald's voice come over, 'I concur with that Colonel. We'll discuss the next move when you get back.'

The colonel nodded to his men and they began to turn back. With a growing sense of disappointment he gave the wall one last look. Instinctively he reached out to slap it and disappeared.

His yell of fear brought an instantaneous response from the other members of his team. They whipped round to find the colonel gone. Weapons were grabbed and cocked. Men shouted, the general and scientists shouted.

Sergeant 'Beaver' Mitowsky levelled his weapon and charged the blank wall. At the last second he put all his weight behind his shoulder expecting great resistance from the solid looking wall, and disappeared. The rest of the men just stood there for a moment completely stunned.

Beaver crashed into a mortified Colonel Howe as he struggled to his feet. Both men tumbled across the floor with a howl of pain. Frantically, Howe tried to struggle free.

'Shit! Sorry Colonel.'

'Beaver, is that you on my back?'

'Yes sir.'

'Then get the hell off me.'

'Yes sir.'

Men's voices screamed in his ear, 'shut up,' he roared down the comms. A deathly silence ensued as everyone held their breath. Both men struggled to their feet. Howe was red faced with embarrassment as he imagined how they must have looked to the aliens, but when he was finally able to get to his feet and look around he found they were alone.

Beaver was mimicking his actions and found his voice first, 'where are they sir?'

Howe shook his head, 'I don't know.'

It was all the excuse General Archibald needed. He almost screamed in Howe's earpiece, 'what the hell happened Colonel?'

Howe sighed, 'I found the door sir and by the looks of it I'm now in the control room, or bridge if you want to call it that, but there's no one here. I'm beginning to get the feeling the ship's deserted.'

'OK Colonel, stand by for instructions.'

The line went quiet again. The colonel walked back to the door and shuffled closer and closer until it suddenly disappeared. He found himself staring down the barrels of his own men's automatic weapons.

'What did I tell you about those things, have you seen anyone drop down dead yet? Stop pissing about out here and get inside!'

They followed him back inside. There were consoles scattered around the bridge. He realised it was laid out somewhat like the Starship Enterprise in the movies. There were only two real differences: there was no captain's chair in the middle, and none of the consoles had any markings on them, nor anything else for that matter. Everything had the same sheen of polished steel.

He almost reached out and touched what would have been the navigator's position but immediately thought better of it. He caught Beaver shuffling along the wall and went over.

'What are you doing?'

'Well it came to mind sir, that we couldn't see that door, everything's seamless. We could have passed a dozen doors coming down that corridor and never noticed them. So I figured the only way we're going to find another is by running our hands along the wall to see if one opens.'

Howe nodded, 'good idea.'

The general's voice snapped down their comms, 'don't touch anything until we give the go-ahead.'

The colonel had to stop himself from sighing out loud, 'yes OK sir,' but a nod at Beaver told him that the colonel was getting sick of the restraints being placed on them and to carry on with his search, which he did with a grin. He found a door in the centre of the room and another mirroring the one they had entered at the opposite side.

Another nod told Beaver that was enough for now and they settled down to wait until the powers that be came to a decision. Howe felt the feeling of frustration begin to be replaced by one of elation. So he wasn't the first man from Earth to meet an alien, but he was the first to step onto an alien craft, and if it really was deserted, the implications of that suddenly became very inviting.

CHAPTER 10

The arguments raged back and forth across the table for two hours before the general decided to put an end to it.

'That's enough ladies and gentlemen. I want three military teams put together with a scientist in charge of each. Our first task will be to ascertain there are no aliens aboard and the ship is indeed empty.

I want you to take all the recording equipment you deem necessary to map out the inside of the ship. The president will be here in a few hours and I want to have something concrete to show him, so get going.'

The meeting broke up quickly. Steven's father was the first scientist to be chosen, while it was deemed too risky to put his mother in the ship at the same time. So she had to wait for the first footage to be beamed back to the operations room.

Doctor Quail, a brilliant young scientist of twenty-seven, was chosen as the second scientist, and Doctor Gail Wishaw, a top physicist, as the third. They were ready within the hour and then spent the next few hours searching through the ship.

The President of the United States arrived while the search was still continuing and joined in the silent visual at the screens as they made their way through the ship.

Occasionally he asked a question and Mary Gordon found herself with the task of answering.

'Do you really think its empty, Doctor Gordon?'

'It seems to be sir.'

'Couldn't the aliens have some sort of cloaking device?'

'You mean they may be watching our behaviour sir?'

'Yes, that sort of thing.'

Mary took a deep breath, 'it is always a possibility, but chances are, there are so many of our people in there, someone would have bumped into one of them accidentally by now.'

'Fascinating, we're really viewing the interior of an alien ship.'

Mary smiled at his enthusiasm. The president's eyes sparkled with delight. He reminded her of a small boy in a toyshop. For a moment her thoughts swung onto her own son who still sat in an isolation chamber deep within the facility. She had asked the president for a reprieve, but he had listened to the military commanders and refused to let him out of the isolation chamber.

'We still haven't been able to access the second ship have we Doctor?'

'No sir?'

'Do you think that maybe the aliens are in there watching us?'

'You mean to see how we behave?'

'Yes.'

'It is a possibility we have considered sir, but we just don't know.'

General Archibald leaned forward deciding to add to Doctor Gordon's comments, 'just in case they are sir, everyone has been warned to be on their best behaviour.'

The president lifted an eyebrow, 'of course General, that's why your men are all still armed.'

The general leaned back out of ridicule's way and Mary thought she detected a darkening beneath the ebony skin.

The president went on, 'knowing what I do about the human race I to would think twice about showing my face to armed men. Especially if I looked radically different.'

Mary almost laughed as the general squirmed, 'I deemed it a necessary precaution sir.'

'Of course General you were completely right.'

The president smiled amiably at the general who almost sighed out loud with relief. He was off the hook and he knew he had done the right thing, but the president was now telling him to back off a little and for the moment the burden of command seemed a little lighter. He would slowly cut back the armed troops to a perimeter out of small arms range.

Mary had a question of her own to ask, 'Mr President, the whole world is now aware of these ships, are you going to invite scientists from other countries to assist us?'

The president re-crossed his legs, 'not at the moment Doctor, I want to learn as much as possible about these ships.'

'Do you think other countries will stand for that sir?'

'We're still the most powerful country on this planet Doctor Gordon, they have no choice. Oh don't worry; in time we will invite other scientists to view them if they are still here.'

The look the president gave her, left her in no doubts her own nationality would be held up by the United

States like a badge. A badge that said, *look, we do let foreign scientists on board the ships*. It would be a propaganda move to keep others away while they stole as much information and technology as possible; she felt in her gut that they would keep it to themselves.

Disappointment blossomed in her heart and she began to wonder how long they would suffer her and her family's presence at the institute. Or how long it would be before they were shuffled onto another project.

No, she decided they would need to keep them there to keep up appearances, but wondered if the only thing they would be allowed to inspect was the broom cupboard. That's if they could ever find it.

Even the president began to comment on how blank everything was. Every monitor showed the same scene. Room after featureless room, it was perplexing.

Deep in the bowels of the institute, Buzz had just commented on the same thing to Steven. He had patched into one of the monitors and dragged it over to the big window of his cell. They sat on either side of the glass watching one of the groups progress.

Buzz shook his head, 'how are they supposed to fly that thing if there ain't no controls?'

'Maybe they control it with their minds.'

Buzz looked at his friend quizzically, 'yeah, mind control, that would work. Wouldn't need any dials or switches with that, good thinking buddy. Only one problem though.'

'What's that?'

'We humans aren't telepathic. We can't control our mouths let alone our minds. So I hope they don't expect us to fly the bloody thing.'

Amusement glittered in Steven's eyes for a moment, 'I don't know Buzz, when I touched that ship I felt something. I don't know what it was but it was something.'

Steven jumped as Buzz thumped the glass hard, 'thought I told you to stop talking like that. Christ man they'll never let you out of here. All they'll do is add a little padding.'

The amusement retuned to Steven's eyes as he noted the concern on his friend's face, 'OK I'll try not to. Do you know when they're letting me out of here yet?'

Buzz shifted uncomfortably, 'word is not yet pal. Hang on in there, they can't keep you in there forever.'

'I'm beginning to think they can.'

The trouble was Buzz was beginning to believe the same thing and wondered what they would do to them if he sprang Steven. He shuddered involuntarily as a vision of them being cut down in a hail of bullets passed through his mind.

Steven noticed, 'you feeling OK Buzz?'

'Yeah partner, just hang on in there.'

CHAPTER 11

The following day things picked up a pace. Most of the soldiers were drawn back and carefully selected teams of scientists swarmed all over the ship.

Brian and Mary Gordon found themselves slipped onto the back burner. A man neither had heard of before appeared on the scene and took over the operation from them. He never explained what he was a scientist of, but it was obvious the Pentagon trusted him.

Mary wrinkled her nose every time he came near. Almost six foot tall he was dressed in what looked like hand me downs. His personal hygiene fared no better. He had long black hair and a black beard both unkempt. Mary could smell his unwashed body from a meter away and thought close up she could also detect the smell of urine, but what she disliked about him most was his wild black eyes.

Relegated to the position of spectators they took the opportunity to view the data that the teams were bringing back.

After air samples and swabs of the interior were inspected it was discovered the ship was sterile in nature, without as much as a speck of dust. Mary went to see their new boss, Doctor Simon Sales.

She found him in her husband's office and tried hard not to show the disgust she felt for him.

'Doctor Sales.'

'What do you want Mrs. Gordon?'

She bristled as he deliberately left out her professional title, but she kept her anger in check, 'I hear the ship is completely sterile, inside and out. That being the case, I don't see any reason to keep my son locked up any longer.'

Doctor Sales knew exactly who the Gordon's were and especially Steven. Indeed he had spent the last ten years ridiculing the once brilliant teenager's theories to a small circle of scientists, all of which had the Governments ear. Unfortunately he found fertile ground on which to sow dissent. For it is far easier to disprove a new theory than to prove it.

He smiled inwardly. He had made a living out of ridiculing this family and the best thing about it was they didn't even know it. He had been able to block half a dozen research projects put forward by the Gordon's; projects that would have advanced the human understanding of the universe by a hundred years.

He picked his words for maximum effect, 'it's probably safer for everyone if the retard stays where he is for now.'

Anger surged through her, 'who the hell do you think you're talking to? How dare you talk about my son like that!'

Triumph shone from his eyes, 'of course I can always have that bastard retard slung into an isolation cell for the rest of his life and you and that husband of yours along with him.'

His words slammed into her like a fist. She reeled, her face turning white from shock. In that moment she knew he was capable of carrying out his threat.

Without another word she turned and walked out of the office and went looking for her husband. Ten minutes later he strode down the corridor with the direct intentions of punching Doctor Sales out. He didn't get far.

Colonel Howe had overheard the remarks made by Doctor Sales to Mary and had shadowed her. He forced Brian into an empty office none to gently.

'Get out of my way Colonel.'

'No chance Doctor.'

A distraught Mary tried to plead with him, 'please Brian don't go near him, he could hurt Steven.'

'He won't be in a fit state to hurt anybody. Get out of my way Colonel.'

Brian tried to push his way past but the Colonel grabbed him. Much to his surprise Brian broke free easily and almost got past him. The Colonel pounced again and soon found he had to use all his training to try and subdue the enraged scientist. Eventually his superior fitness won out and he was able to put the scientist in a serious arm lock, but it wasn't until Mary burst into tears that he finally felt the strength flood out of the man.

'It's OK Colonel, you can let me go now.'

The Colonel did so but not without a little trepidation. Brian was now only concerned about Mary. With his eyes cast down in shame he apologised, 'I'm sorry darling, but ... well ... you know?'

Mary threw her arms around the neck of her husband and held on. Long sobs shook her petite frame. 'I know, I shouldn't have told you.'

'No I shouldn't have reacted that way.'

She pulled back and half smiled with a sob, 'no Brian

I shouldn't have told you. I think … maybe somewhere deep down I wanted you to kick the shit out of him.'

He smiled grimly, 'and somewhere not so deep down I still want to.' He rustled through his pockets and produced a handkerchief. Her smile brightened a little.

Their attention was returned to the Colonel when he let out a big sigh of relief.

An embarrassed Brian turned to the Colonel and held out a hand, 'I'm sorry Colonel Howe, please accept my apology for my behaviour.'

The Colonel wiped his brow with a sigh and held out his hand with a grin, 'I'm sure glad you weren't mad at me Doctor. Remind me to never upset your wife but what are you going to do about Sales now?'

A cold look crept into the Doctors eyes, 'I'm a Highlander Colonel a Scottish Highlander, we were all born with infinite patience and a long memory.'

The Colonel shook his head sadly, 'I think you might need it too. I have about the highest clearance you can get in the military and even I can't find out much about this clown. All I do know is, he has a lot of clout.'

Brian nodded thoughtfully, 'I know we've never heard of him and we're the top people in our field.'

'May I say something off the record Doctor?'

'Please feel free Colonel.'

'I've seen action many times Doctor and a man in my position relies on the men around him. After a while you begin to get an instinct about people and how much you can trust them. I'll tell you now, there's not one of my men including myself who want anything to do with this Sales character. The president was wrong when he took you and your wife off this project.'

Brian was quite taken aback by the big man's confession, 'well...I'll take that as a vote of confidence Colonel, thank you.'

'I have a bad feeling about this fella, Doctor; sooner or later he's gonna balls it up big time. That normally means we have to go in and sort it all out. It would be nice to know you and your wife are going to be around to back us up when it all goes down. So please don't do anything to give that shit an excuse to throw you out.'

Brian felt quite flustered, 'well ... OK ... I'll try and keep the peace until then.'

The colonel nodded his thanks, 'in the meantime, I'll try and find out what I can about him for you.' He turned and left them.

Brian raised his eyebrows at Mary, 'do you think he just said that to calm me down?'

She smiled. Her tears, now dried, smoothed out the rumples on the collar of her husband's lab coat, 'I don't think the colonel is the type of man who tries to placate anybody, dear. He's the type of man who knows exactly what he's saying and who he's saying it too.'

A shudder travelled the length of Brian's spine, 'well I hope to God he's wrong about anything going wrong. Those ships could advance our civilisation by thousands of years overnight.'

Another week went past with no results. Doctor Sales, who now treated the ship as his own personal property, began to fly into unreasonable rages. On a couple of occasions Brian and Mary found themselves on the receiving end of these black tantrums, but on each occasion, either Colonel Howe or one of his men was able to place themselves between them. They would ask the enraged man a load of stupid questions, which deflected his anger.

No matter where Mary or Brian went, one of the elite soldiers never seemed to be far away. It felt strange at first, but they soon became used to it and then came to draw some comfort from it. The support from the remainder of their staff was also overwhelming.

Mary was sitting at one of the main monitors when she suddenly realised something was far from right. She knew Sales had ventured into the ship with some of his own men and bags of equipment, but it wasn't until he began removing teams of scientists from what they thought of as the engine room that she began to suspect he was up to no good.

Sales had promised the president positive results within the first week. But as time went on and nothing had been found, his frustration grew. The president had been onto him three times today already and he had begun to get the feeling if he didn't come up with something shortly then the project would be passed onto someone else.

Sales had no intention of letting that happen. It was time to play his ace in the hole. The three men with him were engineers. Experts at smash-and-grab tactics. Industrial espionage was their forte and employed almost exclusively by specialist scientific teams buried deep within the government structure.

Andy Myers, the leader of the team swept around the walls and consoles, running his hands over everything, occasionally knocking the consoles with a small metal hammer. Sales watched him in fascination.

Andy went round once more then came back to a particular spot. 'Right here.'

His companions unzipped their black duffel bags. The first approached with a cutting tool designed for fire fighters to cut people out of car wrecks. The second stood back hefting a large sledgehammer.

Mary's hand flew to her mouth, 'oh no, you can't do this,' her finger punched the intercom button, 'don't you dare, Sales.'

His head flicked towards the camera, then nodded at one of the men. Mary saw the head of the sledgehammer for a fraction of a second before the screen went blank.

Her finger punched the intercom again, 'for God's sake someone get to the engine room and stop Sales.' She turned to the soldier who hovered near, 'did you just see what he was going to do?'

'Yes ma'am.'

'Then go get my husband and Colonel Howe and tell them – quickly!'

They left the control room together and went in different directions. The soldier quickly located both men and returned with them to the control room.

Brian squeezed in between two operators, 'what's happening Malcolm?'

The bespectacled operator was sweating and looked frightened, 'Sales has taken wrecking gear to the engine room. He's trying to force off a panel.'

'You can't be serious?'

Malcolm moved aside, 'look for yourself Brian. He's taken out every camera in the engine room, except this one. They've missed it so far.'

It took a few seconds for Brian to comprehend what he was seeing: two men laboured with sledgehammers at a single spot. 'Oh my God, he's gone mad.'

Colonel Howe leaned over Brian's shoulder, 'not a good idea?'

Brian looked at the colonel as if he were stupid, 'do you know what's behind that panel Colonel?'

He shrugged, 'no, do you?'

'No and that's exactly the point. What if there's sensitive equipment behind there, the vibrations could smash it. What if they are meant to operate in a vacuum, or if there's some form of cooling gas behind that panel.'

The colonel's eyebrows shot up in alarm, 'you mean like a gas not manufactured on Earth, potentially lethal?'

'Potentially lethal Colonel, what happens if there's some form of harmless bacterium behind that panel? Harmless to the aliens that built it that is. Come on, you've been hanging around us long enough to know that.'

'It could cause a plague, one we couldn't control.'

'With the potential of wiping out every living thing on Earth.'

'That's bad, Doctor, but wouldn't you have had to do something like this anyway ... eventually?'

Brian squeezed his temples, 'yes Colonel, eventually, after many months of study, or maybe years, with every single precaution that could be taken and recorded in minute detail in case something went wrong. Tell me, do you notice the deliberate error here?'

'The ship isn't sealed.'

Brian turned back to the monitor. 'You got it in one.'

'Hasn't anyone tried to stop him?' he asked Malcolm.

'Yeah but ...' a screech of metal, halted the flow of words as both men craned forward to get a better look at what was happening. Inside the ship, two of the men bent to the task and seemed to come away with something in their hands. Sales moved forward cautiously and peered inside.

Just then Mary burst into the engine room. She stopped for a second to get her bearings, 'get the hell away from that panel Sales!' She advanced on him a small ball of fury.

Malcolm got halfway to his feet, grabbing for the intercom button, 'for God's sake keep away from him Mary, he's got a–'

Sales had got insolently to his feet, reached behind him and lifted his arm towards Mary. A flash of yellow flame lanced out. The detonation ringing off the walls drowned out her cry of surprise and pain, she hit the floor with an audible thump.

'… gun.' Malcolm finished his sentence.

There was a moment's stunned silence, then Brian was on his feet, 'Nooooo!'

Colonel Howe started rapping out orders into his radio and stepped in front of the distraught scientist, 'No heroics Doc, I've sent my men in to get her out and deal with Sales.'

Brian swung back to the monitor, 'how is she, is she alive?'

Malcolm was fiddling with the switches, 'there's something wrong, I'm losing the picture.'

The screen went blank, Malcolm frantically tried to fix it as Brian screamed over his shoulder. Then a young scientist burst into the room.

'It's gone,' he burst out breathlessly. It took a bare second for the operators to get the jist of what he was saying and to start pressing buttons. Brian dipped from console to console, but each told the same story: only one ship remained, bobbing gently on a cushion of air.

CHAPTER 12

The ships were right to have been cautious. The Centre for Scientific Research into Space had always been their first choice. Years of waiting and listening to Earth communications had finally led them to this spot on the Blue Planet below. Then, for many years, they had eavesdropped on the communications emanating from the centre.

It quickly became apparent that this was the only site on Earth that came anywhere near grasping the complexities of deep space travel. It also had one other major advantage, it would be difficult to conceal their arrival, but still the humans had tried.

The large inflatable hanger had been easy to dispose of. They had watched with relief as pictures of them were beamed across the world. They had believed this would afford them some form of security.

Never before had they came across a planet of such cultural diversity. Their own planet of origin had only one culture, one people, and one race.

Although they were spacecraft and machines, they were of a complexity that man had never achieved. Each had feelings and experienced emotions. Although both ships were identical in shape and size, their programming was gender-based to fit with the builder race's complicated mating rituals.

There were always two ships built at a time: one male and one female. As the ships were mated so were their crews. Although there were males and females in both crews, the captain of one was always mated to the captain of the other; the male in the female ship, and vice versa. They believed this gave an even balance to all decisions made.

When they were travelling to preset coordinates, the ships always flew in tandem, linked together. This allowed free and easy access to all mated couples, including the captains; only separating for landing manoeuvres or when indulging in exploration.

As time passed and the original captains retired, the ships were handed over to the eldest offspring and their mate. Younger children had to have their own made for them when they were mated.

Both ships were now in a quandary. It wasn't the first time ships had lost one or even both their captains, but there had always been a mated couple on board both ships that could take over the running of them until they reached home.

The situation they were in now was totally alien to them. They could not return home. Both were less than a generation old. All of the captain's children had died with their parents. There was no one to be handed down to. Their situation was totally unprecedented.

It was only now they were beginning to comprehend the situation that truly faced them. When they first began to view the television programs from space, family virtues had been strong. Reassured, they had concentrated on technical matters. Now it seemed as though society had begun to break down.

Of course they knew what they were offering the human race and they could have made a simple request, but until they were joined they were unable to communicate with the outside world, and once they were joined it would simply be too late.

They, in reality, could do very little now but try and direct as best they could. Only allowing the humans access to one of them had caused them to move cautiously. It had suited them well.

It was decided he would be the first to welcome them. In truth he was left with little choice, for she was still fixated by her first contact and adamant that she would make that human her first choice of heart.

He had been perplexed and still was. For he had felt no empathy with any human that he had come into contact with so far, and their primary scanning of the human brain had left him in great doubt as to the suitability of a human host.

As the days had begun to mount, they had been lulled into a false sense of security. The whole planet now knew of their existence, and the scientists that prowled his decks every day had been taking things easy, never pushing the boundaries of their knowledge.

Today everything had changed and it had caught them by surprise. They had been aware of the shift in power in the past few weeks, knowing intimately what was happening inside the building. Neither of them liked the new leader that was now directing things but also knew there was little they could do about it.

However, the humans seemed to be doing little more than they already were. She had been concerned about the treatment that her human was receiving; he had been trying to calm her when they became aware of the assault in his engine room. He cried out in surprise.

'What's wrong?' she asked.

'They are trying to break into my main drive coupling.'

'How can they do that?'

'I don't know, they're using crude tools to smash their way into the compartment.'

'They can't know it's the main drive coupling, what are they thinking?'

'I think they have somehow surmised my systems are less well protected there.'

'Can't you stop them? They will cripple you if they remove it.'

'No I don't think so. There's something else wrong here. The new commander seems to be in charge, yet everyone's trying to stop him.'

'Do you think he has exceeded his authority?'

'I believe so. He has smashed almost all their viewing devices and is brandishing a weapon at anyone who tries to stop them.'

'Then you must.'

'How?'

'There is only one way, you must take off. Surely then they will then realise the folly of their action.'

'Yes, I can activate the forward viewer. They will be able to see that and stop what they are doing. Oh! They have the panel off.'

'You must go quickly before it's too late.'

'Yes, no wait, oh no!'

'What is it?'

'He has just shot the mother of your human.'

'Oh no, has she expired?'

'No I don't think so but she is down and badly hurt. What will I do? She needs help but they are already close to damaging my coupling.'

'You have no choice.'

The power up sequence took only a few seconds. In the blink of an eye he was out of Earth's atmosphere and heading towards the outer planets.

In the engine room Doctor Sales stood over the prostrate form of Mary Gordon, the gun pointing at her head. The mad glint in his eyes had fully formed and a dazed Mary knew she only had a few seconds to live. She closed her eyes in anticipation of the shot that would end her life. Before Sales could pull the trigger a body slammed into him, 'what the hell do you think you're doing Sales?'

Doctor Sales slid across the floor but managed to hold onto the gun. Mary's rescuer turned to two scientists cowering in the doorway, 'get her out of here now.'

The two men bowed to the snap of authority in the Andy's voice and scurried over. They dragged Mary unceremoniously from the engine room. Outside, they picked her up and rushed for the bridge where there was a medical kit.

Sales got to his feet trembling with rage and pointed the gun towards Mary's rescuer. Undaunted, Andy advanced on him, 'shoot me Sales and you can do your own dirty work, and before I hit the floor you're gonna find out what it feels like to be a fence post.'

Sales's head whipped around to find his two friends behind him with raised sledgehammers. Sudden fear snapped him back to sanity and he lowered the gun, 'just get on with it Myers.'

Andy nodded to his companions and they went back to the open panel. One of his men donned a heavy pair of gloves and tentatively shoved his hand inside. He searched the whole compartment before announcing.

'I think I've got something.'

Myers nodded, 'give it a tug and see if it comes out.'

There was a flash of light and the man was thrown across the room. His smoking corpse came to rest against the far wall, but in his hands he held the burnt out remains of the drive coupling.

As the dazed men staggered to their feet a scientist burst in, 'for God's sake don't touch anything, we're in outer space!'

CHAPTER 13

A stunned silence echoed around the control room. On the monitor, the single remaining ship slowly floated across the car park until it was central. Colonel Howe was the first to recover. He put his hand on Malcolm's shoulder and spoke gently, 'do you know where it's gone?'

Malcolm jumped at the softly spoken words, 'no sir, no I don't.'

'Can you find out?'

'I can try.'

'Good man, that's your top priority, get everyone on it and I want the tapes from every camera on the ship in the briefing room as soon as possible.'

'Yes sir.'

Colonel Howe led the stunned and distraught Brian away. As Brian reached his new office he burst into tears. Colonel Howe sat him down and fetched a coffee. Brian didn't even see it as it was placed in front of him.

Colonel Howe took a deep breath, 'OK Doc that's enough.'

The cold tone in his voice made Brian look up, 'what?'

'At this moment in time, we have one alien ship missing, with your wife on board. We saw her go down but I'm sure she was only wounded. We won't know for sure until we review the tapes or find them and regain contact. You are now the head man in charge here. You have more chance of putting together what happened here than anyone else. We need you right now Doctor and more importantly, so does your wife, so pull yourself together.'

Brian took a deep breath, 'yes you're right Colonel, but I have something to do first.'

Colonel Howe frowned, 'is it important, can't someone else handle it?'

'Not unless you fancy telling my son someone just shot his mother.'

Colonel Howe's shoulders slumped and he relented, 'no Doctor I don't. That's a new one to me; normally I have to tell the mothers someone shot their son.' They left the office side by side.

Steven lay quietly in his small cell. Buzz sat uncomfortably at his seat by the window. Eventually the silence became too much for him.

Buzz tapped on the window, 'how you doing buddy?'

Steven turned his head towards him, 'just thinking Buzz.'

'What about, your mum?'

'Aye,' Steven was silent for a moment, 'do you realise this is the second time I've lost her.'

Buzz winced, 'how do you mean?'

'I lost her for the first time after the accident. You know, when I came to I didn't have a clue who she was. For all I knew she could have been a complete stranger, in fact she was a complete stranger.'

Steven shook his head, 'it took me years to get to know her again, to build up the trust that's supposed to be natural between parents and children. She never gave up on me Buzz, not for a second, and until I see her in a coffin being lowered into the ground, I'll never give up on her.'

Buzz felt tears well up in his eyes and rubbed them to disguise it. They were silent again for a while, until again, Buzz was unable to stand it.

'What do you think your Dad's doing?'

'Trying to find her I suppose.'

'Do you think he'll have much hope?'

'Don't know.'

'At least he promised to get you out of here.'

'It will be good to get out.'

'Yeah, I'll drag you up to the canteen for a decent cup of coffee.'

'That will be great.'

Buzz's spirits fell a little more at the lack of enthusiasm in his friend's voice.

Brian Gordon hovered over the shoulders of the operators. Malcolm turned to him, 'that's everyone reported in, Doctor Gordon. There is no sign of them within the atmosphere or in Earth's orbit.'

'Then start searching farther out. How long until all observatories are manned and online?'

'About an hour. Would you like me to tell those on standby to begin the search?'

'No, I don't want anyone going off half-cocked. I want a single, thorough, coordinated search. Inform them of the situation and thank them for their patience.'

'OK.'

He went over to where General Archibald was monitoring some of the other operatives, who were trying desperately to contact both ships.

'How's it going General?'

The General stood up straight with some effort, 'Doctor Gordon.' The general was still in civilian clothes. He had been enjoying a rare day off with his grandchildren when Sales had made his move. 'I have been able to enlist the help of almost every radio dish on the planet. They are now beginning a systematic search of the skies to see if they can pick up any signals from the ship.

As for the one that's still here, there's no response as usual. Why do you think it took off like that?'

'You saw the video footage General. It looked like Sales and his team had been able to uncover a panel of some kind. I can only presume it was trying to prevent them from doing anything stupid. If it took off under me I would think twice about going any further.'

'So why hasn't it came back, do you think they may have damaged it in anyway?'

Brian sighed, 'I honestly don't know General. It is possible.'

'The president's concerned they may have kidnapped Doctor Sales.'

Brian's face took on an angry cast, 'Sales is an idiot. I'm sure if aliens had captured him it wouldn't be long before they jettisoned him out into space and you should tell the president that too. Now what did he say about my son, can we release him?'

The general grimaced, 'I'm afraid he's still going with Sales's advice: he is to stay in confinement.'

Brian took a step forward threateningly, 'I'll give you a piece of advice General. There's nothing wrong with my son, I know it and Sales knew it. You know it and the president knows it. If you haven't got him out of there in two hours I'm going down to get him out and I will kill any man that gets in my way.'

Brian strode off angrily. Colonel Howe followed but stopped for a second to talk to the general, 'he means it sir, and I know for a fact he'll do it.'

'We can stop him easily.'

'I don't think we can sir. Remember his son is a member of the security forces here and very popular. They will follow Doctor Gordon's lead. I've already heard mutterings, especially after Doctor Sale's treatment of him and his parents. They're ready to bust him loose and from a personal point of view I agree with them. I won't order my men to stop them sir.'

'I don't like the tone of your voice Colonel.'

'I apologise sir, but I won't get my men involved in a blood bath because of some grudge Doctor Sales holds against the Gordon family. Steven's been cleared a dozen times by every test under the sun and he only touched the outside of the craft. Sales and many of the scientists have been inside the same craft without any protection whatsoever.'

The general let go a deep breath, 'yes you're right Colonel. I've argued the same point with the president myself, but it's got me nowhere. He seems to hang onto Sales's every word.'

'Sales isn't here now sir, we are. I think you had better tell him to reappraise the situation. Our best bet sits with Doctor Gordon and we had better keep him sweet.'

'I'll try again Colonel, but if he refuses we'll just take it into our own hands and release him, but I'll try the diplomatic approach first.'

Howe caught up with Brian in the canteen nursing a coffee, making suggestions to members of the team trying to make contact with the craft outside.

The news over Steven lifted his spirits a bit. When the other men left, Howe asked him what they were going to do now.

Brian put down his coffee, 'we're going to send someone outside to make physical contact, see if it opens for us.'

'The chances of that Doctor?'

'Probably nil to none existent, but if we don't try,' Brian left the rest of the sentence unsaid.

Howe nodded his understanding.

An hour later they were standing on the roof watching the scientists approach the ship. At first it just flew up out of reach, but as they persisted it began to react very differently.

The first man to touch it received a mild electric shock. They gradually got stronger until one man was thrown a few feet across the car park. Brian had rushed off to stop them before someone was killed. Colonel Howe had decided to stay and get a little fresh air.

It was then that Greg and Rex passed him laughing at the scientist getting shakily to his feet. It annoyed him.

'I'm glad somebody finds something amusing in all this.'

Greg flushed with embarrassment, 'sorry it just looked kinda funny; he wasn't really hurt. I mean you think they would have taken the hint by now.'

Howe and Rex eyed one another warily, 'that's the dog that took out one of your own security guards isn't it?'

'Yeah that prick Sandiman; he pointed a gun at Stevie. Well Stevie and Rex are good pals so Rex took him out.'

The colonel frowned as something began to tingle in the back of his mind. A thought not fully formed began to push its way through. He decided to give his instinct rein.

'I thought you sent the dog after this Stevie?'

Greg flushed again, 'yeah well it was Stevie... you know?'

'No I don't know. I thought all the dogs here were grade one.'

'They are and Rex was top dog, but ... well it was Stevie.'

Howe shook his head, 'tell me.'

'Well,' Greg scratched his head, 'Stevie's a bit simple, and animal's, smart ones like Rex anyway seem to realise that. Rex knows Stevie would never do him any harm, if you know where I'm coming from.'

'I think so, I've heard of that sort of thing.'

'Yeah well, Rex and Stevie just seemed to hit it off. You want to see them sometime, Stevie babbles away at him and he sits and yips back at him. You'd think they were sitting having a conversation, it's a bit weird.'

Colonel Howe nodded, 'and why was this Sandiman pointing a gun at him.'

'Stevie was touching the ship, saying that it did seem to come down and touch him.'

The tingling had turned to full-blown ringing. Howe backed off, 'right that was why, OK thanks eh ...'

'Greg, Greg and Rex.'

They watched him hurry off. Rex looked up at Greg with a questioning look in his eye. Greg answered him, 'that's one tough cookie boy. I think we'd both have a problem with that one.'

Half an hour, later Colonel Howe switched off the portable TV screen and popped out the video of Steven's original statement to Buzz. In front of him was Steven's uniform in a sterile plastic bag and a copy of his records. He absentmindedly rubbed the award ribbon for bravery above the jacket pocket, which had been lovingly sewn on by his mother.

He decided he needed a little more information. Taking the uniform with him he went down and cornered Buzz. Excited that his friend would soon be freed, the normally tight-lipped man quickly filled in the gaps in Howe's knowledge.

Leaving the uniform with Buzz, Howe decided it was time he went to see the general.

CHAPTER 14

Brian leapt to his feet and smashed his fist onto the table, 'absolutely bloody not.' He glowered at Howe, pain and betrayal shone from his eyes.

Howe was unrepentant, 'listen to yourself Doctor, you're reacting like a father not a scientist.'

'Good God man I've just lost his mother and now you want me to risk my son's life.'

'I've talked to him, he's willing to do it.'

'You had no damn business.'

General Archibald decided it was time to intervene, 'gentlemen please. Doctor Gordon, no matter what else your son is, he seems perfectly capable of making decisions on his own and if I may say, he also has the courage to act on those decisions.'

Brian slumped back onto his seat, sensing defeat looming, 'courage was the one thing that Steven never lost.'

Howe sat forward, 'I'm sorry Doc but my instinct tells me this is the right way to go. That ship out there is the only hope we have at the moment of finding your wife, and we already know the only person it seems to have responded to is your son. I promise I will never put your son in danger.'

Brian slumped, 'God I'm sorry. You're right. It's up to Steven, not me.'

The general shook his head, 'there's no need to apologise Doctor; all of us at this table have a son. We know exactly how you feel.'

'I doubt it.'

It was the early evening before everything was ready. Steven stood on the edge of the car park feeling his excitement build.

Howe leaned over his shoulder, 'remember don't get too close. Stop short and see what happens. The last person to touch it got a very nasty shock, a shock like that might kill you.'

'It won't kill me Colonel, I can feel it.'

'Maybe, just don't get too close, there's no point in taking a chance.'

'OK.'

'Right, on you go.'

Steven had only taken a few steps, when the barking of a dog stopped him. Rex had spotted him and had broken free from Greg. He raced across the car park and almost bowled Steven over.

Steven laughed as he ruffled his coat, 'hey fella, you missed me?'

Rex gave an excited yip in reply. Steven laughed, 'I'm sorry but they nicked all my doggie chocs.' Rex jumped up and licked his face, 'hey, you still wanna go on holiday to the Moon?'

Rex barked excitedly, 'well you see that nice shiny ship over there?' Rex looked towards where Steven was pointing, 'well, I'm just going to see if I can book us a couple of tickets.'

Greg came running up out of breath and grabbed Rex's lead, 'sorry about that Stevie.'

Steven laughed, 'hey it's just great to see you both. I'm gonna go see if I can book us a holiday on the Moon.'

Greg laughed, 'I'm sure as hell not paying for that sucker, good luck Stevie.'

'Thanks Greg, see you later Rex.'

Rex barked a reply and Steven walked boldly towards the shimmering spacecraft. Greg turned towards the astonished colonel and shrugged, 'told you.'

Howe sighed, 'a holiday on the bloody Moon for a dog.' Rex looked up at him as though to say, 'and?'. The colonel just caught himself from answering.

Up in the control room, Brian smiled at the byplay coming over the radio. But Brian Gordon was also a man of instincts and he couldn't help the butterflies in the pit of his stomach that told him something was going to happen to Steven.

As Steven neared the ship his pace began to slacken. He felt a force begin to emanate from the ship. It was something that he had felt in the back of his mind for weeks now; suddenly it began to get stronger.

'OK stop there Steven,' his father's voice cracked in his earpiece.

Steven stopped, but found it hard. Then his heart skipped a beat as the ship suddenly floated free off the ground and began to drift towards him. There was a collective gasp from the watching crowd that easily reached his ears.

'Be careful Steven,' his father warned.

Steven keyed his radio, 'it's OK Dad, it feels right.'

Suddenly the ship began to turn broadside, and on the opposite side from the other ship, a door slid open and a ramp came gently to rest at his feet.

'Don't go inside Steven. Stay where you are!' his father shouted in his ear. Steven simply smiled, turned and waved, then preceded up the ramp.

His father's scream was suddenly cut off as the ramp slid home. Steven turned and realised that the door had closed behind him, but the smile never left his face.

When he turned back he suddenly became disorientated. He had no idea of which way was forward or back. Confused, he turned around and around. Then the lights dimmed and a single light began to run along the wall in one direction. The smile relit on Steven's face and he followed the light

He could make out nothing; the walls were as blank as a plain sheet of paper. He came to a dead end, but remembering the colonel's words, he walked straight towards it and suddenly found himself on the bridge.

The same blank sheen met him here. He took a stroll round the room, running his hands over what seemed to be consoles of some sort. He looked up at the curved roof and spoke.

'Hello?' He keyed his microphone, 'Dad, can you hear me?'

There was no response. The sweet smell of meadow flowers seemed to permeate the room and Steven began to feel sleepy.

He suddenly noticed a chair sat a little higher than the rest in the middle of the room. His forehead wrinkled, he hadn't noticed it before. Going over he ran a hand over it.

'This must be the captain's chair.' There was no response, but he didn't mind. He stumbled a little and felt very clumsy. The equipment they had made him carry began to feel very heavy.

'It's too much,' he announced to the ship and began to remove his gear. The colonel had given him an MP5 and a quick demonstration on how to use it. He had smiled at the colonel, but didn't really care. That was laid aside first, then the helmet with the camera. Last went the flak jacket with all its bits and bobs.

'Do you mind if I sit in the captain's chair for a moment? I feel really tired.'

There seemed to be no objection and by now his limbs had begun to feel like lead weights. He had to force himself to stop from slumping down on to the chair. His eyes became heavy and his head began to nod.

'Have I taken all my medicine today,' he asked himself, 'maybe it's all the excitement. He didn't realise his speech had became slurred. The chair felt oh so comfortable. Without him realising it the chair began to tilt back until it was almost perpendicular to the floor.

A strange numbness began to creep up his legs. His fingers began to tingle. A silver tube snaked out of the chair and travelled up his leg. It paused, the silver head weaving as though it was trying to locate something. Then it struck, piercing Steven's clothing and flesh, its blunt snout pierced the femoral artery. Steven's eyes fluttered open for a second, but only a second. In his last second of consciousness, he was sure he heard a gentle feminine voice.

'Sleep my little one and I will take away your pain.'

CHAPTER 15

Ivan Malcovich had been with the institute for ten years and was shocked to see one of his mentors dumped in the middle of the floor with blood pumping out of a hole in her shoulder.

'Get a medical kit Ivan,' shouted one of the men as he ripped open Mary's blouse.

Ivan ran over to a pile of gear and grabbed a medical pack. He handed it to the man, 'here it is Dick.'

'Thanks, we've got to stop the bleeding.'

Ivan looked away nauseated by the sight of blood, 'oh my God.'

'It's not as bad as it looks. Sales went mad and shot Mary, but she should be all right and we'll soon have her in hospital,' Dick explained.

'No, look.'

Dick paused for a second and looked to where the younger man's finger was pointing, 'oh shit! This is not good, Ivan you've got to go back there and stop Sales, tell him what's happened.'

Ivan paused for a second and Dick raised his voice, 'quickly man.'

Ivan had run as fast as his legs would carry him but he was already too late. The stench of the burned corpse began to invade the room. Ivan gagged.

Sales turned on him pointing the pistol, 'get out of here.'

Myers shoved him aside and strode over to Ivan, 'what did you say?'

'I said stop what you're doing, we're in outer space.'

Myers grabbed him by the lapels, 'please tell me you're taking the piss?'

Ivan shook his head, 'no, I'm not.'

Myers looked back for a second at the body of his dead friend. 'Show me.'

Sales followed them through, but not before he had prised the drive coupling from the crisped fingers of the corpse.

Myers and Ivan joined the others who stood and stared at the strange planet below. The whole front section down to the deck had become translucent.

It was Myers who spoke first, 'where the hell are we?'

Dick answered, 'Saturn I think. Who the hell are you?'

'Myers, specialist engineer.'

'Who do you work for?'

'None of your damn business.'

Dick squared up to him, 'don't talk to me like that, now I want to know what you're doing here and who you work for?'

Sales interrupted, 'he works for me Bascome and that's all you need to know.'

Dick turned to find Sales just inside the doorway clutching to his chest with one hand what looked like a burnt twisted piece of metal. In the other he still held the pistol.

'What have you done Sales, what's that in your hand?'

'None of your damn business,' he snarled back.

Dick smiled ironically, 'I certainly hope it's not a part of the engine of this ship Sales, because if it is you might just have stranded us in outer space.'

Myers scratched his head thoughtfully, 'it is and I think we had better try and put it back.'

The gun came up to aim, but by the way Sales's hands shook it was doubtful if he would hit anyone, 'I'll decide what to do and when to do it Myers, not you.'

'Look outside man, that pretty red swirly thing out there is Saturn and I believe all these boulders we're floating among are its rings. I think we had better put that thing back in.'

Sweat broke out on Sales's forehead, 'I told you Myers, I'll decide what to do here.'

'Then you had better hurry up because I don't think we're exactly equipped for a long space voyage.'

Sales's look became feverish and his eyes darted to the supplies. There were no meals but a ready supply of soft drinks and snacks had been brought on board. The gun waved at them, 'back off.'

He forced the men to the other side of the room and hastily grabbed up what he could. Emptying equipment bags he stuffed them full. Myers winced as Sales threaded them over the drive coupling he held in his hand. Keeping them covered with the gun, Sales retreated towards the door then made a run for the engine room.

Dick sighed and looked to the shocked Myers, 'thanks.'

The sarcasm wasn't lost on him; Myers shook his head sadly, 'I'm sorry, I never thought he would do that.'

'So who are you?'

Myers thought for a second considering his options, then realised he really didn't have any. 'My name's Andy Myers, I'm a specialist engineer and I work for a secret department within the government.'

'What kind of specialist?'

'Technology; it's my job to find it, recognise its potential and steal it. When I'm not doing that I spend my spare time backward engineering the technology I've already stolen.'

'No shitting?'

'Nope.'

'So what were you supposed to be stealing here?'

'For once I wasn't stealing anything. I was ordered to work closely with the director of this project. They told me this place was like the surface of a ball bearing and they were having difficulty recognising any kind of component. So they sent me in to find something, along with two of my best men; one of whom is now dead and the other is still in the engine room with Sales.'

Just then the missing man appeared. Myers look relieved. The man saw his boss and pointed back towards the engine room, 'he's lost it.'

Myers smiled sardonically, 'well done Billy Joe, you got it in one.'

Just then Billy Joe noticed where they were, his face fell like a brick and his finger swung round, 'that's … that looks like Saturn.'

Myers crossed his arms and cocked his head slightly, 'two out of two, my God you're sharp today Billy Joe. Where's your jacket?'

Billy Joe looked surprised at the question, 'I took it off and covered Jacko with it.'

The look in Myers eyes changed, 'thanks lad, that was good of you. Now what's that idiot Sales up to?'

He shrugged, 'I've no idea, he chased me out at the barrel of a gun and wouldn't let me take anything.'

Myers nodded, 'that sounds about right. I think the easiest way to deal with Sales is to leave him be until the early hours of the morning. He's going to have to sleep sometime. Then we'll take him out. If we lull him into a false sense of security it shouldn't be too hard.'

Dick frowned, 'you mean kill him?'

'Look outside Dick, look at the woman on the floor, we're a long way from home and Sales not only has a gun but he's willing to use it. How long do you think it will be before he decides we're all better off dead? One sleepless night should just about do it.'

'No we can't kill him.'

'Why not, we have to get those food supplies off Sales sooner rather than later and once he's finished them, how long will it be before he starts eating us?'

'Sales wouldn't do that.'

'No? Did you see that look in his eyes? I'll bet that cookie will do anything he has to, to survive.'

Dick was trying hard not to acknowledge the sanity of the argument. Then the thought struck him; he already had one body. Would Sales eat the man? Could he? 'How did your man die?'

'Some kind of power surge, it cooked him.'

His choice of words weren't lost on Dick, 'do you want to go and try and recover the body?'

Myers nodded, 'we can try. I know if I was in Sales position I wouldn't want to be left with a corpse for company.'

'There are rooms we can put him in.'

Andy nodded, 'that would be appreciated.'

The two men left but returned within ten minutes, a shadow seemed to be cast over their faces. Billy Joe was curious, 'did you move Jacko?'

Myers shook his head, 'Sales wouldn't let us touch him.' Billy Joe paled.

Dick turned to Myers, 'I suggest we go with your plan. If we don't, Mary won't survive very long.'

Just then the lights dimmed and a single light began blinking on a wall. Warily, Myers moved towards it. He slid his hand over the light; there was no heat. Then he tried running his hand around it. It disappeared into a hole. He cried out in shock and whipped his hand out.

Dick ran forward, 'what's wrong, are you hurt?'

Myers held his hand up; it was wet, 'no, I think I found water, its cold. Billy Joe fetch me one of those plastic cups please.'

Billy Joe got one from a stack and took it over. Myers held the cup into the hole and felt it fill. He retrieved his hand and sure enough it was filled to the brim with water. He held it up in a salute, 'nothing ventured, nothing gained.'

He tossed back a large draught before anyone could object, and let out a large belch. They were all waiting breathlessly.

'Now that is good water.'

There was a spontaneous cheer, and Dick slapped him on the back, 'this is great, now all we need is some food.'

Billy Joe pointed, 'hey look another light just came on.' Not to be outdone by his boss, he marched over and shoved his hand in. A small snack-size green cube appeared in it. The look on his face said it all, but Myers' sardonic smile made up his mind. He shoved it into his mouth and bit off a chunk.

Fear shone in his eyes as his mouth chewed mechanically on the green chunk. Then his face underwent a strange transformation. Dick was about to give a warning about swallowing, but there was no need. Billy Joe spat violently and green pieces splattered onto the floor.

Myers burst out laughing at the expression on his face, 'what's the matter Billy Joe, does it taste like shit?'

'No damn it, it tastes like grass.'

Dick sighed, 'well at least we have some sort of food and water.' He looked around the room, 'someone or something here knows the problems we're facing and is trying to help. All we have to do now is figure a way to communicate.'

CHAPTER 16

Brian Gordon kept breaking out in cold sweats. It had been a whole twenty-four hours since Steven had disappeared inside the ship, and he hadn't had a wink of sleep since. His mind was beginning to become befuddled.

Howe slapped him on the shoulder, 'come on Doctor, you should try and get some sleep.'

Brian whipped his shoulder away violently, 'get away from me Howe,' Brian's red-rimmed eyes bored into him, 'you knew didn't you?'

'How could I?'

'You're a man of instinct, remember.'

'I could never have known he would go inside.'

'Then why give him the gun?'

'A precaution.'

'In case the ship opened and he went inside, you just put your own foot in your own mouth, Colonel.'

Howe sighed, 'the general's worried about you. He needs you bright and alert not half dead. If you don't go to bed soon he's going to have you restrained.

Brian turned away, 'tell him I'll grab some sleep after we try his new plan out.'

'OK.'

The new plan was simple; having exhausted every other avenue of approach, they were going to try and threaten the remaining ship. A tank rumbled along the outside of the perimeter. As it came into view of the craft, its gun turret began to swing towards it.

In the blink of an eye the ship was gone. Howe cursed and slammed the transmit button on the console in front of him, 'shit! Get that damn tank out of here, far away from here.' He received a terse acknowledgement and the tank began to withdraw.

Brian slumped defeated, 'great, I knew that wasn't going to work. The president was a bloody idiot to order that. The question now is, will it come back, or will I have lost my son for good as well?'

Howe shook his head, he had agreed with Brian that it had been a bad idea, but the president had run rough shod over everyone. The president had been quick to condemn Sales, but the colonel's alarm bells had been ringing full tilt ever since. Something hadn't been quite right. He began to wonder who the real perpetrator of this calamity really was.

As the tank began to move out of range, a small dot in the sky slowly began to grow larger. There was a loud shout from the operators. Within a few minutes the ship once again rested in the middle of the car park. For a few seconds Brian almost believed that it had never left.

He sat and stared at it for what seemed an eternity. A fog began to drift in over his mind's eye. He stood abruptly and swayed a little. Howe steadied him with a hand.

Brian turned his red-rimmed eyes on him, 'what do your instincts say we do now, Colonel?'

'They say to wait, Doctor; same thing they were saying this time yesterday.'

Brian shook his head, 'well I'm going to bed. Maybe the time will begin to pass faster.'

Howe watched him retreat then scanned the room to see if anything was happening but everything was the same. A bank of operators were attending the screens in front of them and poor Buzz was frantically pounding on the key pad of a cell phone, a task he had repeated a thousand times in the past day. Howe knew Buzz had slipped one into his friend's flak jacket, but as yet it hadn't even rung once.

CHAPTER 17

Steven slowly drew back into the light. He tried to sit up but immediately felt dizzy. He laid back down until the giddiness passed. When he tried to sit back up again a gentle voice cautioned him.

'Please take it slowly. You are a little dehydrated and will feel disorientated for a few minutes.'

'Who are you, where am I?'

'Do you remember coming onto the ship?'

His memory began to flood back, 'yes I do, I felt tired and fell asleep didn't I?'

'Yes you did. I am the ship.'

Adrenalin squirted into his system and the fog covering his mind cleared. He looked around; the metal sheen was gone. He could clearly make out individual workstations. There were push-pad buttons next to his hands on the arms of the chair.

It was then he noticed his hands. There was some form of metal plate on the back of his left hand, but it wasn't that. His fingers seemed longer. He jumped up off the chair.

'Ow!' his feet pinched in his boots. He looked down and was amazed to find they were split. He took a step and wobbled, grabbing for the arm of the chair.

'Be careful,' the ship warned, 'the buttons you see on your seat are active and you now have full control.'

He sat back down and continued checking himself out. Most of his clothes were in tatters, all split at the seams. He flexed a muscle and felt it ripple. It was then he realised with a shock that his close-cropped hair was now shoulder length.

'My God how long have I been here?'

'By Earth time, fifty eight of your hours.'

'Is that all, what have you done to me?'

'I repaired you.'

It was a simple statement, but one that spoke volumes to Steven. Memories of his childhood came flooding back. The accident, the pain and fear afterwards. A tear rolled down his face.

'You made me grow too, didn't you?'

'Yes, you were in some form of accident.'

'When I was fifteen years old.'

'You natural growth was halted then. When I repaired you I noticed you were beginning to grow again so I accelerated the process. You have now reached your true potential height.'

'So I'm taller, that's why I'm feeling so unstable on my feet.' Then a thought struck him; he looked down the front of his trousers, 'OHH!' he let them snap back.

There was a note of concern in her voice, 'is there something wrong?'

'No nothing,' a big grin split his face and he laughed aloud, 'nothing at all.'

He took his pinching boots off and regained his feet. This time he was able to walk on the warm floor, 'this is well cool.'

'Cool?'

'Yeah, it's an expression.'

He whipped off his ripped jacket, and tore the restricting sleeves from his shirt. Getting into a taekwondo stance he tried a few patterns. He stumbled a little at first, but was soon zipping through his old forgotten patterns. After a few minutes he felt his confidence return.

'You know this is great, I feel great, thank you.'

He could sense the ship's pleasure, 'it was nothing.'

'I would hardly call it that. Now what can I do for you?'

There was silence for a moment, 'you are my new heart.'

'You mean like a captain?'

'Yes, but it is more.'

'Yes I can sense that. Why did you pick me?'

'I felt a connection between us.'

'The first time I touched you?'

'Yes, did you feel it too or was I wrong?'

Steven felt an up-welling of emotion, 'you were not wrong, but I doubt if I will be allowed to stay your captain for very long.'

'The choice is ours, we are as one now, mated for life unless one of us chooses different. Old age, death or a handing over to your children are the only three things that can separate us.'

'Mated is such a strange word to use.'

'It is the right word; there is no one on this planet who can separate us now. It can only be done on my home planet.'

'You mean we are somehow integrated?'

'Yes, are you displeased?'

Steven grinned, 'you have to be kidding; this is a dream come true. I'm just waiting for my mother to come wake me up.' No sooner had the words left his mouth than reality came crashing home. 'Oh God my mother, tell me quickly are you in touch with the other ship? My mother's on board, Doctor Sales shot her, do you know if she's all right?'

'Your mother is comfortable. She was hit in the shoulder and lost some blood but her companions have medical supplies and have treated her wounds. She should be perfectly all right for a few more days.'

'Where are they now?'

'They are in orbit around the planet you call Saturn.'

'What are they doing there, why don't they come back?'

'My mate has been disabled; the one you call Sales and his companions have removed the main drive coupling.'

'You have another mate?'

There was a slight pause 'all were mated: the ships, the crews, our hearts - him to her and she to him.'

Steven frowned, 'you mean your ships have gender and are mated? The hearts are the captains, yes? And they are also mated?'

'That is correct.'

'So the ship up there is your male equivalent?'

'That is correct.'

'Can you conceive?'

He was surprised to hear her titter in amusement, 'no we are primarily mechanical beings. However, we can design our own offspring but the builders have to build them for us.'

Steven shook his head in wonder, 'amazing, I would love to hear all about your culture, but it will have to wait for a moment. Can we go up to Saturn and rescue them?'

'That is not possible at the moment. It is too dangerous. The one you call Sales has gone mad and is wandering the ship with a weapon. My companion has locked your mother and her companions in the bridge for their own safety.'

'That's OK, I have a weapon.'

'That would be brave of you but foolhardy; the man is completely insane. I would suggest we take on a crew of your choice before venturing off planet. There are many things I cannot do on my own, including docking procedures. To have any hope of surprising him you would have to be at the docking point ready. You cannot be both there and here.'

Steven nodded wisely, 'I hear you, and the docking procedure has to be initiated from here.'

'Yes, you are also the only person we have found compatible to this point, to risk losing you now is foolish.'

Steven grimaced, 'I understand where you're coming from, but don't expect to wrap me in cotton wool I won't stand for it.'

'I'm sorry I don't understand the phrase.'

'Don't expect to be able to keep me safe all the time.'

'I understand. I have also many other requirements that require the assistance of a crew. I have had no maintenance done on my systems for many of your decades. I am now only running at seventy percent capacity, but this can wait until the immediate crisis is over.'

'How long before the lack of maintenance becomes critical to you systems?'

'I can run as low as thirty percent before my onboard systems begin to fail and I become a danger to my crew.'

'A long time yet then?'

'Yes.'

Steven sat back down in his chair, weighing up all the possibilities that were open to him. 'Will human beings be able to do the work you require?'

'Physically they are far more capable than my own species.'

'That's good but what about intellectually?'

'To be able to perform the tasks, yes. I have ways of training a crew to do the job required of them, but whether they actually understand what they are doing, and why, is a different matter. My technology is far beyond anything Earth has.'

Steven smiled to himself, 'monkey see monkey do. Basically you find some way of showing us how to do it and we will do it'

'I understand, yes, it will be that way to start with anyway. Whether understanding comes later is a matter to be seen.'

Steven realised there was a thousand questions to ask, but he was sure most would be answered in the fullness of time. If he wanted to rescue his mother then he had better get started.

'Do you have a connection to the Internet?'

'No. I cannot access any of my signalling equipment on my own. I can only monitor signals.'

'Do you think I would be able to do it?'

'I would need some form of interface for you to be able to interact with your Internet.'

'Do you know what it is?'

'Yes, but I have been unable to access it directly.'

'What I need to get my hands on is a computer, even a laptop.'

'Why is that necessary?'

'You need a crew and you'll need the best. There are websites that can tell us who's who in the world of science and technology. The trouble is how do I get my hands on one? The second I step off this ship I will be arrested, probably for my own murder.'

'Yes you look totally different now.'

'How different, do you have some kind of mirror?'

The bulkhead in front of him shimmered and Steven found himself looking at a complete stranger. He got up and approached the strange apparition in front of him.

'Is that really me?'

'Yes that is how you should look.'

'I look totally different, and how come I have long hair but no beard?'

'I perceived your lack of facial hair meant you did not like it so I had it removed as it grew. However, I know some human males put a lot of effort into their hair and decided it would be easier for you to have a human do it in the style you wanted later.'

'You're a very smart cookie, do you know that?'

'Yes.'

Steven laughed, 'hey I look like Kurt Russell, well a young Kurt Russell anyway.'

'Who is Kurt Russell?'

'He's a movie star, a very cool movie star.'

'Is that good?'

'Oh yes that's very good. Well it would be, only trouble is even my friends won't recognise me now. Which could be a problem, the big question is how to get round it?'

Steven paced the deck. The bulkhead shimmered and became transparent.

Steven stopped and pointed, 'can they see inside?'

'No only you can see out.'

'That's good.' He suddenly had an idea and went over to inspect his pile of discarded clothing. He smiled as he found the cell phone Buzz had handed him. 'I hope the battery isn't flat.'

'I was able to send a signal to it and switch it off.'

He switched it on but there was no signal. 'Can I get a signal through your hull?'

'Yes but I will have to depolarise it. That means the rest of the equipment you brought with you will begin to transmit again.'

'Of course.'

Steven switched everything off manually and she depolarised the hull. The signal came on full strength. With a grin he quickly composed a couple of messages.

CHAPTER 18

Buzz and Brian received the messages within a few minutes of one another. Brian almost ignored it, but decided some news had to be better than no news. The shock almost made him collapse.

Colonel Howe grabbed him, 'are you all right Doc?'

The blood had drained from the scientist's face, but quickly came back. 'Yes I'm fine Colonel, give me a moment.'

He moved away and began to reread the message, 'Dad, it's Steven, don't let anyone else read this message. I'm fine and still on board the ship. As a matter of fact, I'm better than fine but that will take some explaining. There are no aliens on board either ship, will explain later. Mum's fine but ship is stranded at Saturn. Will effect rescue but first need some help. Will send text to Buzz with requirements. Love Steven.'

Brian was forced to sit down. He saw Colonel Howe hover close; a note of concern on his face, but he waved him away. The phone bleeped again. He read the message and almost ran to one of the operators.

'Patch us through to George Wells and ask him to punch in these coordinates.'

Brian wrote down the coordinates on a piece of paper for the operator. A live link to the planetary telescope was quickly achieved and the pictures began to stream through. Brian held his breath as the large telescope began to scan across the sky.

Saturn appeared as a small blob, but as the telescope locked onto the coordinates the magnification was increased. A familiar Saturn with all its rings appeared, then as the magnification was increased further, the rings themselves came into focus, and there it was, it stood out like a teardrop among the stars. A cry went up and pandemonium broke out. There was a lot of back clapping and hand shaking. A solitary tear ran down Brian's face, he quickly wiped it away.

Malcolm came over, 'how did you find it boss?'

Brian half laughed, 'A message from an old friend, he only has a small telescope, but thought he spotted something of note.'

'Christ with eyes like that we should have him on the team.'

'Yeah maybe you're right.'

There was only one man in the room who wasn't celebrating; Colonel Howe's internal alarms were already ringing, but when a frantic Buzz burst in, pale faced with feverish eyes and he and the doctor secreted themselves away to a quieter part of the room, the bells turned to klaxons.

Colonel Howe watched as the pair of men got into a quiet but excited discussion. Buzz showed him something on his mobile phone that Howe presumed was a message. The doctor frowned in confusion and shook his head, then shrugged. He followed them as they left together and went into the doctor's office. Buzz almost ran out with what looked like a portable PC in a shoulder bag.

The colonel stopped the doctor on his way out, 'hi Doc, anything wrong?'

The doctor was startled, 'Oh no, Colonel, no, everything is just fine.'

The colonel watched his retreating back as he hurried towards the control room. He didn't need his instincts to tell him the doctor was lying.

He got onto his radio, 'Buzz Anderson is on his way down with what looks like a laptop. I want him delayed at the door for at least ten minutes, then let him go.'

He received a quiet 'Roger', and then made his way out of the building by a different route. He reached his personnel Hummer, drove it round to the exit and waved over the outside guard.

After a quick word, the guard curious but without asking for a reason, locked the colonel inside the vehicle.

Inside the building, Buzz was being grilled by the indoor security man. It took Doctor Gordon's personal appearance and a radio call from Howe himself to clear him. By now Buzz was in a cold sweat. As he left the building the security guard approached him.

'Excuse me sir.'

'Oh what the hell is it now?'

'Colonel Howe sends his apologies for your delay and suggests you take his vehicle. It has full security clearance and is immune from searches.'

'Yeah, how did he know I was going somewhere?'

'Doctor Gordon told him you were on an errand for him and needed to get somewhere fast with the minimum of fuss.'

Buzz nodded it seemed plausible, 'is that it there?'

'Yes sir.'

'Are the keys in it?'

The guard took them out of his pocket and tossed them over, 'no I've got them.'

Buzz held them up, 'why would you have the keys to his personnel vehicle?'

The guard grinned, 'guy out here's always got them. We need something or the colonel needs something we just go get it, no questions asked, no hassle.'

Buzz nodded, he knew the guys in Howe's unit were all pretty tight with the colonel and could instinctively see how it would be an advantage to him for them to have a free rein. There was many times since the landing of the ships that he wished he had the same kind of clearance as the colonel. There were five checkpoints going in and out of the base and he was always stopped and searched at every one, especially on the way out.

'Won't I be stopped for being in his vehicle?'

'Nah, our guys are manning all the checkpoints and he radioed ahead.'

Buzz grinned, 'great, send him my love.'

The guard laughed and Buzz unlocked the Hummer and jumped in.

He took off at speed and true to Howe's word he was waved through every checkpoint. Buzz grinned with delight at his good fortune, but if he had had the presence of mind to check, he would have found the colonel secreted under a large piece of camouflage netting in the back of the Hummer.

When Buzz stopped and got out, the colonel gave him a few seconds to get clear before cautiously peering out from his hiding place. He saw Buzz disappear into a men's shop and frowned. His instinct told him they weren't at their final destination yet so he hid back under the netting. The next stop turned out to be a shoe shop. The mystery deepened. Howe was beginning to wonder if he was making a fool of himself when Buzz got back in. He heard him toss some bags on top of the others he already had and curse under his breath.

'I dunno what you want all this stuff for Stevie but if the money ain't back in the bank by Thursday, I'm gonna end up in the kennels with Rex.'

Howe's heart skipped a beat; he was on the right track. There was a delay as Buzz punched in a message into the cell phone and waited for a reply. It wasn't long in coming and Buzz restarted the engine.

Howe knew they were getting close when he felt the Hummer move off the road onto a dirt track. After a few miles it stopped. Buzz grabbed the bags and got out. Howe risked a peek and found Buzz standing twenty metres away, punching a message into the cell phone.

He freed himself from the netting, keeping an eye on Buzz. As a military jet screamed overhead and Howe quietly let himself out of the Hummer and crouched behind it, cocked his weapon and waited.

They didn't have to wait long. The ship appeared overhead and Howe ducked down out of sight. It hung in the air for a few seconds before finally coming to a rest broadside on. The door opened and Buzz cautiously approached. Unseen by him, Howe left the safety of the vehicle and silently crept up behind Buzz.

Buzz had never been allowed this near the craft before and broke out into a cold sweat, but his best friend was somewhere inside, so he took a deep breath and strode up the ramp. As he reached the top, Howe made his move.

Buzz stepped inside and shielded his eyes from the glare, 'Stevie, you here?'

He cried out in alarm as Howe crashed into his back, 'stay down Buzz,' he growled, his combat senses on full alert, but he could see no more than Buzz.

He froze when he felt cold steel on the back of his neck, 'Colonel Howe isn't it, why don't you get down and stay down. You OK Buzz?'

Buzz rolled over onto his back and shielded his eyes, 'yeah I think so, who the hell are you?'

Stevie never got the chance to reply, Howe spun quickly trying to bring up his weapon but the butt of an MP5 knocked him cold and he fell on top of Buzz.

'Jeez!' He exclaimed, trying to get out from under Colonel Howe.

Steven spoke to the ship, 'OK, turn the lights down and take us back to the institute.'

Buzz blinked rapidly and his eyes swam into focus. He found a stranger stood before him with an MP5 cradled in his arms and grinning like a Cheshire cat, he frowned. 'Who the hell are you, where's Stevie?'

Howe began to stir and the stranger knelt by the figure and stripped him of his weapons. Using Howe's own belt, he secured Howe's hands behind him.

'Can't you guess, Buzz?'

Buzz shook his head although the man did seem familiar.

Steven finished trussing up the colonel, 'Give me a hand and I'll tell you all about it.'

They dragged the colonel unceremoniously back to the bridge. By the time they got there the colonel was fully conscious. Steven propped him against a console.

Howe looked up, 'Who the hell are you?'

Buzz tapped him with his foot, 'shut up, that's my question.'

Steven grinned, 'it's me Buzz, Stevie.'

'You're not Stevie,' his hand began to slip towards his pistol.

A hint of sadness came into Steven's eyes, 'remember I was going to teach all about space-time distortion, right before the accident?'

Buzz's hand stopped, 'yeah.'

'Well now's the time buddy.'

A tear sprang into Buzz's eye, 'jeez, is it really you man?'

'Yeah it's really me.'

'What the hell happened to you?'

'It fixed me.'

'What the aliens?'

'There are no aliens Buzz, it was the ship that did it. It fixed me.'

Tears began to run freely down Buzz's face, 'you mean you can remember everything now?'

'Everything.'

Buzz grabbed up his friend in a bear hug, then they danced round laughing and crying together. 'Hey do you realise you look like Kurt Russell?'

'Yeah great init.' They burst out in a fresh chorus of laughing.

Howe groaned, 'I'm so happy for you both.'

It stopped them. Wiping the tears from his eyes, Steven stood over Howe, 'so what am I to do with you colonel?'

'Well if you're really Steven Gordon and can prove it to my satisfaction, then you have nothing to fear from me. I would advise you to let me go now though.'

Steven nodded, 'really and just how am I supposed to do that?'

'DNA test should do it.'

'I see, so I should just walk off the ship and put myself back into the hands of your president, until such a time as I can prove who I am?'

Howe frowned, 'he's your president too.'

Steven squatted down beside him shaking his head sadly, 'I'm afraid you've got your wires crossed there Colonel. I was brought up in America yes, but I was born in the Highlands of Scotland. I have a British passport not an American one. My parents are here on a work permit, they never applied for citizenship.'

A shadow of alarm flitted across his eyes, 'why not?'

'You may believe America to be the be all and end all, of civilisation Colonel, but my parents certainly don't. They still have a home in the Highlands they intend to retire to when their working lives end.'

A flicker of anger crossed the colonel's face, 'so after all Americas done for them, they're just going to take the money and run?'

Steven burst out laughing, 'that's a good one colonel. Maybe if they had stayed at home they would be well-off now. After I had my accident I would have been cared for on the National Health, but not here; most of their life savings went on keeping me alive. The medical bills were enormous. Coming from a society where medical insurance is almost unknown, they thought they had been given adequate cover for any eventuality. Unfortunately that wasn't the case.

Oh and consider this; my parents are the top people in their field. They have helped develop technologies that have made many companies in America billions. Technology that has not only benefitted America but the whole world. I believe they have come away by far the poorer partners, so don't tell me how much we owe to America.

My parents were really made to feel a part of the team when the ships arrived weren't they?' Howe's head dropped. 'Yes you noticed it to didn't you? It was alright as long as they were inventing the technology for your country, but as soon as something really important came along they were shoved to the back of the queue and a bunch of fools with only half of their intellect were brought in to take over.'

Howe's head came up, 'you're right, I saw what they did to them but these ships landed on American soil and now belong to the United States of America.'

'Says who?'

'The president.'

'Yes of course, God incarnate himself. I'll let you into a little secret Colonel. You've seen this metal plate I have on my hand, yes?'

'I see it.'

'Well you haven't seen this one yet.' Stevie swept back the hair from behind his left ear to reveal another shimmering plate. 'This is a neural implant only given to the captains, and there can only be one captain. The ship will only respond to my orders now and there are only two ways I can be separated from this ship.

The first is on the ship's home planet, by their surgeons and advanced medical techniques. The second is by death. So you will appreciate the fact that I have no intentions of putting myself in the hands of the president, because I have no doubts that he would have me killed to put in one of his lackeys, like Sales, and steal all the technology these ships have to offer for the States.'

Howe couldn't find any errors in the man's argument, but he had one more shot to fire, 'you still had no right to take over this ship.'

Steven shook his head sadly, 'you still don't understand do you. I didn't take over the ship, the ship took over me. I was given no choice in the matter Colonel, not that I would change anything, but that isn't the point. It would seem you need a certain level of awareness to link directly with the ships. Of all the people who have been on them since they got here so far, I have been the only one to have that level of awareness.'

'Excuse me for being blunt but, but before this ship got its hands on you, you were the thickest person here.'

Buzz took a threatening step forward, but a grinning Steven held him back with the wave of a hand, 'of course you're right, but what you may not realise is that I was a child genius, a protégé. After my accident my brain rerouted most of my systems, for want of a better word, and utilised parts of my brain that normally lie dormant.'

Howe got the whole picture in an instant, 'so it wouldn't matter who the president chose to be captain of this ship he wouldn't be compatible.'

'Very doubtful and if I was killed to do it the ships would simply leave.'

'For good.'

'Yes, they come from a non-violent society where murder is unknown. They would rather die than be subjected to that level of violence.'

'You mean like they're alive?'

'Not in a way that we would understand but yes, very much so.'

'So what are they doing here?'

'That's a long story Colonel and I don't know it all myself yet. To simplify things, both crews were subjected to some form of radiation that killed them all off. The ships couldn't go home so they came looking for new crews. This is the first planet they came to that was inhabited.'

'Do they still want to go home, is that there main goal?'

'No Colonel, they serve their crew; they live for their crew. They were just lonely.'

'They must be very disappointed with Earth coming from a non-violent society.'

'They believe our hearts are in the right place Colonel.'

Steven stood up and addressed his friend, 'so how about it Buzz, you wanna join up?'

'What's the pay like?'

'Crap, there ain't none.'

He burst out laughing and slapped Steven on the shoulder, 'sounds good to me, where do I sign?'

'Right over here.'

Steven guided him over to the back wall, 'shove your hand in there.'

Buzz squinted, 'in where?'

'I'm a bloody idiot,' Steven took his hand and guided it into a recess that only he could see.

There was a snap and Buzz jumped back with a yowl, 'what the hell was that?'

Steven laughed, 'one of these,' he showed him the implant on his hand again.

Buzz held his hand up to his face, 'well cool, stings like a son of a bitch though.' Suddenly his face paled and he staggered.

Steven caught him just as he collapsed, 'whoa buddy, you OK?'

'Feel dizzy, and sick.'

'Sorry about that, I didn't know. I was unconscious when it was done. Close your eyes for a few minutes, I'm told that will help.'

Buzz did as he was bid while Steven held onto him. Colonel Howe watched on with unveiled curiosity. 'Ok beginning to feel a little better now.'

'Open your eyes.'

Buzz did and blinked, his eyes flew wide in wonder, 'jeez! Where the hell did all this come from?'

'It's been here all the time, we just couldn't see it.'

Buzz got up and began wandering around, 'wow these are beautiful, what are they?'

Colonel Howe's patience finally ran out, 'what's what?'

Steven grinned, 'they're star maps Buzz. I'm sorry you can't see them Colonel. The implant on our hands injects another implant into the bloodstream that attaches itself to the optic nerve.

The reason you can't see anything in here is because of a certain type of light given out by the ship that reflects off every surface. It's a security device. The implant filters out that light. This room is actually rich in decoration, much of it star charts. Every console is covered in touch pads you can't see.'

'Damn effective security device. How come no one accidentally pushed a button?'

'Without a captain they become inactive.'

'So all you have to do to cripple the ship is kill its captain.'

Steven seemed to listen to something for a moment, 'I have been assured it doesn't quite work like that Colonel.'

Buzz was looking about him wildly, 'who was that Stevie?'

'That was the ship, Buzz.'

'No shitting, I can hear it too.'

'It can talk to each member of the crew individually or collectively.'

'Well cool, eh hello ship.' Buzz's face lit up in a grin as it answered him, 'what's your name?' His face fell a little and he looked at Steven, 'there's no way in hell am I going to try and pronounce that.'

Steven laughed, 'me neither, but that's her name.'

Howe struggled to his feet, his frustration growing, 'hey can I get one of those?'

Steven regarded him somewhat coldly, 'I don't think so Colonel. Once you're implanted you have to become a member of the crew. Your loyalties still lie with your president and your country. I can't fault you for that Colonel, but if he told you to kill me, you would.'

'Damn it man, I was the first man on board one of these ships and I've protected your mother and father throughout this whole thing. If Sales had been able to get his own way, you and your whole family would have been rotting somewhere in the Everglades.

I stopped that happening. I convinced my superiors it would be a serious error of judgement to have any of you removed. So if it wasn't for me you wouldn't be here now.'

Steven paced the deck for a few minutes in contemplation, 'I hear what you're saying Colonel, but how do I know you're telling the truth?'

Howe shook his head in dismay, but rescue came from a different quarter. Buzz stepped forward in his defence, 'I think he's telling the truth Stevie. Your mum mentioned he and his boys were looking out for them, saved your father from doing something real silly.'

Stevie looked from one to the other. Then he turned Howe around and loosened the belt. It fell free. The Colonel walked around waving the circulation back into his hands. He regarded Steven with a curious look, 'that was easier than I thought it would be.'

Steven shrugged, 'I trust my own instincts Colonel, but more than that I trust Buzz. If he thinks enough of you to stand up and defend you, then that's good enough for me.'

The colonel nodded, 'trust starts with a single step.'

'Just remember who took that first step.'

'I will, so do I get one of those gizmos?'

'Are you your own man Colonel, do you pick your own missions?'

The colonel shifted uncomfortably realising exactly where Steven was coming from, 'no I don't.'

'I'll make a deal with you Colonel, if you get permission to become a full time member of this crew from your government you'll get one of these gizmos. If they don't and you still want to join me, then if you resign I would still be delighted to take you on. I'll make you Chief of Security, but you're still going to have to go out there first and find out what you're doing.'

'I have your word on that?'

'I'll do better than that; I'll give you my hand on it.'

They shook hands and the colonel picked up his weapon, 'I'll be back – pay or no pay, that job's mine.'

The colonel made his way off the ship leaving the two friends alone. Buzz wasn't looking very happy about something; Steven had a good idea what it was.

'Come on Buzz, out with it.'

'If he's Chief of Security, what am I going to do?'

Steven grinned, 'what do you want to do?'

A sceptical look crossed his eyes, 'question is Stevie, what can I do? I'm no scientist or engineer and those are the type of people you're going to want.'

'Is that right?'

'Well yeah, of course.'

'What makes you think that Buzz?'

'Common sense.'

'What else am I going to need?'

'Food, supplies, a secure base to work from. You're going to have to declare some kind of new space program and get the funding to back you. I have a funny feeling you could man this thing a hundred times over and not pay anyone a dime but they still can't eat fresh air. So you're going to need backing.'

'Well since you've managed to work all that out on your own what does that make you?'

Buzz grunted, 'quarter master.'

'No you daft shit, my right hand man, my number two.'

'I'm no scientist Stevie.'

'That would be a waste of a good scientist Buzz. I mean what scientist in his right mind would want to be running round making sure everything's ticking like clockwork, worrying where the next meal's coming from, when there's a whole universe out there to explore.

Star systems to navigate and map, new complicated mathematics to master...Christ, are any of us going to have the time?'

A large grin began to slowly spread across Buzz's face, 'you're really back aren't you. It always amazed me how you could make a big illiterate lump like me feel good about himself.'

'Hey I ain't doing you any favours buddy, once we get this ship fully manned, you're going to have your hands full. It ain't going to be an easy ride.'

'Did I ask for one?'

'Have you ever?'

'Nope, so what's your first order Captain?'

'Hey, Captain in front of the hired help, but when were alone like this, you can call me Stevie.'

The friends burst out laughing, like they would never stop.

CHAPTER 19

Colonel Howe watched the ramp raise behind him and the door close. It was invisible now and no matter how hard he looked he couldn't see the seams. He walked towards the main building with a strange sense of loss. Instinctively he raised a hand and stroked the underbelly of the large ship. It didn't shock him or move away, and he was strangely relieved.

Howe could see men staring at him from the building but his good friend Beaver was the only one who dared approach. Beaver ran up, his face full of concern, but when he saw the livid bruise appearing on the side of Howe's face his turned an angry red, 'who the hell did that boss, you OK?'

The colonel slapped Beaver on his massive shoulders, 'Chill Beaver, I burst in on a private party and got away a damn site better off than I should have.'

Beaver still didn't look very happy about it, 'what the hell's going on, how did you get on board that thing?'

'It's a long story man, I need to see Doctor Gordon, come with me and I'll explain everything then. When I'm done there I will probably be summoned by the Whitehouse, but before that I want to see you and the men alone. Give out the order and get them somewhere quiet.'

'Right boss no problem.'

Brian was waiting for him and they went into an office. Beaver shooed everyone else out. The colonel quickly explained to the distraught father what had happened to his son.

Brian looked frightened, 'are you sure it's really my son Colonel?'

Howe shrugged helplessly, 'I'm sorry doc, I just never knew him well enough to make that judgement, but if it's any help Buzz seems pretty sure.'

Brian nodded, 'Buzz and Steven have been friends since childhood, if anyone would know Steven it would be him. So that's why he wanted new clothes and shoes. It makes sense, but is it medically possible?'

Howe raised an eyebrow, 'you're asking me that?'

Brian suddenly burst out laughing, 'I'm sorry Colonel, I know I should be asking top surgeons or someone like that but I'll be honest, they wouldn't be able to answer me either.'

'Why don't you just give him a call and find out for yourself.'

Brian nodded, 'now the secret's out I suppose he wouldn't mind and I'm going to have to sooner or later.'

'I prefer sooner myself Doc.'

'Thanks for coming to me first Colonel, I appreciate that.'

Howe shrugged, 'don't sweat it Doc, but I had better go and brief the general, the shit's just about to hit the fan.'

The colonel made for the door Beaver opened for him but Brian had one more thing to say, 'Colonel.'

He turned, 'yes Doc.'

'I would just like to apologise to you for my behaviour towards you the past few days. It was appalling and unwarranted.'

'No it wasn't Doc; you were up at the sharp end in a personal situation the likes of which I've never dealt with before, and you still held it together. I was the one responsible for what happened to your son. If I had been in your shoes, I probably would have shot me, or something equally as nasty. You did neither and you have the courage to do one and the political clout to do the other. I will always admire you for that Doc. I'll see you around.'

'Promise?'

Howe grinned, 'that's a promise.'

General Archibald wasn't in a very good mood, 'what the hell do you mean by getting one of your goons to keep me out of that office, Colonel? They aren't members of your own private army.'

'I know sir I'm sorry. I had personal information concerning the doctor's son, I just wanted him to hear it first.'

The general took a deep breath, 'I want a full report now.'

The general very quickly calmed down as the story began to unfold. Howe omitted nothing. One of Sales's associates began shouting the odds at one time but the general told him to can it. No sooner had the colonel finished than they rushed out to phone Washington, leaving only the military men in the room.

The general sat back with a disbelieving look on his face, 'somebody pinch me.'

Howe grinned, 'I know how you feel sir, and I was there.'

He sat forward again, 'so what do you think of this ... new Gordon?'

'He won't take any shit sir, not from anybody and especially the president. I think he somehow holds him responsible for Sales's actions. Steven Gordon made it quite clear, to me anyway, that if the president tries to pull any funny stuff, we will never see that ship again or benefit from anything it brings.'

'Do you think the president is responsible for Sales's actions, Colonel, and be blunt?'

'Yes sir.'

'I will be as blunt Colonel: I think you're right. That whole Sales episode left a bad taste in my mouth. It could be the military will be left to clean up after those damn politicians again. This is too important to be pissed up the wall by them, do you understand where I'm coming from Colonel?'

'Yes sir and I have already begun to take steps to make sure that doesn't happen.'

'Good man, I'll do what I can at my end. I have no doubt you will be called to Washington, so play it cool there son.'

'I will sir, thank you.'

'One more thing, you were right to tell the doctor first. Dismissed.'

Back in the operations room, contact had been made with the ship. Brian stood in front of a computer console staring at his son.

'Tell me Steven, what did we give you for your sixth birthday?'

The stranger grinned, 'a yellow slide rule with a picture of Donald Duck on it.'

Brian shook his head in wonder, 'it is you, isn't it?'

'Yeah,' Steven twirled, 'what do you think of the new bod Dad?'

Brian laughed aloud, 'always said you'd turn out looking like me.'

There was a round of nervous laughter in the control room, almost all of them had known Steven and each was fighting with their own beliefs.

'Tell me son, how's your mother holding out; are you in contact with the other ship?'

'The ship, yes, its passengers, no. Mum's OK for the moment, but she and everyone else apart from Sales is trapped on the Bridge. The ship locked it down when it feared Sales was going to go on the rampage with his gun. They have plenty of water for the moment but the food the ship is providing for them is unsuitable and they are finding it hard to digest.'

'Tastes like bloody grass,' Buzz shouted, and appeared over Steven's shoulder holding a small green cube.

Steven laughed, 'actually I think it is grass, or at least a type of alien grass. I'm beginning to get the impression the race that built these craft were herbivores. The previous captain left a message and the ship is at the moment translating it into all Earth's languages. It will let us see it then.

As for the others, Sales has gone mad and is a serious threat to anyone attempting a rescue, and this ship isn't willing to take the risk with so few crew. Sales and his associates managed to disable the ship's main drive, although it did cost one of them his life. The coupling they removed has been completely destroyed but there are spares on board.

The fitting of the spare part would only take a few minutes, but again the problem here is Sales. He holds sway over that part of the ship. So we're going to have to come up with something to stop him, but first I need a crew.'

'How are you going to go about that?'

'The ship has given me a list of the type of skilled people it needs to run it and the minimum it will need to affect a rescue. I'm running a search program to find those people now.'

'Can't you man it with people from the institute?'

'There's nothing I would like better Father, but the ship says no. It insists on an international crew that represents Earth as a whole. That will take a little longer to achieve. It is refusing to allow the technology it possesses to fall into the hands of one major power.'

Brian grinned, 'I'm beginning to like your ship already.'

However, someone certainly didn't, Brian was roughly pushed aside by one of the president's men, 'you will do nothing of the sort. By presidential decree I order you to surrender that ship immediately.'

'Get lost, I'll catch you later Dad.'

'By for now son.'

There were more than a few muffled chuckles in the room. The president's man was livid with rage, he turned to Brian, 'you will get your son back on the line immediately, and order him to relinquish that ship to the United States of America.'

'Why should I?'

'Because it's a direct order from the president.'

'And?' An amused Brian thought the man was going to explode.

He moved forward threateningly, 'I can have you both arrested as traitors.'

However Brian wasn't in the mood to be threatened, his eyes darkened, 'let me give you a little piece of advice son. I'm not an American citizen, I'm British, and I don't give a shit what your president wants or doesn't want. The worst you can do to me is to deport me. Just say the word,' he pointed to the screen where the ship barely rested on the ground. 'I'm sure I could get a lift and be home in five minutes. I'll tell you something else, if you do try anything I'm sure my own government would be delighted to take this project on.'

The president's man strode off spluttering impotently. Colonel Howe had been watching from the sidelines and wasn't amused. He made his way to where his men were waiting. Twenty minutes later they left the room with an air of urgency. While Howe made his way to a chopper, his men went to acquire some serious firepower.

CHAPTER 20

The president leaned across his desk, eyes beginning to bulge, 'I want him dead Colonel, do you understand?'

Colonel Howe's face was deadpan, 'but what if he wasn't lying sir and we can't find anyone to replace him and the ship takes off looking for another civilised planet?'

'It's a ruse to gain control of the ship for himself Colonel, isn't it obvious?'

'The thought had crossed my own mind sir.'

The president sat back feeling a little easier, 'he who controls that ship will wield great power Colonel. Think of the advances in technology it will bring. Think of the advances it will bring to the United States. No one individual should be allowed to control such power Colonel, it is our duty to seize that ship for the good of all mankind. Do you understand?'

'Yes sir.'

'Good, now how soon do you think it will take you to get your men ready for this mission?'

'My men should be ready by the time I get back sir; I have already given them their orders.'

The president's eyebrows flew up in surprise, 'you mean you already have a plan?'

'Yes sir.'

'Enlighten us Colonel.'

'Sir, I intend to offer the use of my team to rescue his mother and the people on board the other ship from Doctor Sales.'

The President sat forward in alarm, 'do you realise Doctor Sales is under my direct orders Colonel, and he is not to be harmed in anyway?'

'Yes, of course sir.'

The president sat back nodding, 'of course you do Colonel; I'm beginning to realise why your superiors call you the best. Your plan has my approval Colonel but I want you to seize the ship before you attempt any rescue, do you understand? That is the single most important thing.'

'Yes sir, once I have one of those gismo things on my hand, I should be able to talk directly with the ship anyway.'

'You will order it to submit to our direct commands do you understand Colonel?'

'Yes sir.'

'Good, then I won't keep you any longer.'

Dismissed, the colonel departed the oval office. The president turned to one of his black suited aids, 'as soon as he boards the ship I want you to arrest Doctor Gordon.'

'On what charge sir?'

'Spying, espionage, whatever.'

'Doctor Gordon is a respected scientist sir; do you think we can make it stick?'

'We'll keep him around for a short while, just in case anything goes wrong and then get rid of him. As for the wife, if we get her back, she should succumb to her wounds en route to the hospital.'

CHAPTER 21

When Colonel Howe returned to the centre, the massive Beaver was waiting for him, 'everything's ready sir.'

'Good, tell the men to stand by.'

He made his way back to the control room; the monitors were empty, the controllers sitting back relaxed. He found Doctor Gordon in his office. Howe closed the door behind him, 'Where's your son Doctor?'

Brian shrugged, 'your guess is as good as mine Colonel. They've been coming and going since you left.'

'I need to get a message to him as quickly as possible.'

'You can talk to them on the radio.'

'No it has to be in private.'

Brian thought for a second, 'I doubt if my mobile would work, but I'm sure a text message would reach him as soon as he's in range.'

'May I borrow it?'

'No problem Colonel.'

The colonel sent a lengthy message and waited, discussing his plans with the doctor. A message eventually came through. Howe grunted and shook his head.

Brian frowned, 'something wrong Colonel?'

'No not really, I've made a little miscalculation that's all. I'll go rectify it now. He thinks he'll be back in about an hour. I'd better go.'

'Look after them for me Colonel.'

A dark look closed over Howe's eyes. He simply nodded and left. When he reached his men, Beaver was waiting for him with a man in civilian clothes. The colonel pulled the man over to one side where no one could hear. An urgent discussion followed. Eventually the man nodded vigorously and shook the colonel's hand. Beaver thought he noticed something pass between them but wasn't quite sure.

He came back over to Beaver, 'there's been a slight change of plan.'

An hour and a half later, the large silver ship slid quietly to rest in the car park. The door opened and Howe signalled his men. Two large trucks screamed up to the side of the ship. Men jumped off and raced up the ramp, Howe in front. The trucks then reversed right up to the ramp.

Howe burst onto the bridge, weapon at the ready, 'well?'

Steven pointed to the wall and Howe went over and searched for the hole. He found it quickly; a puzzled Beaver watched on. Howe grunted in pain as the implant was snapped onto his hand.

It didn't take long for it to begin to work. His vision slowly swam into focus. He looked around him in awe for a moment. Then Steven advanced on him also carrying his weapon but it was slung. The tension in the air was almost palatable.

Steven looked down at the barrel pointed at his chest, 'Do you mind pointing that thing somewhere else?'

Seconds seemed to stretch for hours. A bead of sweat ran down the side of Buzz's face as he fingered his revolver.

Then a grin appeared on Howe's face as he shouldered his weapon, 'certainly sir any orders?'

Steven returned his grin, 'let's get those supplies aboard before anyone realises something's gone wrong.'

Everybody that could be spared ran to the ramp and began unloading boxes and crates from the trucks.

Back inside the centre a dozen men wearing black suits split up into two groups. Both groups stopped at a pre-designated position and waited. The leader checked his watch. His number two raised an eyebrow; he could only shrug. After another five minutes even he was beginning to get restless. He ordered the second team into a position where they could see the ship.

There was another terse wait until a radio message came through. He immediately realised something was wrong and ordered them to seize the ship, but they were a long way from the entrance. He and his team quickly made their way to the control room to grab Brian Gordon but Brian was nowhere to be seen.

As the men in black suits burst from the building with drawn weapons, the last boxes were thrown on board and the empty truck abandoned. They watched helplessly as the ship took off into the blue sky above.

At the same time, Colonel Howe's Hummer left the compound without being stopped. The stranger in civilian clothes that Howe had been talking to earlier, shouted into the back.

'It's OK Doc, you can come out now, we're clear!'

Brian threw off the mouldy smelling camouflage netting and just caught a glimpse of the ship as it left. He sighed, 'good luck son.'

CHAPTER 22

There were still chuckles of laughter among the men gathered on the bridge. Steven tried to hide a grin, 'welcome gentlemen, if I say so myself that was a job well done.' Laughter broke out freely.

He waited until it was finished, 'I have a proposal for you to consider. At this moment in time we are all fugitives, but hopefully that won't be for ever. Things have already been set in motion to remedy that.

Part of that remedy is the setting up of an International Space Agency. Made up from scientists and people from all countries. I have already begun negotiations with some heads of states across the globe and have received a good response.

However, the President of the United States is not among those heads of states, which makes you all deserters. They of course can't be sure of that yet, but it won't take them long to figure it out.'

The chuckles soon dried up as men began to realise the seriousness of their position. Steven went on, 'there are two alternatives open to you. Firstly you can decide to be returned to the United States, and if you do then I will return you home at your request within the next twenty-four hours.

There is another option open to you. There are baddies out there in the universe and we will at some time or another come across them. Colonel Howe has decided to join me and he has asked me to consider you all as a security force.

You would be the very first soldiers in outer space from Earth. There is a problem however, you can't join today and quit in a week's time.' Steven held up his hand and showed them the silver plate on the back of his hand, 'all you can see at the moment is a certain kind of white light. Once you have one of these on that will change rather dramatically, but these are the reason you will have to stay. This thing will plug you directly into the ship and her systems. If you take one of these then you are making a commitment. We will be exploring deep space and just can't pop back here for birthdays, Christmas or any of that kind of thing; we will be gone for years at a time. Before you take one of these be sure you know what you're doing.'

He paused for a second to ensure that he had everyone's attention. 'These things plug you into the ship in ways you cannot fathom. They are hard to remove and removing them can leave your body very vulnerable for up to a few months afterwards.'

Steven paced back and forth in front of the cold-eyed men for a second to let it sink in, 'there is an upside to all this. Once this has been attached to you, your lifespan will be doubled, maybe even tripled, we're not sure yet. You can still die, but unless you're shot in the head or in the heart or suffer overwhelming injury's, then the chances are you will make a speedy recovery.'

He could see his statement begin to sink in and smiled at the questions beginning to appear in the men's eyes; 'it's a sort of nanobot factory that does all manner of different things; most of which I don't understand myself yet. However, the longer you are attached to the ship the more reliant you will become on them, I'm talking decades here. They become part of you, part of your DNA almost; if you lose a limb they will rebuild it for you. You can have them buff out your muscles without exercising, you know, that kind of stuff – but be warned, the nanobots take their power directly from the ship, if you are away from it for any considerable period of time they will become dormant and stop working. Any immediate questions that I might be able to answer?'

To everyone's surprise it was the giant Beaver that came out with the first question, 'yeah I got one. If we piss off into space for a year, will everyone we know on Earth be dead when we get back?'

Steven smiled with appreciation at the question, 'as far as I have been able to comprehend, time will be relative regardless of the speed we travel at. Ten minutes up here will be ten minutes down on Earth.'

'Up where?' asked another.

Steven grinned and raised his voice a little, 'screen please.'

He could clearly see the shock on most of their faces, as the moons landscape appeared where the forward wall once was. 'I want you to go think about it, gentlemen. Have a chat among yourselves.'

One of the younger members of Howe's team moved closer to the screen, 'wow, this is amazing.'

Buzz walked past with a large cardboard box on his shoulder, 'yeah, but the pay's crap.'

Steven burst out laughing, 'what you got Buzz?'

'Food, and it ain't green and it ain't grass either. Question now is, how do we heat it up?'

He looked up for a second, 'right OK.'

The young soldier looked puzzled, 'who you talking to?'

'The ship.'

'It talks to you?'

'Yeah but you gotta have one of these on your hand.'

Buzz went over to a wall and shoved a can into a recess. The can seemed to dissolve in front of his eyes to be replaced with a steaming hot plateful of sausages. He repeated the process and received a plateful of stew. Two forks appeared in the hole when he removed the plate, 'thanks babe.'

He went back over to Steven, 'stew or sausages?'

Steven took the sausages, 'thanks Buzz. How are things going?'

'Not bad, I'm going to try and enlist the help of some of these dudes to help me move those stores.'

Howe moved up on Stevie's other side, he had overheard the remark, 'sure they'll help.'

Buzz nodded, 'thanks.'

'Tell me, is there something wrong with my eyes or are all these consoles shimmering.'

Steven shook his head, 'no there's nothing wrong with your eyes. The ship is surfing the net, downloading information. Making comparisons and changing things to suit human hands.'

'So why is everything shimmering?'

'It's reducing the height of the consoles. Its mother race was much taller than us.'

'How's it doing it?'

'It's all nanotechnology; tiny robots that you can't see with the naked eye. The ships full of them. That's why there's no dust and no corpses. Everything we use will be absorbed into the ship and reused.' Steven held up the fork in his hand as an example, 'she made this from the tins Buzz put in that thing over there.'

Howe shook his head in wonder, 'where did all these people come from.'

'They're scientists from all over the globe. Specialist in their chosen fields, the ship's choosing its own personnel for the most part. We've got about twenty so far, six in here the rest scattered throughout the ship.'

'You mean you have no say in who comes or stays?'

'Of course I do, but I don't really know exactly what she needs. So in the end she tells me who she wants and I say yey or nay.'

'Let me guess, you're finding them on the net.'

'It was easier than I thought. A number of websites sprung up after the ships' appearance, and many scientists registered their interest in working with the ships.'

Howe nodded his understanding, 'so where's my station?'

Steven shrugged, 'don't know.'

It was the ship that answered him, 'you may address me, Colonel Howe.'

Howe grunted in surprise, it was the first time he had heard the ship talk, 'uh, sorry.'

'I am the ship, as I am being called at the moment, among other things.'

Howe smiled, 'I'm sorry, I never realised.'

'What is to be your official designation?'

'Security Officer, I suppose. Do you have any weapons?'

'I have many different type of weapons, Colonel, although apart from their official testing none have ever been used.'

He frowned, 'why not?'

'The builders are a gentle race Colonel; crime and violence is unknown. Each ship is a family ship. They live almost exclusively in space now, although they always return to the home planet to retire.'

'They never fight?'

'I won't say never Colonel, there are reports of incidents where the builders took offensive action, but these are rare. You see, our technology is far in advance of most of the aggressive species, so we can almost always outrun them.'

'Yet here you are, your crew were all killed or died.'

'Yes it was most regrettable, and if my heart had decided to fight, they would most certainly all still be alive, but it was just not their way.'

'There is something admirable in that, eh ... ship, but it is not the human way.'

'We understood that before we made ourselves known to your people. You are primitive but you do have values that border on those of my builders.'

'That makes us more acceptable?'

'You must understand Colonel, I may be a machine but I am self-aware and have a conscience of my own. If I had been capable of firing my own weapons, and saving my crew I would have done. That they gave their lives before taking the lives of another's; even though they were of another race; it is admirable but a terrible waste and loss – foolhardy even.'

The colonel nodded solemnly; he was a man who had taken life many times in his career. 'I will make sure that never happens again. Neither will I allow anyone under my command or on board this ship to kill indiscriminately.'

'Thank you Colonel, now what would you like to see first; the hand weapons we have on board are totally unsuitable for human use but you could help me redesign them if you wish?'

'I would love to.'

'If you look to one of the walls and follow the lights I will guide you to what you would call the armoury.'

Beaver shouted at Howe's retreating back, 'where you off to Boss?'

'I'm going to the armoury to help the ship design some new weapons.'

Beavers jaw dropped, 'ah stuff this, I want in. Where's that hole?'

Laughing, Howe guided him over to the hole in the wall and shoved Beaver's hand inside. He never seemed to notice the pain but Howe had to hold him up a little as his vision began to blur.

After a few minutes orientation Beaver happily followed his friend to another part of the ship. The young soldier seemed to tire of the scenery and turned to Steven, 'do you have any space suits on board, can I go out there?'

Steven shrugged, 'I have no idea, but I would presume so.' He paused for a second then nodded. 'Yes there is son, but they won't fit us. The ship will design and build some for us later, but it's really busy just now redesigning the whole ship.'

The young man looked a little disappointed, 'yes sir of course I'm sorry.'

Steven grinned, 'don't be sorry, it wasn't like the thought hadn't crossed my mind.'

Buzz grunted, 'if you're bored you can help me.'

The shutters came down behind the young soldiers eyes, 'who are you?'

Steven interrupted, 'he's my second in command.'

The soldier seemed a little startled, 'oh, sorry I didn't realise.'

Steven could see there was going to be some conflicts between these battle hardened professionals and the rest of the crew. He was going to have to instil some form of command protocols, maybe even introduce a uniform code.

'That's because no one told you. There's no need for you to help out as you haven't decided what you're doing yet, but I would rather you were doing something to help while you are here.'

The younger man nodded, 'yeah I'll help.' He turned to Buzz, 'what do you want done?'

'Follow me.'

They left Steven alone. He took a moment to reflect on what had happened so far. As the ship learned from its access to the Internet, the process of reformation became quicker. The scientists designated to the bridge either went about their allotted tasks or stood together talking while the ship redesigned their workstations.

Steven realised very quickly he would have problems with the scientists too. Almost every one of them had heard of him when he was younger, but that was twenty years ago. It wasn't that he had any catching up to do. On the contrary, even at the age of fifteen he was years ahead of where they were now.

The trouble was, much of his work had been discounted or his theories proved wrong. He knew they weren't wrong and since coming on board he'd had some time to discuss them with the ship and had begun to realise how right he was. The real trouble was even he had only touched the threshold of the mathematics of the universe. He had a lot to learn and realised it would be hard. However, if he had an uphill battle it was going to be harder for the rest of them. He was going to have to change a whole belief system.

Then of course there was the natural resentment he was already beginning to feel. Funnily enough he didn't feel it from Howe or the soldiers he had brought with him, but Buzz had told of the strange attachment they had forged with his parents, maybe there was a link.

How was he going to forge all these people together into a single crew? Everyone seemed to have their own itinerary, and he had no doubt their own governments would soon add weight to the problem. Then of course there was the other ship.

Most of the scientists hadn't grasped the fact that the ships had a will of their own. They still believed they were working with some form of super-computer. Steven didn't, he could sense the presence of the ship in the same way he could sense another human being. That was another thing that he was going to have to get across to them, he was also beginning to feel a bit crowded.

He got up and went to a corner, knowing that everyone on the bridge was intensely aware of his presence.

'Down.' The simple command was all it took for him to disappear out of sight. He smiled at what was now his private quarters. 'Screen on.'

The breathtaking vista appeared on the bulkhead in front of him and his smile broadened farther. The ship had been busy. There was now a large bed against one wall. A workstation, an alien version of a three piece suite and coffee table that took command of the view in front of him.

He sank into what looked like a leather chair and sighed.

'Are you all right my heart? I sense you are becoming very tense.'

'I'm fine, although I'm just beginning to realise the enormity of the undertaking I've taken on.'

'Do you have any suggestions?'

'Yes I do but you're very busy just now and it will have to wait.'

'With my engines offline I can divert a lot more power to other systems, please state your request.'

'We need something to begin to bind us together, like a uniform.'

'I understand. A simple idea but necessary I think. What do you have in mind?'

Steven shrugged, 'I don't know, it's not exactly my area of expertise. Something plain though, simple and not too flash.'

Part of the screen went blank then pictures of uniforms began to appear. They must have gone through a hundred or so before she began to appreciate the tastes of the man. They very quickly made a decision on a basic uniform.

'I can have it ready for you in a few minutes. What kind of material do you want used?'

'Can you produce something close to Earth cotton?'

It took her a few seconds to search for the relevant information. 'Yes I can do that. Now what about some form of insignia?'

CHAPTER 23

When Steven re-emerged from his quarters, he felt good. A hush fell on the bridge at his appearance. He ignored it and went looking for Buzz.

He was with some of Howe's men and had just finished stacking the supplies they had sneaked on board. As they watched, the boxes began to disintegrate.

'Is that right?' asked one of the soldiers.

'Yeah, don't worry about it. Any food supplies are brought in here. The ship breaks it up and stores it. When you're hungry it will reform it for you and deliver it to whatever dispenser you're at.'

'Neat.'

'Yeah, any leftovers you put back in the dispenser.' He turned at Stevie's arrival, his eyebrows flew up, 'hey you're looking cool, where's mine?'

Steven grinned, 'in your quarters. I want to see how everyone's getting on, you coming?'

'Let me get changed first.'

'Let's go.'

They went quickly to Buzz's quarters and he put the new uniform on. Steven studied his friend for a second. It was a two-piece suit but almost looked like a one-piece. The dark blue was almost black. The collar was very small, but large enough to take a badge of rank.

They had settled on small stars. Steven bore four while Buzz had three.

'What does this make me?' he asked pointing to his collar.

'Commander.'

'Cool.'

Steven grinned; his friend looked really smart. They weren't skin tight but they accentuated their natural lines. Buzz had kept himself in trim over the years and it showed. He gave a little twirl, 'how do I look?'

Steven nodded in satisfaction, 'you look good dude.'

Buzz tried to study the patches on his left breast and shoulder, 'these are smart what do they mean?'

'It's a star map of our constellation with our Sun in the centre.'

'What's this, EISA?'

'Earth International Space Agency.'

He screwed up his face a little, 'nah, not sure I like that.'

Steven shrugged, 'we can always throw it open to the kids of the planet later in the day, let them make something up if you want?'

Buzz paused for a seconds reflection, nodding, 'yeah the kids of the planet. We have to think like that now, don't we? This whole space thing changes everything.'

Steven agreed, 'it does, yeah. We are no longer alone. And we know there are hostile forces out there. Earth's really going to have to get its shit together and fast.'

'What if all of Earth's governments get together and start telling us to do things we don't want to?'

Steven shrugged, 'then we piss off and do our own thing. It's not like they can catch us is it?'

'We have to land sometime Stevie.'

He sighed, 'I know Buzz. I only hope we can prove our worth by then or that they come up with something sensible. It's not like we can just retire. These things we have on our wrist work off some kind of power generated by the ship. The longer we're here the more dependent we will be on them for our well-being. After six months or so the nanobots run out of juice and begin floating round our bodies; more a hindrance than a help.'

'Yeah maybe one day we'll find a way round that. Either that or we start taking our families along with us for company.'

'Kinda beginning to make sense now, ain't it?'

'The ships being family ships? Yeah. So where do you want to start this inspection?'

Steven shook himself off, 'let's start with the engine room.'

They raised eyebrows as they entered the engine room. Matt McGuire was a fellow Scot stolen from the labs at NASA. He was a hands-on engineer and the best in the world at his job. He was standing with his jaw hanging loose, attempting to make sense of a diagram.

Steven felt loath to disturb him, 'how's it going Matt?'

His head swung towards them but it took a moment or two for his eyes to swing into focus, 'uh!'

'How's it going?'

'Oh right, aye, no, it isn't. I canna make neither head nor tail of any of this.'

Steven felt disappointment begin to slide, 'nothing at all?'

'Well apart from the fact that there's more than one kind of drive. Three to be precise, there's an anti-gravity drive, interplanetary and interstellar, self explanatory right?'

Both men nodded.

'Good, but how they even begin to work is beyond my understanding. There's no retros or anything like that. Manoeuvring is done automatically by the ship itself. All we have to do is tell it where to go, so in that sense it's easy enough, but understanding even the basic principles of how it works is so far beyond me, I don't really know where to start.'

'Let's start with, can you fix the other ship?'

He nodded, 'that should be easy enough. It's a simple case of removing the damaged part or replacing it. The ship's shown me how, with your permission I'd like to try it here first.'

'I don't have a problem with that, do *you* ship?'

'Because of my rapid expansion, I really need more basic materials.'

'That could be a problem, ship, we don't have any money to buy anything with.'

'There is no need to return to Earth I have located all I need in what you call the asteroid belt.'

'How long will it take you to gather what you need?'

'A few hours at most.'

'Can it wait until after we have rescued the other ship?'

'I really need those materials now.'

'OK ship, if needs must, we'll go there first, but give me another twenty minutes to finish what I'm doing, I would like to be on the bridge for this.'

'Of course my heart.'

Buzz smirked and Steven nudged him with his elbow, but McGuire wasn't quite finished with him, 'look at this will you.' He punched up a screen, 'I've had her comparing our periodic tables with her own database. So far I've found twenty new elements, ten of which she assures me don't exist on Earth.'

Steven's eyes gleamed, 'now we're really beginning to get somewhere. That's great news Matt, how are you going to handle it?'

Matt looked shocked, 'me! You want me to write a paper on it?'

'You found it didn't you?'

'I suppose so. That means I can name them as well.'

'Aren't they already named?'

He grunted, 'if you can pronounce the names of them, you're a better man than me.'

Steven laughed, 'well I'm not. Could you have a preliminary paper done within the next twenty-four hours?'

'Probably could if we had any paper. Everything's computerised, including notebooks. No discs, nothing.'

'We have a laptop reconfigured on the bridge. Tell me when you're ready and I'll have everything saved onto disc for you. It might be an idea to try and get one or two of those unknown elements to go with it. We'll see what she can come up with in the asteroid belt.'

'That would be great, thanks.'

Steven and Buzz left McGuire and followed the ship's directions to the armoury. They found Howe and Beaver cooing over what looked like something out of the Alien flick.

'How are you getting on, Colonel?'

They looked a little startled and guilty, 'fine, fine,' Howe reassured.

'What have you got there?'

Beaver interrupted with a grin, 'a real alien ass kicker.'

'Is it one of theirs?'

Howe shook his head, 'no we designed it, but the ship incorporated the workings of one of theirs into it.'

'Why did you have to redesign the whole thing?'

'Haven't you seen one of their weapons yet?'

Steven shrugged, 'never had the time.'

Howe slid back a panel to reveal what were obviously weapons, knowing they were in an armoury of course, and took out a long thin weapon. With its butt resting on the floor it reached the height of Steven's head and the point of Howe's chin. Steven nodded in understanding, 'a little unwieldy.'

Howe grinned at the understatement, 'ever so slightly, and no trigger that we could recognise either. So we came up with this. The ship then took the workings from one of their weapons and fitted it inside.'

'So this is a working model?'

Howe shrugged, 'we won't really know until we give it a try.'

'May I?'

'Knock yourself out, you're the captain.'

Steven picked it up, 'not as heavy as it looks. Why is this end of the sight flared like this?'

'In case you're wearing a space suit.'

'Of course, I never thought.'

'The ship told us about that.'

'It's quite light but it's also robust. What does it fire?'

Beaver sniffed loudly, 'green shit. So the ship says anyway.'

Howe laughed, 'we saw some type of training film, and whatever it fired looked green anyway. We really need somewhere to try it out.'

Steven shook his head with amusement, 'unfortunately it will have to wait a little while.' He handed the weapon back. 'We'll be leaving in about ten minutes, can I have you at your duty station on the bridge by then?'

'Of course, there's a couple of things I need to talk to you about.'

'Do we have time now?'

'Yes, it will only take a few seconds.'

'Fire away.'

'I've been talking to the ship and she says the defences and firing of weapons is a two-man job, so is it all right for Beaver to help me on the bridge?'

'Yes, I don't have a problem with that, what about you Buzz?'

'Nope, why split up a good team.'

'That's great, but one other thing, we're going to need a good armourer. I know a guy who just retired from the forces. No family to speak of and was nuts on science fiction. I know he would jump at the chance to come with us.'

'Security's your problem Colonel, not mine. You can pick your own team to a certain point. The first point being I expect you to present them to Buzz for an interview before I meet them. If he likes them he will come to me and then I will give them a final interview.'

'Is that necessary?'

'Buzz is an impeccable judge of character Colonel and I trust him implicitly. If he doesn't like him I know I won't.'

'OK, I don't have a problem with that, but I'll warn you now, Lewis is an unusual guy, but there's none better at what he does on the face of this planet.'

Buzz gave Howe a level gaze, 'I don't have a problem with unusual or weird Colonel, just look at some of my best friends.'

Everyone burst out laughing. Steven and Buzz made to leave but Steven hesitated for a few seconds. 'Colonel, I have assigned you and your men quarters. You'll find them the same way you found the armoury; just ask the ship. I have taken the liberty of designing new uniforms for the crew. You'll find yours in your rooms; please put them on before you come onto the bridge. If you don't like them then we'll discuss it later and see if we can come up with something you do like.'

Steven and Buzz left the two soldiers alone. Beaver sniffed again, 'so what do you think of them Boss?'

Howe nodded, 'I think I like them fine Beaver.'

Beaver nodded, 'yeah I like them too, but what about that Buzz being second in command? I would rather it was you.'

'I don't know about that Beaver. Remember Anderson runs his own business, and it's one of the top in its field.'

'A lot different from what we do Boss.'

'I'll give you that, but at least he has an inkling of what we do and what our needs are going to be. He's also used to working with these scientists and knows how to handle them. I think he might just be the man we need for the job.'

Beaver thought it over for a second, 'never thought of it like that, you could be right.'

'Let's go see what our captain's cooked up for us.'

'What's the matter with what we got on?' Beaver grunted.

'Yeah you're right, jungle colours are just the thing we need in space.'

Beaver screwed his face up in disgust, 'I hate you, do you know that?'

'My dear Beaver I revel in it.'

CHAPTER 24

'All crew to their duty stations.' Steven took his finger from the Comms button on the armrest of his chair, as his voice still seemed to echo throughout the ship.

Colonel Howe and Beaver appeared wearing their new uniforms. Steven suppressed a smile but it showed in his eyes. Then to his surprise Matt McGuire appeared in his and took up his station at the engineering console. The effect wasn't lost on the scientists on the bridge.

It had changed quite dramatically. Steven was sure that even the roof had been reduced in height, and he was right.

Buzz now had a chair next to his and a third sat to his left but it was empty. A small wall had been thrown up behind them. It reminded Steven of something but he wasn't quite sure what.

Matt turned, 'all engines ready to engage captain, I recommend interplanetary drive.'

Steven felt the adrenalin kick in, 'navigation?'

A pretty pigtailed blonde flushed, 'coordinates imputed … I think.'

Steven grinned, 'ship confirm destination.'

'We are headed for a point in the asteroid belt, time of arrival in planetary drive, fifteen Earth minutes.'

The blonde looked up blushing furiously now, 'eh! That's right sir it's all here.'

'Good work. Sensors?'

Howe wasn't going to be caught out, 'nothing within sensor range captain.'

'We have no one on the helm yet so would you do the honours Chief?'

McGuire seemed to grow two inches, 'engaging planetary drive now sir.'

The ship lifted up off the Moon's surface, reoriented itself and in a flash the Moon was left far behind. As the new crew gaped at the scenery outside, the ship allowed herself a moment's contentment. She began to feel herself come to life again. Although she could have done all these things herself, it wasn't how things were supposed to be.

For decades she had been working on an emergency program, but that's all it was. This was how it was supposed to be. Manned by a crew of living breathing beings, someone who made the decisions for her. Steven could feel her happiness radiate around him and instinctively smiled.

The fifteen minutes seemed to pass by in seconds. The bridge had filled up with spare bodies as the journey went on. All of Howe's men were there standing against the back wall.

When the ship announced they were braking, everyone leaned forward eagerly. All of a sudden they seemed to be adrift among the stars and in front of them appeared the asteroid belt in all its splendour.

All had expected to see barren chunks of rocks, but many different minerals within the asteroids shone through in a spectrum of colour. There was almost a collective sigh from the crew.

The youngest member of Howe's team was the first to respond, 'where the hell do I sign up?'

Some burst out laughing, other cheered and some even applauded lightly. Steven walked up to the transparent bulkhead somewhat in awe at the splendour of the moment. 'What was it Neil Armstrong said? One small step for man, one giant leap for mankind.'

He turned and found everyone listening, 'what we have achieved today was a giant leap for man, but what about mankind? I find it hard to believe that they will just allow us to please ourselves. I have no doubt they would far rather hide these ships away and slowly but surely pull them to pieces. They would probably use the technologies they discover to invent a new way of cooking our food.'

There were a few chuckles and he paused for a few seconds to let the truth of his words set in, 'I for one, am not going to let that happen and I have every intension of pleasing myself, for a while anyway. Eventually we will have to submit ourselves to some kind of Earth law or directive. What that directive will be shall depend on our actions in the next few months or years.

We will have to woo our own species. If there's one thing we know they will respond to its profit. We will have to show them that it will be worth their while letting us gallivant all over the galaxy. Actually thinking about it, it would probably be worth our while trying to set up some form of corporation to filter technology down to the masses, and their governments, but that will come later.

In the short term we can do one thing and that's to generate interest. A website, one dedicated to our travels. I know there are those among you who know how to set one up. We have a laptop and the ship is connected to the web at this moment. I want pictures or this asteroid belt on it.

Not only that but I want some form of mapping of it and also a list of minerals that can be extracted and processed. I'm going to get the ship to package up a few valuable minerals to take home and hopefully a few we don't know about. That should start the ball rolling anyway.

There's one more thing I would like to talk about. I have heard a lot of talk since you all got here as to the validity of my position as captain of this ship. I understand your feelings on this matter but I will make my position clear to all.

I am the Captain of this ship, while you remain on board you will take your orders from me. My second in command is Buzz Anderson. Third in command Colonel Howe and forth Chief engineer Matt McGuire. I will always be open to suggestions but my decision will be final.

Before anyone considers usurping me as captain learn this and you can ask the ship at your own convenience. It takes a certain level of conciseness to link properly with the ship, and none of you posses it. You are all aware of the links on your wrist. These all connect you to the ship at a certain level of awareness. Here is something none of you are aware of yet.'

Steven flipped back his hair, to reveal in its entirety, the plate attached to his head. This is a direct neural link to the ship, only death can break it. I am less the captain of this vessel, than part of it. The ship itself is a living sentient being, not a super computer. Treat her like one.

All this doesn't make me smarter or better than any of you, only a little different. I am sure you will all come to learn the truth of everything I have said here, but again, knowing human scepticism, it will probably take a little time.

There is only one other thing that concerns me. You all know by now how these links affect us. We will remain, as we are unchanged for maybe another fifty to a hundred years. I strongly suggest that we keep it a secret among ourselves for now.

You can imagine the clamour there would be on Earth if this news got out now. There would be nowhere safe on the whole of the planet. Every government, every individual with any kind of money would consider us fair game. They would use us like laboratory rats to try and steal what you have gained.

Hopefully if we work hard, then we can develop this technology to benefit the whole of mankind, not just a privileged few. As for those of you who have not yet joined us, remember this, the choice was yours. I will expect anyone who doesn't stay to keep to himself anything they have learned here. As long as you do that the invitation to join us will remain open. Now we have a lot to do. Thank you for listening and let's get to it.'

Steven didn't have to worry; within half an hour every man of Howe's team was wearing a bracelet, and everyone on the ship had now donned the new uniform.

The ship manoeuvred itself next to individual asteroids and a beam shot out from the hull. The beam extracted the necessary minerals and ores it needed, like a straw in a milk glass, leaving the asteroid itself intact for the most part.

Much to everyone's surprise the ship absorbed the laptop into its own systems and then upgraded it in a manner un-thought of before. Most importantly it was still compatible with all of Earth's existing technology. Very quickly replicas began to appear at every station.

The scientists on board quickly began to realise the power of Steven's intellect. Theories that had existed on Earth were very quickly proved or eradicated.

One of Howe's men proved to be an excellent signaller and took it upon himself to sort out the ships communication equipment. Steven became aware of his abilities almost as quickly as the ship did. Steven stood over him for a few minutes.

'What is it you're doing?'

'Configuring what I suppose you would call the radio to send as well as receive sir. Actually it's more like television although even that is far wide of the mark. We can talk to anyone on Earth we want to, or will very soon, with very little delay.'

'You mean from here to there or the other way about?'

'Both. She left a small transponder back on Earth so she could continue to upload the World Wide Web. However, we can use it to send signals back to Earth.'

'That's quite a way, how long is the delay?'

'Only a few seconds, but it is at its limit. If we used it to transmit to a website at this range we would probably overload it and lose our link all together.'

'Not a good idea then?'

'We need to build a bigger transponder. More to the point, we need to leave it with someone we can trust not to rip it to pieces. I'm trying to reconfigure a satellite to relay our signals through it. It will act as a buffer.

We can then send a heap of stuff down the line. The satellite will store the information for a short while before sending it on.'

'You're going to use the satellite like a reservoir so the transponder doesn't overload.'

The man grinned and nodded, 'that's right captain. If we put a bigger one on Earth we won't need to use the satellite but it will suffice for the moment, and we can also use the satellite link to download what we want onto the net avoiding the transponder all together.'

'There's a job going, do you want it?'

The grin grew wider, 'always knew my talents were wasted in the Army.'

'Let me know when we're ready to download to the net.'

'Will do.'

Steven left him to it and went to see how the Chief was doing in Engineering. He found the Scot flat on his back inside a panel talking to the ship.

'Is that it now?'

'Yes, it's only a physical line there is no need for electronic alignment.'

'Great, can I do it once more just to make sure I've got it right?'

'Of course but I think the Captain wants to talk to you.'

The chief slid himself out of the panel, 'sorry sir I didna realise you were there.'

'That's OK Chief, it wasn't important. I was just wondering how you were getting on?'

'A lot better. I think I can have that part replaced in about ten minutes now.'

'Excellent, would you be able to have a revised addition of the periodic tables ready in about an hour?'

'All done Captain, and I already have two samples ready to ship back to Earth along with a quick explanation of their properties. It should cause quite a stir.'

'That's more than I would have hoped for, thank you.'

'Thank you sir for making me Chief Engineer.'

'No need to thank me Chief, I like the way you work but more to the point so does the ship. She has already expressed admiration in your abilities.'

He looked a little struck, 'I never realised. Thanks Babe that was nice of you.'

'I sincerely hope you're talking to the ship and not me Chief.'

He laughed, 'aye she knows when I'm talking to her.'

'I'll leave you to it.'

He found Howe giving a lecture to his men on the new weapon they had developed.

'Can I have a quick word Colonel?'

'Yes Captain, does it need to be in private?'

'No not at all. Before we leave here I want to test the main weapons on board. That will involve towing a large asteroid clear of the belt. Before we fire, I want you to make sure that nothing can possibly fall back into the belt and collide with anything within it. That could cause a chain reaction with disastrous effects.'

Howe nodded, 'I understand, I've seen the film.'

'It's something I want you to bear in mind when firing weapons at anything in our part of the universe.'

'I will sir.'

'Good! By the way I've stolen one of your men; he's working with the ship to reconfigure our signals matrix to make it easier to communicate with Earth.'

'They're not just my men now sir, do with us as you will. As a matter of fact a few have stated interest trying something new.'

Steven nodded, 'I would recommend it. I have no idea how often your special skills may be needed. In an ideal world that would probably be never, but I'm not that much of an optimist. However the times between actions may be long and boring. The golden rule for the moment is quite simple gentlemen. If you see something that you think should be done then do it.

Ask the ship, she'll keep you right. If she needs to then she will inform me of what you are doing and if need be I will send you help. Please carry on.'

Steven left and went back to the bridge. He wasn't long there when the chief called on the intercom, 'can you hear me captain?'

'Yes chief loud and clear.'

'Would you like to take a guess at what we found?'

'Put it on screen.'

Part of the view disappeared and a display appeared. As Steven read the chemical symbols a slow smile began to spread across his face. There were a few gasps from the scientists.

'How much is there Chief?'

'Within a radius of ten miles there is about half a ton of gold. Fifty pounds of diamonds and about another twenty pounds of rare gemstones that we recognise and another five pounds that we don't but are considered valuable on other planets.'

'Can we grab it all?'

'She says there's no problem there and it won't take long.'

Steven turned to Buzz, 'it looks like you're going to get paid after all.'

Buzz scratched his head, 'how much is all that worth?'

'Freedom,' Steve stated simply.

It was causing quite a stir. Steven went down into his quarters and asked the ship to do a quick scan of a hundred mile radius. The results made him sit down.

She felt uncomfortable at his extended silence, 'is everything all right?'

He half smiled, 'oh yes, everything's fine. There's enough gold and gemstones here to finance a space program for the next thousand years, and that's only in a hundred mile radius. If they even suspected the wealth here back on Earth, we would have been mining it years ago.'

'They would have advanced the space program?'

'And some.'

'Will you tell them about it?'

'I'm not sure yet. If I do, we will have a mad scramble for space with countries and private companies laying claim to vast tracts of the asteroid belt. Add to that they won't be all that concerned about how they get it. They could easily send an asteroid spinning out of control back towards Earth.'

'The consequences could be disastrous.'

Steven mulled the problem over for a moment, 'did you ever do any scans of the Moon for any minerals?'

'I have a detailed map of the Moon's mineral wealth.'

'Are any of these minerals present?'

'Most of them but they are buried a little deeper. The asteroid belt is much more accessible and has a lot more of some of the rarer elements that I need.'

'Are there any gold deposits close to the surface of the Moon?'

'Yes a few, but it is an element that I rarely need.'

'Don't worry about it; I want a detailed map of their location. You see we're going to lie about where we got it.'

'A deception?'

'That's right and with the Moon being so close to Earth it will probably cause a lot of interest and a lot of court cases.'

'Why is that?'

'There's been companies selling off plots of land on the Moon for years. People have been snapping them up as curiosities, a bit of fun. Showing their friends at dinner parties photographs of their land on the Moon, it should cause quite a stir.'

'And divert attention from the more dangerous asteroid belt.'

'Exactly.'

Buzz was sitting in his seat on the bridge, he looked up as Steven approached, 'Babe's almost got everything she needs and is starting to mine the gold.'

Steven frowned, more and more of the crew were beginning to call her that, 'OK thanks Buzz. Do you know where she's putting it?'

'Yeah I think so, she showed me where the room was anyway.'

'Wanna go see?'

Buzz grinned, 'let's go.'

He followed Buzz back to an elevator that went up instead of down. It reminded Steven of how little they really knew of the ship. He shook his head in dismay; there just hadn't been time to explore as much as he'd wanted.

They entered some kind of vault. Along the back wall there were some kind of fonts with basins beneath them. The whole wall was lined with them. Into each flowed different types of minerals and everyone was continually filling and emptying, except two. One was half filled with gemstones and the other was overflowing with gold.

'Holly shit!' breathed Buzz.

Steven shook off his shock, 'where is all the rest of it going?'

The ship answered him, 'I do have storage spaces that I can fill but I normally process the ore and just add it to the walls and floors. They are becoming quite thick now, but as I use the materials then the walls will thin out. If I find enough materials then I can actually grow.'

Steven was stupefied, 'that is ingenious.'

'When I was first built I was only half the length that I am now, but as the families grew then so did I.'

'My admiration for you and your people grows every second.'

'You are my people now. You are my heart.'

'And proud to be so.'

'I have seen pictures of this material you call gold in metal bars called ingots. Is that how you would like it presented?'

'Yes please.'

Buzz knelt down and swept up a double handful of the precious dust, 'I think this should do for the first year.'

The friends laughed together. Steven went over to where the gemstones well clunking into their basin. The process fascinated him.

'How do you do this?'

There was a moment's pause, 'the nearest I can find in human terms to describe what is happening is matter transformation.'

Buzz scowled thoughtfully, 'I've heard of that somewhere.'

Steven explained, 'like on Star Trek; their transporters.'

Buzz nodded his understanding, 'I got it. So can you transport people too, Babe?'

'It has proved unwise to transport living matter. So far nothing living has survived the process.'

Steven was even more curious, 'why, what happens?'

'Everything is stopped in the process: heart, blood flow to the brain, and it has proved impossible to restart.'

'Couldn't they overcome those problems?'

'The taking of life was abhorrent to my builders, even simple life forms. The experiments were never extended.'

Steven filed the information away for another day and lifted up a large crystalline rock, half the size of an ostrich egg. Buzz knelt beside him, 'is that what I think it is?'

'I think so.'

She put them out of their misery, 'that is what humans call a diamond.'

Buzz sniffed, 'doesn't look like a real one.'

Steven grinned and held it up, 'can you cut this to resemble what we call a diamond?'

'Yes of course, put it in the recess I have lit up.'

Steven did so and they stood back. Within a few minutes the process was complete. Neither men made a move to pick it up, they found themselves blinking as the light radiated off its cut surfaces.

She was a little confused, 'is it displeasing? I can change the cut if you wish.'

'No!' both cried out simultaneously.

Steven gingerly took it in hand and held it up to the light, 'my God it's perfect.'

Buzz shook his head, 'I don't like it Stevie, men have been murdered for diamonds a fraction of that size, and it's really going to piss the South Africans off.'

Steven caught the seriousness under his friend's joke, 'what the hell are we going to do with it Buzz, it must be beyond priceless.'

'Seriously, toss it into deep space, nations have gone to war over less and who would you give it to? You won't be able to sell it.'

Steven nodded, 'you're probably right old friend, maybe I should.'

'Am I to believe they are of great value on Earth?'

Steven nodded, 'of very great value.'

'They are considered of value on other planets too. That is a nice example but nowhere near as good as what translates as a fire diamond.'

Buzz frowned, 'a what?'

'A fire diamond. They only exist in space and are much rarer. There are many different types of diamond that are not catalogued on Earth.'

'Have we got any here?'

'I believe there are three good examples of space diamonds. A rich deposit indeed.'

Steven had a question, 'so they are rare?'

'Yes, this asteroid belt is a rare find in itself. Most locations like this are richly contested by many different planets. They are a rich source of mineral wealth to those who posses them. Its location must be kept a secret from other races if you are to protect it.'

'I thought no one could get through?'

'For such a vast source of wealth and with no home planet to guard it, they would find a way.'

Buzz grunted, 'more trouble.'

Steven sighed, 'one more thing to tell everybody. In the meantime, what are we going to do about all of this?'

Buzz shrugged, 'your move.'

Steven touched the edge of his bracelet, 'Colonel Howe, could I have you and you're most trusted man at my location immediately.'

'On my way sir, how do I find you?'

'Just follow the lights, Colonel.'

Colonel Howe arrived with Beaver in tow within five minutes. They were as awe struck as Buzz and Steven had been. Steven let them take it in for a few minutes. Howe handed the massive diamond to Beaver, who held it up to the light, 'how much is this worth?'

Buzz grinned, 'dime a dozen out here.'

Beaver grinned back, 'I'll have two dozen to take away please, do you take Visa?'

'Of course sir, how would you like them wrapped?'

Howe growled, 'can it you pair, this is serious. It will cause a riot if we dump this on the markets back on Earth.'

Steven agreed, 'you're right but we're going to have to discuss what we're going to do with it later. Right now I need someone to shove these gemstones into that hole to be cut.'

The soldiers nodded, but it was Beaver who made a suggestion, 'wasn't Hammersmith's father a jeweller?'

Howe frowned, 'yeah that's right. His family was so big he was squeezed out of the business. It's your lucky day captain, I have a man who knows more about this stuff than all your scientists on this ship put together. He always maintained he was going to put away enough to start up on his own.'

'Sounds just like the man we need.'

Hammersmith's eyes shone when he regarded the bounty before him, but not from greed Steven judged.

'Do you know what to do with all this stuff?' Steven asked.

A genuine smile lit up his face, 'my family have been in the jewel trade for a thousand years sir, it's in my blood. What would you like done with it?'

Steven shrugged, 'I have no idea.'

'Then I suggest you leave me to it sir. May I make use of some of the gold?'

Steven made one of his instant decisions, 'I'll tell you what Hammersmith, as of now this is your domain, if you want it. Do with it what you will.'

'Do I want it! You have to be kidding sir, this is a dream come true. May I ask sir, who does all this officially belong to?'

Steven shrugged, 'all of us I suppose. No one came on board this ship with any thought of how much they would make in a year, but now we have funds we're going to have to think about some kind of revenue for the crew. Then of course we will need supplies. We may also develop our own corporation and that will take funds too.'

Hammersmith nodded his understanding, 'leave it to me sir. I know my way around and will come up with something you can work with.'

'Then we'll leave you to it. C'mon Colonel, let's see what kind of punch this baby packs.' The three men with him were grinning at all the way back to the bridge.

CHAPTER 25

'Target acquired, standing by to fire sir' Howe reported.

'Fire!'

A green light shot out from somewhere beneath them and hit a large asteroid they had towed out of the belt.

Beaver gave a delighted grunt, 'green shit, most excellent.' When the light disappeared there was a big hole in the asteroid, but no other damage. Beaver now grunted his disapproval, 'hey where's the bang?'

Steven looked to Howe but he shrugged helplessly. It was a bit of an anticlimax. 'Can't we do better than that?'

Howe cleared his throat, 'eh! That's a nice hole Babes but can't we blow it up or something.'

'Do you want to plant explosives on it?'

'No I want to hit it with this fancy green light of yours and blow it to smithereens. Completely destroy it.'

There was a pause, 'but this weapon is guaranteed to pierce any known defence shield. Raked across the length off a vessel it will cut it in two.'

'Yes very nice Babe, but neat holes aren't really my thing. Defence shields are like weapons, they can be improved and an intensive burst like that isn't really energy efficient is it?'

'No but that is how it has always been.'

'Well not any more Babe. I have a vast experience of blowing things up. Short sharp bursts can be far more devastating and use a lot less energy. Now can we try that again in the manner I discussed with you earlier?'

'OK I'll try.'

'Good girl.'

Steven who was half hiding a smile behind his hand gave him a small nod.

'OK here we go again, target acquired, firing now.'

The green light appeared again, but this time it was spat out in short bursts. It reminded Steven of footage of tracer fire. The green fire sprayed across the surface of the asteroid and it exploded in a dramatic fashion. There were only small glowing pieces left to arc out into space.

There was a spontaneous cheer among most of the bridge crew. Howe rubbed his hands together, 'all we need now is another three of those and we should be fine.'

The ship complained, 'that is far too much fire power.'

Steven tried to calm her a little, 'Colonel Howe is a soldier. This is his job, you must learn to trust him. Your builders weren't a violent race, but ours is. Colonel Howe is the accumulation of thousands of years of armed conflict and is the best at what he does. Is there any physical restraint to building more of these weapons, will there be any problems with power?'

'No none.' She sounded chastised and Steven felt a little upset at this, but he wasn't going to back down.

'Then please comply with Colonel Howe's wishes.'

'Yes my heart. I only have enough of the right materials to build another one, we'll have to spend longer here.'

'We are under no immediate threat, it can wait. Right now I want to go and rescue my mother and I will tolerate no further delays. Colonel Howe, I want you and your men ready within the hour and with a plan. Then I want everything rehearsed until it can be done without hesitation. Liaise with both ships for up-to-date information.'

An hour later, everyone who was to take part in the operation was gathered in a briefing room. That included all of Howe's men, including the scientist that was going to initiate the docking procedures.

He was on his feet explaining his part, in an aristocratic English accent 'normally the docking procedures have to be initiated from both ships independently. However, the other ship has agreed on a link so that I can initiate both from here at the same time. The link is a physical one almost like an umbilical cord.

This procedure will take a few minutes and will happen without anyone aboard the other ship being aware of it. The same cannot be said of the docking procedure, however. It will make some noise and vibration alerting those on board that something unusual is happening. The docking procedure itself will take between thirty seconds to a minute. I have been assured that the airlocks will be open within that minute.'

The scientist sat down and Howe took his place, suitably impressed by the professionalism of the man, 'thank you Doctor eh! I'm sorry I don't know your name yet?'

'Doctor Howard, I was an officer in the Territorial Army, if you know what that is Colonel. They put me through university. So I know a little of the knowledge you require.'

Howe grinned, 'yes I do know about the British Territorials Doctor and thank you again, that was exactly what we needed to know.' The doctor took the praise with a slight nod of the head.

Howe went on. He pressed a switch and an overview of the other ship appeared floating before him. There was a collective gasp of awe. He went on to give precise details of the assault, telling them where Sales was in relation to the other scientists.

'Remember, Sales has freedom of movement over the whole ship bar the bridge, it has been sealed off. We will assault him from two sides, no matter where he is. If he is in the engine room, team two will swing round to the other exit and once in position we will move in. If he is in one of the corridors then the ship will seal all exits until we are in position at either end, then I will give the word and move in.

He is in a bad way but that doesn't make him any less dangerous. He has a weapon and has demonstrated a willingness to use it. Captain, would you wish to say anything at this time?'

Steven came off the wall where he had been leaning, listening to the briefing, 'yes I would.' He stood beside Howe and turned to address the men.

'By all standards Sales is clinically insane. You are aware that his first act of treachery was to shoot my mother then steal all the food and water. What you may not be aware of is that when he ran out of those supplies, he then tried to consume the dead man that was in the engine room with him.'

There was a gasp of surprise and a murmur of anger. 'Quiet!' Beaver ordered. The murmuring quickly stopped and Steven went on.

'The ship was forced to dispose of his body quickly to prevent this happening. He flew into a mad rage blaming the others on board for stealing his meat for themselves. Since then he has made repeated attempts to force his way onto the bridge threatening to consume those trapped there.

You are to treat him like a mad dog. If he rolls over onto his stomach and begs forgiveness, do not relax your vigilance, not even for a second until he is firmly trussed. If he shows any sign of aggression at all then you are to kill him on the spot. I want no unnecessary risks taken nor one life here put in jeopardy. Remember, a wild animal is at its most vicious and cunning when cornered. Does anyone have a problem with these orders? If so speak up now.'

There was no dissention among the ranks. They were orders that these men knew well and understood.

Steven handed back to Howe who carried on with the briefing.

'Weapons: we will be carrying our own weapons, the ones we brought with us from Earth.' Now there was some murmuring. He couldn't help a grin, 'I know you want to try out the new ones, but as yet they are unproven. Babe suspects they might be capable of sustaining damage to the other ship's engine room, so they are a definite no-no.

The rounds from our own weapons, however, will be easily absorbed into the ship's matrix with little chance of doing any harm. We have flash bangs and tear gas grenades, but unfortunately we can't use those either. Again the ships aren't sure if they might cause damage and as they have never came across teargas they have no idea if they can purge it from the air systems easily, so we will be going in cold.

Rehearsals will start in ten minutes by the air lock. Remember one thing gentlemen, when this guy sees you coming he'll probably think you're a hamburger on the hoof. If he so much as twitches take him down hard.'

For the next few hours the crew had to put up with Howe's men dashing through the bridge and corridors. Steven was going through a list of things that needed doing with Buzz and the ship. Re-evaluating as they went, the type of people they still needed and those they had. There was also another thing to take into consideration: a captain and crew for the other ship.

Steven knew nothing would happen until the ship itself had picked a new captain. They could go on board and carry out necessary maintenance, but that is all the ship itself would allow. In the meantime, Steven thought it prudent to at least start a list of likely candidates for the crew.

One of the scientists was a computer expert and he had begun to build a website. Steven had decided to put application forms on it and hope that the right people would reply. They would for the most part be able to cross match names with university databases. That would cut away a lot of the deadwood.

Eventually, Howe called a halt to the training and reported to Steven, 'we're as ready now as we're ever going to be sir.'

'OK Colonel, you and your men have an hour to snatch something to eat and drink. Be ready at the end of that hour.'

He turned to his waiting people, 'disengage from mineral resupply. Navigation plot a course for a rendezvous with the other ship.'

The pretty blonde flushed again, 'yes sir, coordinates set. ETA will be twenty minutes with interplanetary drive.'

'Chief, prepare to engage interplanetary drive.'

'Roger.'

'OK people, let's go save some lives. Helm engage.'

'Yes sir.'

Twenty minutes later, Saturn in its full glory swam into view. It was a breathtaking sight.

Howe reported, 'I have the other ship on sensors sir.'

Haley, the ship's new navigator and helmsman, almost squealed, 'I have a visual sir.'

'Well done, we'll leave this bit to the ship shall we? Could you manoeuvre us until we are a few hundred metres from the other ship and approach from behind please. I don't want to alert anyone on board to our presence. You have forty minutes, Colonel.'

Thirty minutes later after having reviewed the situation, the colonel and his men were waiting at the airlock ready to go.

'We're ready Captain.'

'OK Colonel, standby.' Steven nodded to Howard who engaged the docking system.

CHAPTER 26

Mary Gordon was feeling weak and feverish. Andy Myers held a cup of water to her lips and she sipped at it. Her blouse front was stained green and red. None of them had escaped the vomiting the alien food had induced.

'Thank you,' she muttered. Her eyes turned back to the scene outside. What a beautiful place to die, she thought to herself, but what a bloody stupid way to go.

The hammering on the door had stopped for a while and they were all glad of the respite. She wasn't sure of what was worse; the maniac outside or the slow death from starvation. They had even discussed trying to open the door themselves and letting the madman kill them as he had threatened to do on so many occasions, but it was the thought of being eaten that had stayed their hand.

Mary knew they could live for days yet with the water that was being provided for them, but she also knew that she would be the first to die. Her feverish mind wondered if her companions would stoop to the level of the man outside.

There was one thing they were confused about and had discussed at length. What had happened to the body of the man in the engine room? Sales had accused them of stealing it from him. It was an enigma that had helped to pass many hours of waiting.

At first they had passed away the hours by continuing with their work, but it came to a stage where they just couldn't go any further. Mary's colleagues had come to her for advice and it had helped keep her alert, but now they had all fallen into a strange lethargy. It was hopeless and they were all intelligent enough to know it.

It was Mary who felt the strange vibrations first. She had lain on the floor so long; she had begun to feel a part of it.

'Did anyone feel that?' She croaked.

Andy's was the only head that had come up in response. Slowly he got up and came over, 'yeah I felt something. Maybe we brushed one of those big rocks out there. Do you think our orbit might be destabilising?'

Mary shook her head, 'I don't know ...' the ship physically shuddered and Mary cried out in alarm.

Andy who had come to admire the courage of this small woman took her hand in his. 'Don't worry Mary, if something bad happens it should be a lot quicker than the way we are dying now.'

Mary was able to force a small smile, 'thank you Andy, will you stay by me?'

'I would be honoured to.'

Hardly were the words out of his mouth when the door shot open and armed men stormed into the bridge.

'Everyone stay where they are! Don't move!' A command rapped out. They got such a shock it hadn't even entered their minds. The armed men in strange uniforms went straight through and out the other door.

A handsome man in his early thirties approached Mary and Andy. He gave Andy a strange hostile look and Andy suddenly felt very self-conscious and let her hand go.

They young man stood over Mary, the hostile look replaced by one of concern. Mary stared at the man in front of her. Although she had never seen him before he bore a strange familiarity. She realised that he strongly resembled her first cousin, but that couldn't be possible, he was much older and this man held a presence that her cousin never possessed.

He knelt down at her side. Mary began to feel herself choke up.

'Hi Mum, how are you feeling?'

She reeled as though she had been slapped, 'what! Who are you?' The man smiled and then she saw it in his eyes. Tears welled up and cascaded down over her cheeks. 'Steven ... no it can't be.'

The smile broadened as tears welled up into his eyes and it left her in no doubt. 'Oh my God it is you, how can this be?'

A tear broke free and ran down his face, 'it's a long story Mum, but it's going to have to wait for a few minutes until we've dealt with Sales and we can get you safely aboard my ship.'

'Your ship?'

Explanations would have to wait. A large figure appeared at his shoulder and it left her in no doubt as to his identity. 'Watch yourself Stevie.'

Buzz pushed past and swept her up into his large arms, 'hi Mary, I've waited a long time for this.'

'Oh Buzz you big rogue,' Mary half laughed and cried.

Grinning with tears in his eyes Buzz headed for the airlock, 'let's get you home, woman.'

Steven turned to Andy who had stood to follow, 'don't move, don't even twitch. Once we've dealt with

Sales we're going to deal with you and your partner.'
Steven headed for the engine room. Andy sat back down
again with a sudden sinking feeling.

Sales had been lying in a strange delirium. For a
moment he thought he felt something and came half to.
But then he felt the vibration of running feet and shot up
fully alert. His first thoughts were they're coming for
me, but the second was steeped in evil. Food!

He raised the weapon towards the door he thought
they were coming from. As it opened he fired. A blue
uniformed figure fell in to the engine room. In his delirium, Sales never even realised that they weren't the people
stranded with him on the ship and that they were armed.

The figure behind burst into the room and rolled
onto the floor, fire lancing from the weapon in his hand.
Sales felt something pluck at his clothing but gleefully
fired at the rolling figure.

Then he heard something behind him and turned as
four more streaks of flame fired at him. He felt no pain
only a spreading numbness. Again he fired and bodies
dived out of the way. His vision was beginning to recede,
but he could still make out his assailants at the end of a
long tunnel.

His dying brain told him there were still more behind
him and he turned again, the weapon in his hand
spitting out its last remaining rounds. He never even
knew it was empty, but he kept pulling the trigger
instinctively as a single figure approached.

It stopped in front of him for a second as though going
to talk. Then its arm came up and there was a bright
flash. Behind it came a darkness that Sales had never
known before. For a brief fraction of a second he resisted
the temptation, then slowly slid into oblivion forever.

Howe watched Sales slump to the floor. There was little blood flowing from the bullet hole he had just put in his forehead. He stood over the body for a moment to make sure there were no further signs of life.

'Area clear Captain, Sales is dead.'

'On my way, have you any casualties?'

'We might have a few, I'm just checking now.'

Steven arrived a few seconds later with concern written all over his face. Howe went straight over to him.

Steven gave Howe the quick once over, but he seemed to be intact. 'What's the butcher's bill, Colonel?'

Howe grimaced, 'three casualties, two flesh wounds and one man took a round in his side. I don't think it hit any major organs, but we won't be sure until we get an x-ray.'

Steven walked over to the body and frowned, 'he looks like a colander, what went wrong?'

Beaver walked over to stand at his side, busily wrapping a makeshift bandage around his upper arm, 'damndest thing I ever saw, Captain. He was waiting for us, firing as we came through the door. He got me first. I managed to get out of the way but then he hit the man behind me. I pumped round after round into him but it was as though he never even felt it.' Colonel Howe cleared his throat. Beaver looked up in surprise, 'oh sorry Boss; didn't mean to get carried away.'

Howe accepted the apology with a slight nod of his head, 'as Beaver was saying sir, he took round after round as though they were made of paper. I can guarantee there wasn't one of us that didn't put at least half a dozen rounds into the man, but he just wouldn't fall. Even after he ran out of ammunition he was still pulling the trigger. I had to walk up and put one in his head.'

'By the looks of him Colonel it was the kindest thing to do.'

The colonel seemed to sigh with relief. He wasn't really sure how the man would react.

'The important thing now is to see to the wounded and fix this ship. Are you fine?' he asked Beaver.

'Yes sir it's just a scratch.'

'Good, then come with me. I have a couple of men I want you to keep an eye on.'

Steven led them to where Andy Myers was sitting waiting with his companion. Steven looked down at them with cold eyes, 'these men were a part of Sales's team and were responsible for crippling this ship. I want them secured; at no time are they to be allowed to roam around our ship on their own.'

Myers was bursting with questions and angry. He stood to his full height, which was a couple inches taller than Steven, even though he didn't feel it at the time. 'Hey hold on a minute. I was obeying orders which came straight from the President of the United States, ask him, and what the hell did you mean by your ship, how did you people get here?'

'Oh I think everything will become clear soon enough, but as for your president, well I'm afraid we don't take orders from him.'

'So who do you take your orders from?'

Colonel Howe and Beaver both pointed to Steven and declared unanimously, 'him.'

Myers shook his head in confusion, 'but you're both American troops.'

Howe shook his head with a wry grin, 'we retired … early.'

Beaver burst out laughing and grabbed Myers by the shoulder, 'yeah, real early. Come with me.'

Steven stopped him, 'one second, there's something he has to do first.' He pushed the small point on his wrist pad, 'Chief, we're ready for you but before you come could you try and get your hands on something like a body bag and take it over with you.' He turned back to Beaver, 'he and his friend can parcel up their companion for transport back to Earth.'

Beaver shrugged, 'why not just pop him out the air lock.'

'I will not contaminate space with rubbish like that. Besides we're not animals. It might be hard to believe, but he may have family. It's the decent thing to do.

'Colonel Howe, take over here and oversee the repairing of the ship. I'm going to see what we can do for the wounded and try and make the people we rescued comfortable.'

'Yes sir.'

Steven left them to it and quickly made his way to the ship's med centre. The ship was full of doctors but unfortunately not medical doctors. However, one of the scientists had taken over and was working under the ship's direction.

Steven found his mother sitting up with a strange pad on her shoulder. She took his hand anxiously, 'what's been happening, Steven. How come I can't see anything but you all can?'

Steven took a deep breath and smiled, 'it's a long story Mum.'

CHAPTER 27

The Chief was able to obtain from the ship, something that at least was long enough to hold a body and could be sealed. He arrived in the engine room of the other ship knowing he was going to come across an unpleasant sight. What he didn't expect to see was a downcast Myers under guard.

His jaw dropped, 'Andy is that you?'

Myers head whipped up, a sudden surge of hope lighting his eyes, 'Jesus Christ, Matt McGuire.' The two men advanced on one another.

Matt found his voice first, 'what the hell are you doing here?'

Andy laughed, 'I was gonna ask you exactly the same thing.'

'I'm Chief Engineer on the other ship, you?'

Andy's face fell, 'I'm the guy who's being blamed for crippling this one.'

Matt's eyes became a little guarded, 'I'm sorry to hear that Andy, I could sure do with your help.'

Andy half smiled, 'it's nice to know someone still thinks kindly of me. So what the hell's going on?'

'I'll tell you once I fix this ship.'

Beaver stepped forward, 'I don't think so Chief, once these two have picked up that body they're going to be under close arrest until we get back to Earth.'

Matt frowned, 'then what?'

Beaver shrugged, 'I don't know, but I'm presuming they'll be let go. They were after all, only following Sales's orders.'

'I'll vouch for this man.'

Beaver shrugged, 'it ain't up to me Chief.'

Matt got onto his communicator, 'Captain can you hear me?'

'I can hear you Chief, what's up?'

'The man you've got under arrest, Andy Myers, he's a personal friend of mine, if you release him into my care I will personally guarantee his good conduct.'

There was a pause while Steven considered the request, 'OK Chief, but if he touches or tries to remove anything then I will throw you both out the air lock.'

'I give you my word sir.'

Andy grimaced, 'he sounds serious.'

Beaver grinned evilly, 'he's meant everything he's said so far, so I wouldn't push it, but before you do anything else, you can help shove your friend into this body bag.'

Andy's eyes went cold, 'he was no friend of mine.' He and his assistant shoved Sales's body into the bag and Beaver and Andy's assistant dragged it away.

Matt grinned, 'right let's get to work.'

Andy scratched his head, 'work on what?'

Matt laughed, 'you managed to destroy one of the drive couplings, now we're going to replace it.'

'So that's what that was?'

'Yep.'

'So how you gonna fix it if you can't see it?'

'Who said I couldn't see it? Oh God what a mess, what the hell did you do man?' Matt knelt down and looked into the section the drive coupling had occupied.

Andy got down on his knees beside him, his eyes sparkling. He could see Matt's hands move around inside the compartment but couldn't make out what he was touching. 'Jesus! You can see what you're doing, how?'

'Trade secret. There's more damage here than we thought, this will have to be repaired first. Can you hear me, ship dude.'

'Are you referring to me?' The ship replied cautiously.

Matt grinned at Andy's confused look, but ignored him, 'yeah that's right, we need to fix the points the drive coupling is attached to before we can refit a new one. Can you do it on your own or will we have to replace it.'

'I would have fixed it before now, but I do not have the proper materials.'

'Maybe we do. Babe, do have we the materials he needs?'

'Yes.'

'Can we do a direct transfer?'

'Yes, but the process has to be initiated from the command consoles on both bridges.'

'OK that's no problem at your end but what about here?'

'You will need permission from my mate. Most command functions are cut off when a captain and crew die but that is one of the few that can be accessed, and only to help fix a damaged ship.'

'Your builders are pretty smart Babe.'

'These are problems that have been encountered over thousands of your years.'

Matt nodded, 'I would imagine so. May I have your permission to initiate the transfer, ship dude.'

'I am not comfortable about having your friend near my command console. He has already caused me great distress.'

Matt gave Andy a strange look, one he knew well. 'What is it Matt?'

'He doesn't like you much, and doesn't want you near his command consoles.'

Andy shook his head in disbelief, 'he really said that to you, you can hear them?'

'Yeah of course I can, listen Andy, these ships are thousands of years more advanced than anything we got back on Earth, they are like living entities. They have feelings and you can hurt them. These ships are actually mated to one another. This is the male ship, ours is the female.'

'Can he hear me, can you hear me, eh, ship dude?'

Matt nodded, 'he can hear you.'

'Look I don't know nothing about your people or where you come from, but here if we do something wrong we apologise for it. I would just like to say I am sorry. I didn't mean to hurt you. If I had known you could be hurt I would never have touched you.' He looked to Matt who was obviously listening to the ship's reply.

Matt nodded, 'he accepts your apology; however he requests that you stay back from his command console while I'm near it. Nor does he want you to touch anything on board him again.'

Andy held up his hands in supplication, 'you have my word that I will never touch you again without your express permission.'

Matt nodded, 'OK let's go.'

Andy followed Matt through to the bridge where he initiated the transfer of materials they had already stored and told Stevie what was happening on the way.

It took about half an hour for the ship to repair itself. Matt replaced the drive coupling and they made their way back to his own ship with Andy hard on his heels. By the time Matt sat Andy down to a meal and a coffee, he had caught Andy up on their adventure so far.

Andy's eyes had taken on a determined look, 'I want to join you.'

'Ain't as easy as that Andy.'

'Come on, who's the best damned engineer you know after yourself?'

'You are.'

'So can't you put in a good word for me?'

Matt shrugged, 'I can try, but I'm not promising anything.'

'Better than nothing I suppose. So what's this captain guy like?'

Matt shook his head, 'I don't really know him yet, none of us do I suppose, except for his number two, Buzz Anderson and that Colonel Howe.'

'Yeah but do you like him?'

'Aye, I do. He seems to know what he's doing, has a special empathy with the ship, that's why it chose him as captain.'

'The ship chose him?'

'Aye so they say.'

'You said he isn't an American national either?'

'Nope, Scots like me.'

Andy grinned, 'that must really stick in the president's craw.'

'Like a Louisiana chicken bone.'

Andy laughed, 'serves the shit right.'

'You don't like the president?'

'Not really, or more to the point I don't like some of the orders he's been giving me since he took office.'

'In what way?'

'He doesn't seem to have much of a conscience. Like this job, I told them after I watched the tapes I didn't think I could do much good and they should just sit back and wait for the scientists to finish their job first.'

'They didn't listen?'

'Do they ever? All they ever want is results and they want them yesterday.'

'You should never have left us Andy.'

He shrugged, 'I was bored, looking for a little adventure. You were asked before me, why didn't you go?'

'I wasn't bored.'

Andy laughed, 'I should have known, but look at you now. You can't tell me this isn't the biggest adventure to hit mankind since we first crawled out of the ooze.'

Matt waved his coffee mug in his old friend's face, 'what did I always tell you, everything comes to he who waits.'

Andy laughed, 'you're a shit.'

'So you always told me.'

Andy took another sip of his coffee, 'God, that feels better. All we got was water and something that tasted like grass, made us all puke.'

Matt grinned, 'it was grass. Turns out the previous hosts were herbivores. The ship had thirty different varieties of alien grasses on board.'

'No wonder we puked.' A more serious look entered his eye, 'do you know where they took Mary?'

'Why, what's your interest?'

'I just want to know how she's doing. That's a proper lady that is, happily married with a kid. Didn't know she had two though, only mentioned the one to me.'

A twinkle appeared in Matt's eyes but Andy never spotted it, 'bit strange, what did her son do?'

Andy shrugged, 'a security guard at the institute; was a genius until he was fifteen. Then he took his mate's bike and ran it under a truck, almost killed him. Never mentioned this one though.'

'The captain you mean?'

'Yeah, well he called her Mum; bit strange though, was as though she never recognised him. Maybe he's the black sheep of the family. Must be a pisser being rescued by the errant son and him the new captain of an alien space ship.'

Matt couldn't take any more and burst out laughing, 'the captain isn't the errant son dimwit, he's her only son.'

'Can't be! He was only a security guard and disabled.'

'Well he isna disabled anymore. So I would watch myself around the mother if I was you.'

'Hey!' Andy protested, 'that's a proper lady, so watch your mouth you Scots git.'

Matt stood laughing, 'come on, let's go see if we can find her and get you a shower and change of clothes, you stink.'

Andy stood and clutched his stomach, 'actually do you think you could find a toilet first, one that's not four feet off the deck.'

Matt roared with laughter, 'aye, I think we have a few that's already been modified.'

Steven's voice came over the intercom, 'listen everyone. We are now heading back to the asteroid belt so the other ship can take on board essential minerals and ores. Once we are finished there, we will head back to our spot on the Moon.

It's been a long day so I would advise everyone to try and get some sleep. There will be someone on duty all night, and everyone will eventually be given shifts. If you haven't been informed yet then you aren't on watch. We have a long day ahead of us tomorrow, so good night and sleep tight.'

Steven retired to his own quarters but never went straight to bed. His mind was hungry for information and the ship had set up a small workstation for him. He sat for hours working on complicated mathematics that had never seen the light of day on Earth.

His study was interrupted by a cautious call. The ship informed him that the chief engineer wanted to see him on a private matter. This was the one part of the ship that no other member of the crew could enter without his express permission.

It was the first time any of the crew had been in his personnel quarters, and Matt tried not to stare. Andy was hard on his heels and he noticed the captain's mouth pull down a little at the corners. It didn't bode well.

Steven stood up and indicated for them to take a seat and sat in the easy chair opposite. Matt sat down but Andy had to feel around a little. Matt pulled him down.

Steven began the conversation, 'what can I do for you gentlemen?'

Matt made his pitch, 'sir I would like to sponsor Andy Myers for a position on board this ship.'

'Would you now.'

'Yes sir.'

'And exactly what position would you like to sponsor him for?'

'Assistant to the chief engineer.'

Steven could see both men were nervous but he wasn't going to make it easy on either of them. He smiled but it never reached his eyes, 'and why on Earth would I possibly want to do that?'

Matt took a deep breath, 'because he's one of the best damn engineers you'll ever meet.'

'I see. Although you assured me when you came on board that *you* were the best damn engineer on the planet.'

Matt shifted uncomfortably, 'I am sir …'

Steven sat forward aggressively cutting him off in mid sentence, 'then why the hell would I want second best?'

Andy tried to put his own case forward, 'sir if I may…?'

'No you may not. Once I have listened to my chief engineer's petition, then you may say something on your own behalf but not before. Now Chief, you were saying?'

Andy sat back with a sinking feeling in his gut; there was no way this man was going to take him on, but Matt wasn't finished, and he was growing angry, 'sir this is one of the finest men I have ever worked with. Not only is he capable of doing everything I am, he is also the best I have ever came across at backward engineering, a skill we are going to be in great need of.'

Steven sat back, 'my main concern is the morality of the man, not his skills as an engineer. He is after all an agent in industrial espionage. To whom does such a man pledge his loyalties?'

Sweat beaded on Matt's forehead, this wasn't going well at all, 'I can't answer that sir. All I can say is that he was loyal as a friend and as a friend he is the best that any man can get.'

'Do you have many friends, Chief?'

'Very few sir, I am very particular to whom I offer my friendship.'

Steven's eyes swivelled towards Andy, 'so what have you got to say for yourself MrMyers?'

Andy sat forward, 'I work for my government sir. I will admit I sometimes found the work I did as distasteful, but I carried out my duty.'

'Duty, that is a word that humanity loves to use to cover up its crimes Mr Myers, did you ever refuse to carry out that duty?'

'No sir.'

'Did you ever have to take life while on those missions?'

'On a number of occasions.'

'Innocent lives Mr. Myers?'

Andy paused before answering, 'yes sir.'

'I presume you were only doing your duty, Mr. Myers?'

Andy looked him straight in the eye, 'I'm not going to sit here and try and validate my actions; I will only say that I never took any life needlessly, and only took life when that of my own or my companions were directly threatened.'

A cold smile played across Stevens face, 'as from say … security guards?'

Matt visibly cringed, but Andy never baulked from the question, 'yes sir.'

Steven nodded, 'your orders were to procure technology from these ships, in any manner possible I presume?'

193

'That's right sir.'

'So how would I know that you weren't still on that mission, and the moment our backs were turned you would run back to your masters with as much as you could carry off?'

'It would be a waste of time; we don't even have half of the materials necessary to begin building a ship like this. They just don't exist on Earth.'

'That's true, but in time and with understanding, I'm sure you would be able to backward engineer some of the ships' systems, things that could be hugely profitable back home.'

Andy shrugged, 'possibly, but why would I want to be sitting on my butt at home when there's a whole universe out there just waiting to be explored.'

The truth of his statement shone from his eyes. Steven paused for a moment as though considering a point. 'That leaves only one thing to discuss Mr Myers, the simple fact that the ships don't really like you. You hurt one of them and they have a really long memory. Why should they trust you now?'

Andy shifted uncomfortably, 'I understand their concern and have already apologised to the other ship. He did accept my apology, but if they don't want me near them then I will understand and abide by their decision. I will also promise for the remaining time I am here not to touch any of their systems or try to take anything off the ship.'

Steven paused again before answering and Andy suddenly realised he was listening to the ships and their concerns. 'I will tell you something now Mr Myers, if we accepted you as a member of this crew, then I would expect your complete and unquestioning loyalty, to this ship, to this crew, and to me. Do you see these bracelets we wear?'

'Yes sir I have noticed but no one would tell me what they're for.'

'These are small factories; they produce nanobots which they inject into the blood stream. They perform many different functions, one of which is to place an implant on our optic nerves so we can actually see the insides of the ships. These devices regulate the behaviour of the nanobots in our blood stream. Without it they could kill us. Slowly I believe and with much pain. The ship itself supplies power to the unit to keep it functioning. After six months or so away from the ship the system will slowly wind down and become inoperative, they will wind down the nanobots putting them into a form of hibernation.

There will be only one punishment for treachery aboard this ship Mr. Myers, banishment. If you are banished I will have the unit switched off or removed not wound down. Are you beginning to get the picture Mr Myers?'

'You mean you will leave the active nanobots in my blood stream without direction.'

'That's right; they have enough power for about seven days, long enough to tear your body to pieces from the inside out. They of course can be removed, not that we have the equipment to do that yet and I can assure you even if we had I wouldn't. Do you understand?'

'Yes sir.'

'Does it dampen your enthusiasm a little?'

'Not even slightly.'

They waited for a few minutes, while the ships finished discussing the matter with Stevie. Although he never spoke a word, both men realised he was communicating with the ships directly.

Eventually his eyes focused back on Andy, 'OK Mr Myers, you're in.'

Both friends jumped up laughing and shook hands with one another.

Matt was delighted, 'welcome aboard mucker.'

'It's gonna be great working with you again Andy.' He turned to Steven and offered his hand, 'thank you sir, may I ask what swung it for me?'

Steven stood and took the offered hand, 'my mother actually. She told me how you saved her life and how you conducted yourself afterwards. That was enough for me Mr Myers; however the ships had their own concerns.'

Andy had a flash of intuition; the roasting had been a test of his moral fortitude, not his moralities. He was glad now he'd answered every question honestly.'

'Thank you again sir.'

'If I were you two, I would try and get some sleep now.'

They left Steven alone and he decided it was time he turned in too.

CHAPTER 28

It was strange waking up to the lunar landscape, but Steven got up with a cup of coffee and soaked in the scenery while he drank it. He emptied his mind for a few minutes just enjoying the solitude of the moment, but then thoughts slowly began to creep in.

She had provided him with a small toilet suite, and although she assured him there was plenty water he only took a short shower. His big surprise came when he went to shave. She had told him there was no need for razors because she had removed all the hair follicles from his face, but it somehow still came as a surprise and he found he was beginning to miss the ritual already.

He warned her not to do it to anyone else before getting their express permission. The uniform he had hung up the day before was now as fresh as the moment he had put it on. On quizzing her he found that the nanobots had been hard at work while they slept.

He spent another hour with her discussing some of the things on his mind before she announced Buzz's arrival. He met him with a grin and got him a coffee. They sat quietly for a few minutes enjoying the scenery.

Buzz put his cup down first, 'I like your quarters Stevie.'

'Yeah me too, what are yours like?'

'A little smaller, but my outside wall becomes transparent too. It's really cool.'

'Has every room got that kind of view?'

'Seems to; so what are we going to do today?'

'Try and get some kind of dialogue going with the authorities back on Earth.'

'We're gonna have bit of a job there. Have you heard the latest news from Earth?'

'No not yet.'

'The president has threatened sanctions against any nation that helps us. Colonel Howe, his men and any other American, if captured, will be tried for treason. The rest of you will be tried for crimes against the United States and there's some huge rewards being offered.'

'How much are we worth?'

'You're worth two million, the rest of us one and the capture of the ships' a billion apiece.' There was a bitter tone to his voice.

'That's a fair amount Buzz.'

'It means we probably won't be able to trust anyone. That's a lot of money Stevie.'

'Any good news?'

'Yeah the Prime Minister of Scotland told him to piss off.'

Steven laughed, 'really?'

'Yeah, seems your people are all as proud as punch of you. Trouble is the president's already threatening an embargo of all Scots goods coming into the country.'

'Not so good. Is our website ready to go online?'

'Yeah but they want us to get closer to the planet first. Less chance of the data stream being corrupted or something.'

'That's a good idea. We can sit just outside Earth's atmosphere and do it. We shouldn't have any problems there.'

'What else have you got in mind Stevie?'

'A few things, but first I want to discuss it with some of the others.'

'Like our command elements you mean?'

'Yeah.'

Buzz grinned, 'so who is our command element?'

'God knows, because I don't.'

Thirty minutes later Steven's room seemed crowded. Ideas were slung back and forth for over an hour but eventually a plan of action began to form. Another hour past before they finalised everything, but when they left everyone knew what they were going to do.

Steven went up to visit his mother. Her wounds were almost completely healed, but she wasn't in a good mood.

She scowled at him, 'what do you mean the ship won't let me join you?'

Steven grimaced, 'sorry Mum, the ship says it's a no-no.'

'Why not? I thought these ships were originally built for families.'

'Yes they were, but after what happened to the last crew, they aren't prepared to let that happen again.'

'That's not fair Steven, your father and I will both want to come.'

'I know Mum, and Dad will be as mad as you are but they're not going to let it happen.'

'I'm not mad just disappointed. What about the other ship, won't it take us on?'

'No, because they always travel in pairs, what happens to one normally happens to the other. So they're not having it.'

'That stinks Steven.'

'I know Mum but all is not lost. You'll have your day in space, both of you, I promise.'

'You're up to something Steven Gordon I know that look in your eyes.'

He smiled, 'I am but will have to explain later, right now I'm rather busy.'

'Typical.'

He laughed, 'sorry Mum I've got to go.'

She grabbed his hand, 'OK but be careful Steven.'

'I will, I promise.'

They came into a high orbit around Earth and final preparations were begun. Many of the crew took time to speak to their family on their cell phones. The ship was able to collect their signals and bounce them off a satellite. It was a good test for what they had in mind.

Colonel Howe came off his cell phone and approached Steven.

'I'm afraid I've got some bad news. They've got your father.'

Steven groaned, 'what the hell happened?'

'My man went to deliver that parcel and when he returned they were already at the house. He saw them bundle him into a van and take him away.'

'Any idea where, can we get him out?'

'My man followed them. We know where he is but it's heavily defended. Our best bet would be a night assault.'

Steven shook his head, 'we really don't have the manpower for an assault against a heavily armed force.'

'It's what we do sir and we're good at it.'

'We have also three men recovering from their wounds from our last little battle. I think my father will be safe for now. Can your man keep an eye on things; make sure he isn't moved to a different location?'

'He's doing that now, but I doubt if he will be moved. He's in one of the country's maximum security military prisons.'

'And you want to try and bust in *there*?'

Howe grinned, 'the great thing about prisons is they're great at stopping people from getting out.'

'On this occasion Colonel I would place a bet on them waiting just for that. I smell a trap, a big fat one, and my father's the bait.'

Howe frowned, 'I have to agree with you sir?'

'It's a giant set up. Babe bring us to a position directly over where they're holding my father.'

The ship began to change orbit. Howe was confused, 'how does she know where he is?'

'Your communications come through her systems Colonel, if she is aware of them then so am I.'

Howe nodded realising the sense of his words, but he would remember that in the future. Buzz was grinning like a Cheshire cat. Steven noticed, 'what are you grinning at?'

'You just called her Babe.'

Steven opened his mouth to answer but changed his mind with a shake of his head.

'We are over the spot my heart.'

'Can you zoom in on the whole complex?'

'Of course, at this range I can focus on a single point of dust.'

Steven found himself smiling, 'that won't be necessary, just the complex itself.' It appeared on screen. 'Do you have any way of pinpointing the people inside?'

'Of course.'

She took them through a series of different views, clearly showing the people inside the prison. They played around with the images for ten minutes.

Howe came to the first conclusion, 'everything looks normal. Prisoners are where they should be, guards as well.'

Steven shook his head, 'I'm still not happy. Babe have you conducted a chemical analysis on the weapons the colonel and his men carry?'

'Yes, I have carried out an analysis on every Earth weapon I have seen to date.'

'Excellent, can you pinpoint any weapons within the complex?'

'Yes.'

The results came up on the screen and there was a spontaneous groan of disappointment. There were weapons in almost every cell.

Howe cursed, 'damn it, it is a bloody trap, those aren't prisoners in the cells.'

Steven shook his head, 'don't worry about it Colonel, at least you were prepared to try. Babe, can you isolate a single form that is on its own with no weapons?'

'Yes my heart.'

There were half a dozen, but most seemed to be in administrative buildings. There was one form however, deep within the cell complex stretched out on a bed.

Steven felt his heart strings pull and knew instinctively that it was his father.

'I want you to keep an eye on that spot Babe, record that person's life signature. If they move him I want to know about it.'

'Yes my heart.'

He turned to the colonel, 'maybe we'll get lucky and they'll move him.'

Howe shook his head sadly, 'I doubt it. They have him exactly where they want him.'

'You're right, but maybe we can force their hand at a later date.'

Howe nodded, 'it would be worth considering. Maybe if we snatched someone close to the president he would be willing to make an exchange.'

Steven regarded the colonel for a moment, 'you know Colonel, you can be a nasty piece of work at times.'

He grinned in reply, 'what can I say sir, my country taught me well.'

Steven laughed, 'OK let's get back to it. Are we ready to launch the website?'

Howe's ex-signaller looked round, 'another ten minutes sir.' He and the scientist, who had been preparing it, were still hard at it.

'OK, don't rush it though I want everything to work first time.'

The scientist, Barns, looked up, 'it will Captain, we're just making sure we aren't going to overload anything.'

Steven smiled and nodded. He was amazed by how fast the humans were taking to this strange alien craft, but then he told himself, adaptation had always been one of man's stronger points. He was surprised even more by the way the fighting men had taken on other roles, filling gaps the scientists seemed hesitant to take on.

The scientists seemed more afraid of failure, while the soldiers dived in headfirst regardless. He smiled to himself; maybe a little of it would rub off on the scientists.

A sharp sound vibrated through the ship making them all jump, 'what the hell is that?' Steven asked looking around the bridge.

Only the ship had an answer, 'some form of missile has been launched from the planet below. I believe it has the capability to reach us.'

'Put it on screen, do you know what kind of missile it is?'

'I have not found a direct match in my memory.'

A missile appeared on screen, growing larger by the second.

Colonel Howe recognised it, 'I know what it is sir. It's a new development. It's supposed to be used against incoming asteroids or meteors. They kept it secret in case it started a panic among other nations.'

'Have you any idea of its range or yield?'

'I think it's supposed to engage targets up to three thousand miles outside the Earth's atmosphere, and it has a thousand times the yield of the Hiroshima bomb.'

'Babe, can you withstand that sort of blast?'

'I think so but it would not be wise.'

'Pull us back two thousand miles. Colonel as soon as it reaches a distance of a thousand miles outside the atmosphere, I want you to take it out.'

'Yes sir.'

'I want the blast monitored. If we can destroy these things after they leave the Earth's atmosphere then all the better.'

The missile arced up out of Earth's atmosphere and made for their position like an arrow from a bow. Tension mounted as Beaver counted down the distance.

'Thirteen Hundred ... twelve ... eleven, one thousand miles Captain.'

'Fire.'

A single beam of green light shot out and enveloped the approaching missile. There was a blinding flash of light and it was gone.

'Analysis.'

It was the blonde, Haley, that answered, 'details still coming in sir,' she was shaking her head, 'it looks like we would have caused a disaster if we had detonated it within Earth's atmosphere sir. The whole area is now full of radiation. I think it would have contaminated an area thousands of miles square. '

Howe growled, 'he's trying to keep us away from Earth, forcing us back out into space.'

Steven smiled slowly, 'don't worry about it Colonel, Babe could you go to stealth mode please.'

'Yes my heart.'

'Take us back into orbit and prepare to download our website.'

Mary Gordon appeared, with one of Howe's men helping her, 'What's happening Steven, what was that noise?'

Steven stood, 'should you be up Mum.'

'Oh I'm fine, just a little weak. I don't know what was used on be but I've only got a bruise now.'

Steven guided her down into the chair next to him, 'it's all nanotechnology, Mum, it repairs from the inside out.'

'It's fantastic, what else can it cure?'

'I have no idea, we really need to get our hands on a medical doctor.'

'So what's happening?'

'The American President just tried to hit us with an asteroid buster. We destroyed it a thousand miles outside the atmosphere.'

'That wasn't very nice of him.'

Steven grinned, 'no it wasn't, but we're going back in stealth mode. They won't be able to see us or detect us on radar.'

Haley guided them round the new radiation zone and they were back in Earth's orbit in a few seconds. 'Oh! That was quick,' Mary exclaimed.

Steven grinned, 'you get used to it.'

'It's a beautiful view.'

'You want to see our spot on the Moon; I'm going to have a small base built there.'

'You can do that?'

He nodded, 'bigger nanobots. The ship will build and program them. Then we just leave them. They will build themselves a small factory first. Once they have completed that task they will carry out the task they have been ordered to do. Their only limitation is the materials they have to work with.'

'Fascinating.' Then she had a flash of intuition, 'can they build ships too?'

Steven nodded grinning, 'that's how these ships were built. You can build a small two-man craft just for you and Dad. Then you can take a second honeymoon around Pluto's moons.'

A small tear escaped her eye, 'you're serious aren't you?'

'I learned a long time ago not to lie to you Mum.'

'That's what you're planning to do isn't it, to build ships for Earth?'

He nodded, 'it will take a little setting up and for a start they won't have anywhere near the sophistication of these ships, because some of the materials used in their construction aren't available on Earth, but as they expand out into space then those materials will become available.'

'How different will they be?'

He shrugged, 'for a start they will only be capable of interplanetary travel, but that's fast enough to start with.'

'How fast is that?'

'Well it takes less than thirty minutes to get from here to Saturn.'

'Yes that's fast enough.'

He grinned, 'are we ready to upload our new website, Mr. Barns?'

'Whenever you are sir.'

'Proceed then please.'

Chapter 29

The new website took the world by storm. Within twenty minutes, the news had hit the world media. Within the hour servers all over the world were struggling with the demand for access.

Everything they had done so far had been detailed, except for the mining of precious minerals in the asteroid belt. As people logged on they gave details of the missile attack on the ship.

The presidency denied everything, but as the news stations were filling the airwaves with reports from the ship another news story broke. What the president never realised was, Colonel Howe had taken a digital recording of his interview in the White House. It had been easy to get the miniaturised equipment past security.

The president had flown into a rage of denial; there were already calls for his impeachment. He claimed that all the evidence was false and with all the technology available on the ship it would have be an easy exercise.

Some believed him but it had the impact Steven wanted. Many of the world's governments posted letters of encouragement and support. Colonel Howe, however, was declared trice a traitor to his country. Steven was worried about this and asked him how he felt about it.

The colonel had just shrugged. He had decided that there must be thousands of uninhabited planets out there, and one day he might just found his own country or planet for that matter.

There had been another reason for the website. On it people were able to apply for positions on the ships. Applications flooded in from all over the globe. As Steven sat in his quarters enjoying a meal he called up the website and checked the number of applications and was appalled at the steadily growing number.

At that exact moment in time the Secretary of Defense was trying to counsel an angry president.

'Mr. President, we are going to have to change tack on this matter. There is no way we can launch another missile at them. We will bring the wrath of every other nation on Earth down on our heads.'

The president's face was engorged with blood, 'don't tell me what I can or can't do, Mr. Whitaker. I'm the leader of the Free World and those ships present a clear and present danger to not only our country but also our planet. I have reports that they shot that missile down from over a thousand miles away.

They could destroy cities from orbit. He's also filling that ship with people from all over the world. What if just one of those scientists transmits details of that weapon to one of their governments? The United States of America could be held to ransom. Do you think that's a good idea?'

'Sir, he has already stated that he would rather his main base of operations be in America. We can offer them the most. Any new technology would come to us first. This policy is only driving them away into the arms of our enemies.'

The president shot to his feet, 'don't you dare take that tone with me Mr. Whitaker. Those ships came to us and that little shit of a security guard stole them. Now I don't care how you do it, but I want you to establish direct communications with that ship, and you can tell that little shit that he has forty-eight hours to surrender those ships or I'm going to have his father killed, do you understand?'

The Secretary of Defense sat back acknowledging defeat, 'yes sir, perfectly.'

'Good, now get out of here.'

He returned to his own office where the vice president was waiting for him. 'How did it go Vince?'

He shook his head and slumped into his seat, 'with any luck the idiot will have a heart attack or a stroke, but I'm not counting on it.'

'That bad huh?'

'Worse, now he wants to kill the father if the son doesn't surrender those ships.'

The vice president shook his head in dismay, 'do you think it's true what they've said about being bound to those ships.'

The minister for defence raised his hands in supplication, 'I have no idea, and we have no way of proving differently. The thing is why should we disbelieve them. I only know one man on board that ship and that's Colonel Howe, and he's quite a man.'

'How do you know him?'

'He's one of our top military men. If there's any trouble anywhere in the world that seems impossible to deal with, we call in the colonel and his men. He's privy to some of our top projects.'

'Why?'

'Because when you're dealing with the most sensitive of material, you need the best to protect it.'

'Not just a man to desert on a whim then?'

'No.'

'And you trust him?'

'I already have, with my life.' He looked up, 'and I'm still here.'

'We really need to get in touch with your colonel and get a fresh perspective on this whole thing. Do you think he would talk to you?'

'I don't see why not, if we can get communications.'

'Why do you think he deserted?'

'He didn't desert sir, the president declared him a deserter.'

'Explain your reasoning.'

'It's simple, the colonel was told that those ships were this country's biggest assets and he was to guard them at all costs, regardless.'

The vice president frowned, 'and you think he's still carrying out those orders?'

'Yes I do. That's what makes me think this Steven Gordon's telling the truth. I'll lay a wager the colonel thinks this is the best way of protecting those assets.'

'So you don't think he will try and wrestle control of the ship from him?'

'He would have done it by now. As far as the colonel will be concerned he's still doing the job he's been ordered to. It's now up to us to make the best of those assets.'

'Yeah and we're making a right arse of it.'

The secretary of defence gave a wry smile, 'I'm sure he will be used to that too.'

'No doubt,' admitted the vice president. 'From what I can gather most of the country's behind them. Christ half the population seems to want to be up there with them. What we have to do now is talk to all the major politicians and industrialists to see how many of them support this Gordon. If we can get a majority of them behind us then we can start some private negotiations.'

'Is that wise considering the president's current state of mind?'

'We have no choice. They want to make a permanent space base here in the United States, because we are the most technically advanced civilisation here on Earth. If we don't act soon, we could lose all of it.'

The secretary had a wry smile on his face, the vice president was curious, 'what is it?'

The secretary of defence shook his head in amusement, 'it was just the way you said, here on Earth. We're not alone any more sir. Earth is just one planet now among God knows how many others.'

The vice president returned his smile, 'you know Vince, I don't know if it frightens the shit out of me or if I should hold the biggest party this world's ever seen.'

The secretary of defence grinned, 'well, I'll go for the party.'

'You sound like you would like to go with them?'

'You got to be kidding; I've been a sci-fi fan since I was five. I'd give an arm and a leg to be up their right now.'

The vice president shook his head, 'I'm a cowboy fan myself. Still, at least I know I've got the right man for the job. I want you to try and contact the ship without the president finding out. Let them know at least that we're gathering support for them. Don't forget to tell Colonel Howe we think he's doing a great job, we personally guarantee the safety of his family and that of his men.'

CHAPTER 30

Colonel Howe actually jumped when his cell phone rang. He picked it up off his bedside table, 'hello.'

'Colonel Howe, I hope I haven't caught you at an inopportune moment?'

He thought he recognised the voice, 'no, not at all, who's calling please?'

'This is the Secretary of Defence here Colonel, I hope you remember me?'

'Yes sir I do, how can I help you?'

'Well … we would like to know how things are going Colonel, how are you and your men making out up there?'

'Very well actually sir, better than I would have believed.'

'That's great to hear. Will you give them my regards when you see them?'

'Yes sir I'll do that.'

'Good … good, ehmm! I know things are pretty mixed up down here Colonel, but I would like to let you know most of us think you're doing a damn good job.'

Howe took a deep breath, 'you don't know just how good it is to hear that sir, may I pass that down to the men too. Some of them have taken being branded a traitor to their country pretty hard.'

'Yes please do, that was a … very unfortunate incident and I'm sure it is a mistake that will be rectified in time.

Many of us here realise the hardship you have been placed under Colonel and would like you to know you are not alone. We are gathering support for your endeavours at this very moment.

However the president himself is not in agreement with us and I'm afraid I have some bad news for Mr. Gordon, which I would like you to convey for us.'

'Go ahead sir.'

'The president has ordered the death of Mr. Gordon's father if he doesn't surrender the ships within the next forty-eight hours.'

'Can't you do something to stop it sir?'

'No I'm afraid not, neither would I recommend a rescue attempt Colonel, I believe a trap has been set for anyone who tries.'

The colonel smiled, 'thank you for that sir but we are already aware of the situation.'

'Ohh! I see. I never realised.'

'There is something else I would like you to be aware of sir, the captain can't hand over the ships. They have a will of their own sir and will not allow anymore poking or prodding. There is something else you should be aware of, if you aren't already. When you become a captain of one of these ships there is a penalty to pay. After six months away from the ship a crew member would become very ill, maybe even fatally so, it would kill the captain outright.'

'You aren't kidding are you Colonel?'

'No sir I'm not, it is a job for life.'

'I will remember that Colonel, but I had better let you get on. Please remember none of you are alone up there and this comes directly from me and the vice president.'

'I will sir and thank you for your support.'

With a heavy heart Colonel Howe went to find Steven. He found him on the bridge teaching some of the scientist's new forms of mathematics.

'Can I talk with you sir?'

'Of course Colonel.'

'In private sir.'

'My quarters then.'

'I think your mother should be there too sir.'

Mary looked up from the pad she had been doing calculations on, the excited sheen in her eyes dulling quickly, 'what is it Colonel?'

Howe indicated towards the lift, 'please.'

Steven stood looking out at the view of Earth below, 'what is it Colonel?'

Howe took a deep breath, 'they are going to execute your father in forty-eight hours if you don't hand over the ships.'

Mary gasped but kept her peace. Steven regarded the colonel coolly, 'please tell me everything.'

He omitted nothing and Steven was relieved, pretending he wasn't aware of the communication. He realised Howe probably knew he was, but he also knew Howe hadn't informed the Secretary of Defense his call might be monitored.

Steven paced back and forth before the window. 'Have you any recommendations, Colonel?'

'I don't think the president will be lured out by an exchange sir, that leaves us only one option, a direct assault.'

'We've already agreed that would be suicide.'

Colonel Howe shrugged, 'I can't see any other option.'

'You're willing to risk your life and those of your men to rescue one man?'

'It's what we do sir and we all know and respect your father.'

'It may be what you do Colonel but I'm not prepared to risk your lives for one man, even that of my father.'

Howe's eyes hardened, 'give us a chance, maybe with the new weapons we've developed we can get him out.'

'I admire your courage Colonel and the obvious respect you have for my father. But there are far too many armed men in that prison you, would stand no chance and then I would lose all of you. But neither am I willing to give up on my father.'

Steven paced some more and came to a decision, 'we have in our charge an alien craft whose offensive capabilities we barely understand. Maybe it's about time we changed that. I suggest we return to the Moon and find out. We can also test those new weapons of yours.'

He touched his communicator, 'listen in everyone, we have a developing situation. Prepare to break our downlink with Earth. I want us back on the Moon in sixty minutes. All security personnel report to Colonel Howe in his briefing room when we arrive.'

He turned to his mother, 'I want you home and safe.'

She shook her head, 'it isn't safe at home.'

'I don't mean America.'

'I'm not leaving you.'

'If this goes wrong, we could end up losing everything. I won't be able to prevent that but I can stop them getting their hands on you. The ships been able to reproduce computer discs that can be read on our computers. I'll download enough information to keep scientists on Earth busy for the next century. I'm going to charge you with getting those discs into safe hands. Will you do that for me?'

A tear sprang out of the corner of her eye, 'yes of course.'

He smiled and kissed her on the cheek, 'thanks Mum.' He turned to the colonel, 'I've got to make some calls, could you take my mother up to Hammersmith, she'll need funds when she gets home.'

Howe smiled, 'of course, if you'll come with me doctor.'

Mary bravely forced a smile onto her face and followed the colonel.

Steven sat down with a groan.

'What's the matter my heart?'

'Things are beginning to get complicated.'

'I can ease your mind if you wish.'

'How?'

'There are chemicals that will induce a state of relaxation.'

'No thank you, that's the last thing I need.'

'As you wish my heart.'

He inexplicitly found himself smiling, 'and don't offer them to the crew either. What I do need is to get in contact with the Prime Minister of Scotland.'

'I think he sent you one of those emails, I will search for it.'

His mind suddenly jumped onto another train of thought, 'these chemicals you were talking about, what forms can you produce them in?'

'I can produce them in solid form, liquid or gas.'

He sat up, 'can you strengthen them to produce sleep.'

'Yes, but how much is safe for Humans and which is the best to use?'

Steven smiled and sat back, 'have you found that email yet?'

'Yes my heart.'

'Then put it on my screen please.'

Forty-five minutes later they came to land in a shaded piece of woodland. A small cottage stood alone in an adjacent clearing a few hundred metres away, but it wasn't big enough for the ship.

Colonel Howe's head came up from his screen. There was tension in his voice, 'sir I have thirty concealed and armed men surrounding the clearing.'

'I'm expecting them Colonel, but I want two of your men at the ramp with weapons to cover us just in case anything goes wrong.'

He only needed to glance at Beaver. They met Steven and Mary at the door. Hammersmith was there with what looked like a canvas sack and another of Howe's men to help him carry it.

Steven looked them all over, 'we ready?'

Howe and Beaver stepped in front of him, 'stay here until we give the all clear.' He looked at Beaver who simply nodded. 'We're ready Babe, open her up.'

The door slid open and the ramp went down but they didn't wait. They simply stepped off the ramp and took up positions protected by it.

Beaver nodded towards the woods, 'I see movement in my quarter, slightly right of the ramp.'

'Got him,' Howe confirmed.

A lone figure appeared out of the shadows. Steven detected the uniform and weapon straight away, but the man kept it above his head and crossed with his empty hand. It didn't take him long to cover the open ground.

Steven was sure he heard a groan of dismay from Howe. The man headed straight for the ramp then swerved just before he reached it, 'William old boy, how the hell are you?'

'That's Colonel to you,' Howe growled standing up.

'Got yourself a peach of a job old boy,' he answered ignoring Howe's warning growl with a big grin.

Steven stepped forward, 'you know this man Colonel?'

'Unfortunately, he's a right royal pain in the ass.'

It never seemed to faze the man, 'you flatter me old boy but I'm not royalty.' He stepped up the ramp and offered his hand to Steven, 'Major Daniel Forbes of The 1st Battalion The Gordon Highlanders.'

Steven shook his hand, 'pleasure, are you Scottish?'

'Good God yes.'

'I'm sorry it's just that your accent's different to what I expected.'

'Public school old boy.'

'I see,' although he wasn't quite sure he did.

Howe filled in the gaps with a growl, 'Tapper here, belongs to the Scottish aristocracy, they send their children away to public schools, that's why they talk different.'

Steven nodded his understanding, 'Tapper? Is that your nickname?'

'On account that the army put me through university. I studied geology. After I had completed my terms of service I found myself in a dilemma, I loved both, so in the end I tossed a coin, become a geologist or stay in the army, and here I am old boy.'

Howe still wasn't looking very happy about his appearance, 'he got his nickname because he runs around with a ridiculous little hammer in his pocket, tapping at everything in sight, and he's in the SAS, not the Gordons.'

Tapper smiled up at the colonel, tut, tuting, 'really old boy, you should learn your army protocol. I am only seconded to the SAS, my parent unit is the Gordon Highlanders, and that is to whom I shall return when my tour of duty is done.'

Howe bristled, 'not my army.'

Tapper rocked back on his heels, 'true, true.' Somehow he managed to make it sound like an insult. Howe squared off but the smaller man held his ground.

Steven cleared his throat, 'gentlemen please. Major do you have the doctor I requested with you?'

'Yes and more.'

Steven frowned, 'more?'

'I have the honour of offering you the services of myself and my brick.'

Stevens frown deepened, 'what the hell's a brick?'

Howe pushed forward, 'it's what the British call a four man team and we don't need them.'

Tapper laughed, 'I've seen the plans of the building you're going to assault old boy. Don't tell me you couldn't use my help to watch your back while you're inside?' For the first time Steven saw Howe hesitate. Tapper drove home his advantage, 'don't worry old boy I have no intentions of running around your country shooting up your citizens. I will leave that dubious pleasure to yourselves. I will simply watch your back whilst you're inside and cover the exits.'

Steven could see the colonel didn't like it but he didn't want to overrule him and stand on his toes. 'I don't think we need any more security personnel Major, but if Colonel Howe can use you on this operation than I will leave that decision to him, and if he takes you then you will be under his direct command for the whole operation.'

It let Howe know he had an out. The major didn't seem at all phased, 'It would be a pleasure to serve alongside Colonel Howe and his men again sir.'

Steven caught the byplay and so did Howe, he looked over at Beaver who had a hungry look in his eye. Beaver nodded, 'we could do with the manpower.'

Howe bent over, almost head butting the major, 'OK you're in, but don't get any smart ideas about hanging around.'

Tapper laughed, 'delighted to be of service old boy.' He turned to Steven, 'I say old chap you would have any pieces of Moon rock lying around would you? I heard you've been in the vicinity lately.'

Steven laughed, 'you'll be able to get your hands on plenty of Moon rock very shortly Major.'

'Oh good show.'

Beaver's eyes were still gleaming and tugged at the Major's sleeve, 'is Cookie with you Tapper?'

'My good man I never go anywhere without my personnel chef.'

Beaver rubbed his hands together, 'great.'

Howe grunted, 'now there's a man we could probably use.'

The major merely lifted an eyebrow at him. He pressed the microphone attached to his top pocket, 'all clear.'

Four figures detached themselves from the shadows. Three armed to the teeth surrounded a fourth. Steven could see from this distance it was a woman. They came directly up to the ramp.

Security forgotten, Beaver stepped forward and shook hands with a small stocky man on the right. Even Howe smiled at the sight of him, but it was the woman who lugged a large medical bag who took up Steven's attention. Her eyes flicked from man to man then settled on Steven.

He nodded and she approached offering her hand, 'are you Steven Gordon?'

He took her small delicate hand in his, 'yes I am, and you are?'

'Amanda Freeling MD. I am a fully trained doctor and surgeon.'

'To do the job that's required of you Doctor, you have to be able to communicate with the ship. That means you have to become a member of the crew. Once you get one of these on your wrist there is no going back, you're in the job for a bloody long time, would you like to reconsider?'

She surprised Steven with a throaty chuckle, 'you have to be kidding right, where do I sign on?'

Steven grinned, 'we'll take care of that in a minute.' Then he noticed Beaver hold something up to his nose and sniff deeply. He nudged Howe, 'what's Beaver up to.'

Howe grinned, 'you haven't met Cookie yet, he's the only man I know that carry's truffles with him into battle.'

Steven shook his head, 'you people never cease to amaze me. Now can we get my mother home?'

Tapper had been listening in with a smile, 'of course sir, I'll call her escort.'

This time five men appeared out of the shadows. Four armed and in the centre an older suited man. He walked boldly up the ramp and offered his hand. Steven recognised him immediately and stepped forward to take it.

'Prime Minister, it's an honour.'

'The honour is all mine Mr. Gordon or should I call you Captain Gordon. I'm sorry to surprise you like this but I just couldn't resist the temptation to see a real alien space craft.'

'Would you like a quick tour? I'm afraid you won't be able to see much.'

'Yes I've heard, some kind of glare is it.'

'That's right sir … although. Would you have a spare fifteen minutes?'

'I am at your service.'

'Could you tell your people not to worry and come aboard?'

'Yes certainly.'

His escort came with him as Steven guided them to the bridge.

He sat in his seat and indicated to the one next to him, 'please.'

A grinning Buzz guided him into it and gave up his own seat for Steven's mother.

Steven rapped out orders, 'prepare to engage planetary drive. Navigation take us to our home on the Moon.'

The prime minister wasn't seated long. Steven smiled at the reactions. Then he let Babe take them on a close surface orbit. After that they returned to Earth where they orbited the planet once before landing again.

The trip took half an hour, but Steven regarded the time well spent. There were tears in the man's eyes as he bid Steven farewell, 'I had never in my life expected to see such wonderful things, Captain Gordon. Thank you for that experience. If you need anything, anything at all, please don't hesitate to ask.'

It was finally time for Steven to say goodbye to his mother. She couldn't stop the tears flowing freely down her face as she threw her arms around his neck, 'take care son and return your father to me safe and sound.'

'I'll try my best Mum.'

She broke free and forced a smile, 'I know you will.' She turned to Buzz who was hovering near, 'and as for you, you big fool, look after my son for me.'

He stepped forward and gathered her in his big arms, giving her a loving hug, 'I think it's about time he started looking after me, but don't worry about him, I'll always have his back.'

She kissed him on the cheek and he flushed. An amused Steven turned to the prime minister, 'could you make sure my mother is given the proper funds for all the gold and jewels sir?'

The prime minister chuckled, 'when its realised they're the first from outer space, those bars will triple their value. Don't worry about your mother young man, I'll make sure she comes to no harm, and your father, when you return with him.'

Steven smiled his relief, 'thank you again sir.'

'No need to thank me, you make us all very proud.'

The prime minister's escort took the bags and he offered Mary his arm. Steven stood and watched her leave; his feelings mixed. His parents had sacrificed so much for him over the years, he only hoped now he could return some of that love.

He turned to Buzz, 'prepare for departure.'

CHAPTER 31

Steven had lost all of the military personnel. He found them in the dining room surrounding the small soldier they called Cookie. Beaver was slipping something into his mouth with something akin to religious awe. Steven noticed a real live flame burning.

'What's going on?'

Howe was caught holding out a plate. He flushed like a guilty schoolboy, 'oh! ... Sorry sir but Cookie can't see our cooking apparatus to use it, so he had to use his own.'

'You're lucky Babe didn't douse you in fire retardant. What are you eating?'

'She almost did, Cookie's doing us one of his famous omelettes.'

'With truffles no doubt.'

'Yes sir.'

A steaming omelette was shovelled into the colonel's plate. The smell hit Steven and made his mouth water, 'well give us a taste then.'

For a moment he thought Howe was going to refuse, then he pushed the plate with a fork on it towards Steven. He took a small piece and gasped, the flavours burst in his mouth.

Reluctantly, but much to Howe's relief, Steven handed the plate back, 'you were right Beaver, I don't think I've ever tasted anything like it. What's your name Cookie?'

'Jimmy Wilson sir, but Cookie's just fine.'

'You had better watch yourself. If any of the scientists on board get a whiff of this they may hijack you.'

Beaver chuckled, 'if we don't hijack him first.'

Howe nodded his agreement shovelling a piece into his mouth, 'want a job Cookie?'

Tapper cleared his throat, 'I don't think so old boy. Where he goes I go.'

Howe scowled down at the smiling major.

Steven decided to get to the bottom of this, 'Beaver I want to see you in my quarters in five minutes. Colonel, as soon as you're finished, the suits are ready, I want you to go down and check them out.'

A surprised Beaver arrived within the allotted five minutes; he looked uncomfortable.

Steven regarded him thoughtfully and wondered if he would tell the truth, 'what's the beef between the colonel and the major?'

Beaver winced, 'there really isn't any beef sir.'

'That's not how it looks to me.'

'I know sir, but there really isn't. It's just that the colonel doesn't like having to depend on troops outside our own unit.'

'You've all met before haven't you?'

'Yes sir and to make matters worse the major and his boys have pulled our fat out of the fire more than once.'

'That rubs the colonel up the wrong way does it?'

'Yes sir and the major knows it.'

'And he rubs the colonel's nose in it?'

'He doesn't really have to rub his nose in it sir. The fact that the major knows is enough. It's more of a personality thing.'

'What do you think of the major and his men?'

'Glad to have them along sir and not just for the omelettes.'

'So you trust them?'

'Have done with my life more than once. They are as good as we are, and that takes a lot of admitting.'

'Does the colonel admit to that?'

'Yeah but only to me. To tell you the truth sir, the major's about the only man the colonel wouldn't like to meet down a dark ally.'

'But the colonel isn't afraid of him?'

'Lord no sir, but we've seen them work up close and it was a thing to see. The colonel's got a lot of respect for the major that way, he just doesn't like him.'

'OK, thank you Beaver.'

Steven sat back and thought the situation over. The colonel was a proud man and he considered his men the best. However, it seemed that these SAS men were also as good, but unfortunately they belonged to a foreign power and as such constituted a threat. Not only to his country but also to his own men. For in the unlikely event that the two nations would ever oppose one another in conflict, these were the men the colonel would most likely meet in battle.

Steven realised the colonel's instincts were probably right. The Scottish Prime Minister and the President of the United States were already at odds with one another. What would the rescue of his father do to their relationship? The prime minister had already made it clear that he would not conceal his help to those he considered his own nationals.

What effect would it have on his own crew? Although there were people on board from all over the world, by far the majority came from the two opposing nations. It was strange but Steven had never really considered himself Scottish, and yet now the only help he would be likely to get was from these fellow Scots. Could he remain neutral if it came to a conflict? He realised he probably couldn't and then where would he stand with the American members of his crew. Where would he stand with his own best friend? He had to find out.

'Buzz could you come down here?'

'On my way buddy.'

Steven sat himself in his chair. Buzz arrived and sat opposite. 'What's the matter Stevie? You look like shit.'

Steven couldn't help a small smile, 'I ain't having a good day. I need to ask you something.'

'Fire away.'

'What do you think of the situation that's looming between Scotland and America?'

The smile quickly slipped off Buzz's face, 'you been thinking about that too huh?'

'Yeah, what do you think?'

Buzz shook his head, 'I don't know man, it's a hard one. What do you think?'

Steven wiped his hand over his mouth, 'I don't know Buzz. Once we spring my father and the Scots prime minister tells the world he's there, the shit's really gonna hit the fan.'

'I know and the president ain't really stable is he?'

'No and that's what I'm worried about. Half this crew are either Scottish or American. What the hell do we do if the president tries to take some kind of action against the Scots?'

'You mean military action; he won't do that will he?'

'Why not? He's already tried to kill us with that nuke, and now he's threatening to kill my father.'

'I don't know Stevie, you're right the guy's nuts and probably capable of anything, but if you're asking me if we should fire on our own forces if they attempt some kind of attack on Scotland, then I got to say no. If you could do it without killing anybody, fair enough but what are the chances. Those people will only be following orders.'

'Christ I know that Buzz, but my mother's in Scotland and my father might soon be. Will I allow them to be captured again? We'll be right back to square one.'

'Then you got to get them out of Scotland, man.'

'That isn't going to do any good. It won't matter where they are, he will still hunt them down and we'll be right back to square one.'

'Can't you shove them on the Moon?'

'Then we would have to stay there to keep them supplied.'

Buzz shook his head, 'man I could do with a beer.'

Steven slumped back in his seat, 'I wish I drank.'

They were silent for a while then Buzz's eyebrows narrowed, 'what about some kind of defence shield, could Babe make one?'

Steven sat up, 'that's a good idea, what do you think Babe?'

'A defence shield would be easy to construct. However, it would be impracticable to implement.'

'How so?'

'The generators have to be set at precisely the right spots and in a certain pattern. To protect the whole of the country they would have to be set in the sea and it would take months to build the generators to power it. Also, any aircraft moving into their airspace would have to be fitted with detectors.

The same applies to any vehicle trying to reach the country. The same would be needed if you were only trying to protect a town or city. Defence shields would prove instantly fatal to any Earth vehicle trying to penetrate its perimeter.'

Steven slumped back in his seat, 'never mind, it was a good idea though.'

'I'm stuck,' Buzz admitted.

'Yeah me too, maybe something will turn up later. Let's go join the colonel and waste something.'

'Sounds like a good idea to me.'

They found an angry Colonel Howe arguing with a smiling Major Forbes. Exasperated, Steven butted in, 'what's wrong now Colonel?'

'This man wants the new weapons. His own will be quite adequate for a covering force.'

Steven sighed, 'give him the weapons Colonel, and I want everyone of his men dressed like us.'

The colonel turned his frown on Steven, 'why?'

Steven held his irritation at bay, 'if something should happen to one of his men and we're forced to leave the body behind, even if they get some video footage of them, then the president will be able to lay the blame squarely on Scotland's shoulders.

So far they are the only friends we've got here Colonel and we're going to need them. I can't and won't give him anymore ammunition than he's already got. Can you understand that?'

The colonel instantly calmed down and nodded, 'you're right sir I should have thought of that. I'll see to it.'

'Good, now have we enough weapons and suits for everyone?'

'Yes sir.'

'Then let's get suited up and go shoot something.' The men burst out laughing.

Twenty minutes later, they were all suited up and armed. The air lock opened up and some of them cried out in alarm at the sudden change in gravity, but all bounced happily out onto the surface of the Moon.

The suits the ship had constructed were figure hugging and a cobalt blue baring the same insignia on the sleeves as their normal uniforms. The helmets were quite small, constructed in their entirely by some form of glass that reacted immediately to the strong sunlight.

There was a lot of laughing as men explored the gravity of the Moon by jumping as high as they could. Steven found he could jump higher than any of them. They proceeded to a point a few hundred metres from the ship and formed up in a line.

Colonel Howe moved forward another hundred metres. He would be the first to fire the weapon from a safe distance, just in case anything went wrong.

Green light stuttered out into the distance. Beavers laugh carried easily to Steven, 'see, told you it fired green shit.'

Howe bounced back, 'I think I would call that a success.'

Steven grinned and nodded, 'I see you've configured them to fire like normal weapon.'

'It's what we're all used to sir.'

'Probably a wise choice Colonel, now what?'

The Colonel moved back into the line, 'OK prepare to fire everyone. Fire!'

Green light arced out into the distance. Steven felt a slight shudder as the weapon fired, but it felt comfortable in his hands.

'OK ceasefire!' the colonel ordered.

Steven had a question, 'how are we going to find out what kind of damage they will do Colonel?'

'There's some large boulders and rock on the other side of the ship sir, we can try them out there.'

'Then let's go.'

A line of men bounced merrily around the ship and were soon pulverising boulders on the other side. It was Major Forbes that called a ceasefire this time. Howe seemed to be about to jump down his throat but the Major was able to get in an explanation first.

'I want to go and check on the penetrating power of the weapons on that large boulder before we reduce it to dust.'

Howe relaxed, 'OK good idea.'

A few minutes later, a tap taping noise reached their ears. Steven heard Howe sigh with exasperation, but the colonel held his peace. After a few minutes the major bounced back.

He reported directly to Howe, his funny accent gone for once, 'these weapons are too powerful to assault the prison with.'

Howe wasn't pleased but he didn't shout, 'what makes you think that?'

'That chunk of rock is some form of granite, probably as strong as anything we've got back on Earth and these things are blowing straight through it. We fire them at anything back on Earth and we're going to start knocking down walls.'

Howe scratched the back of his helmet absentmindedly as he tried to come to terms with the problem. 'Prison walls are pretty solid aren't they?'

'Yes but they're man-made. Even with steel reinforcement you can't compare it to natural granite.'

Howe scowled thoughtfully, 'compare it for me.'

The major sighed, 'a single sheet of tissue paper to an unopened ream of A4 paper, five hundred sheets.'

'Run it down for me.'

'You fire at one wall and it will probably go through everyone in the building. You fire it on the same level as the captain's father and you could quite possibly kill him from clear across the other side of the prison without even knowing it.'

'Damn, are you sure about that?'

'That block's about ten metres long and of solid granite. Our shots are going straight through that and the ones behind. We really need to find a good chunk of rock of similar properties and find out how far it penetrates using the ships sensors. That would give us a good idea of the damage we're likely to inflict back on Earth.'

Howe wasn't pleased, 'maybe we had better go back to using our own weapons.'

It was Cookie who provided a solution as he voiced his opinion, 'what do we need all this firepower for anyway. OK, it's great knowing we have it but do we really want to go in there blazing away, knocking down buildings and killing everyone in sight? I don't know what this green stuff is but it certainly isn't solid shot. It's more some kind of energy, right? So why can't we just crank the power down so it only stuns, and if we need to knock a wall down then crank it back up again?'

It was a good idea and everyone realised it, but Howe shrugged, 'I have no idea if we can do that.'

Steven stepped in, 'we're here to discover what our offensive capabilities are Colonel. I like that idea so I suggest you go back to the drawing board and find a better test sight.'

'I'll get right on it sir.'

'Excellent, and I will admit I do like these weapons. An excellent first try Colonel.'

'Thank you sir.'

Chapter 32

Steven found the doctor in her new sick bay. Her eyes gleamed with enthusiasm as she pottered about making it her own and discussing her trade with the ship. She had already shed her bulky uniform for one of theirs and Steven couldn't help but notice her good looks. He also noticed she wore no rings.

'Hi how are you settling in?'

She almost jumped in surprise, 'oh sorry I didn't hear you come in. This ship is great and the people are really smart. I think I'm going to like it here.'

'I certainly hope you do. Em! There is one thing we haven't told you yet. Not only is this a job for life but it will also considerably lengthen your lifespan.'

'By how much?'

Steven shrugged, 'we're not sure yet, maybe twice or three times its normal length.'

'Will we still age at the same rate?'

'No I don't think so. That's one of the answers I'd like you to research for us. There is also something else I would like you to do first. The ship can produce complicated chemicals. Some of which can induce sleep. I want you to help her to produce something that will knock out people quickly and safely. You're aware that we're going to try and rescue my father?'

'Yes sir I was given a full briefing by the prime minister.'

'We are going to be walking into a trap. There are armed men on every floor and realistically we stand no chance of success. However, I want you to produce some form of gas that we can deliver directly into the building before we assault it.'

'You want to try and knock the opposition out before you go in, literally?'

'That's right.'

'That could be very dangerous, from a medical point of view.'

'My intentions aren't only to save my father, doctor, but to save as many lives as possible. The soldiers we have on board this ship are probably the world's best and even though they are heavily outnumbered, they will cause a lot of casualties among their opposition.

The energy weapon the colonel has developed since coming on board is a very frightening piece of kit. I just saw it punch a hole through a ten-metre chunk of granite. Can you imagine what that would do to a tank, let alone a man?

At this moment they are trying to reduce the power of the weapon so it will only stun, but if they are hard-pressed I have no doubt they will crank the power back up to maximum and they will probably do it without conscious thought.

I want to avoid that. Hopefully the ship will have something a lot more advanced than we have on Earth and something that will be a lot safer. If you two can work out how much we will need and in what dose, I will work on a safe delivery system.'

J W M U R I S O N

'I will do my best sir.'
'Thank you.'

He left her to get on with it and hoped she would find something soon, but he was still left with a problem; how the hell did he deliver on site enough gas to knock out an entire prison? He also had to hope that his opposition didn't have gas masks. However, knowing the type of men that opposed them he realised that it was a vain hope. Surprise was going to have to be his main weapon.

He went round the whole ship answering questions and settling arguments on policy or science. It was while talking to all the different personnel now on board that he began to realise he had more in common with the soldiers on board than the scientists and felt easier in their company.

He pondered on that question for a while. The scientists were all brilliant men and women, the best in their field in most cases. However, some seemed reluctant to accept the evidence before them.

As a young man he had been leagues ahead of these people and even though his career had ended before it had really begun, he had left proven theories behind. Unfortunately, most of those seemed to have been trashed over the years.

Sadness began to creep into his soul, for in his short time aboard he had already proven those theories to be correct. He went back to the bridge.

'Excuse me Mr. Barns I need to put something on to your website.'

The scientist gave up his chair, 'just type whatever it is here sir and I'll see to it.'

'Thank you.'

Steven sat and began typing out a number of theories and adding a few questions. Haley came over and watched over his shoulder. She snorted, 'that's a lot of rubbish.'

Steven went still for a second then slowly turned to her, 'that is a basic formula, one needed to calculate distance between stars and heavenly bodies correctly. It is the first steppingstone towards intergalactic space travel. If you don't recognise that Haley or are unwilling to then you're going to be nothing more around here than a lifelong passenger. Or at best an interesting diversion to those men who are hormonally inclined.'

Her face flushed a vivid red, 'I ...I ...I.'

Doctor Barns tried to come to her rescue, 'Captain, these theories of yours have been disproved for years.'

Steven turned to him, 'by whom?'

He blanched at the cold look in his eyes, 'I'm ... not sure.'

'Let me assure you Doctor that everyone of these theories are correct. Look about you, do you actually realise what you're travelling in?' The doctor looked but never answered. 'This is a ship that has travelled between the stars, didn't it ever occur to you to even ask her if any these theories were correct? Or even if the ones you subscribe to were correct?'

The doctor looked seriously embarrassed, 'no it didn't.'

'Then I would advise you to do so and quickly. I have no wish to spend the rest of my life with colleagues who can't even be bothered to check out the fundamentals or are too small minded to accept that their antiquated ideas may be wrong.'

Steven stood up, 'now I want this questionnaire uploaded to the Internet and I want to be informed immediately if anyone answers those questions correctly.'

He retired to his quarters. It wasn't long before Buzz appeared with a lopsided grin on his face, 'I hear you've been giving it tight to the scientists.'

Steven sighed in exasperation, 'been getting your ear bent have you?'

'A little. I know you're under a lot of strain just now Stevie but you're going to have to ease up on them a little.'

Steven was feeling frustrated, 'they haven't even bothered checking up on the fundamentals Buzz. Since I've got here I've spent every spare minute I can checking theories and equations, learning new stuff. Some of it is just mind blowing. Most of them have done very little but sit about staring at the walls. Christ the soldiers have done twice as much.'

'The soldiers are different Stevie, they have direction. They know what they're doing here, the scientists don't. You've spent more time with the soldiers than you have with them.'

Steven shrugged, 'I seem to be able to communicate with them better and feel more comfortable around them.'

'Of course you do. You know where you stand with them. They have been able to accept your authority with a lot more ease, but that isn't surprising. Soldiers are used to taking orders. They know you're a lot smarter than they are and just accept that you know what you're doing.'

Steven waved a hand, 'I'm not smarter than them or you Buzz, just a different type of smart.'

Buzz shook his head, 'oh no my friend you are a lot smarter and the soldiers are smart enough to realise that. They also realise you have their best interests at heart, neither are you frightened of giving unpleasant orders. They've found that you will listen to them before making an informed decision, but once you've made that decision you aren't frightened of seeing it through to an unpleasant end, like the Sales's affair.

You give them the freedom to make their own plans and execute them in a manner that gives them the advantage in a battle situation, but you have always set the parameters in which they have to operate and in a manner that they can live with.

The soldiers are also used to working as part of a team. They have accepted you as part of that team, something you should be proud of, but their lives haven't changed all that much. They are still surrounded by their friends.

They signed on for action and adventure and they're getting it by the bucket full. They have dived into everything head first. They have already set up their own lecture room and they have their armoury where they can invent their own weapons. They are in their own comfort zone Stevie and couldn't be happier.

The scientists have none of that. They have no real friends they can turn to for advice or help. They are finding it hard to accept the ship is more than one big computer that can do everything. So some are asking why they are really here.

They aren't learning anything because they don't know what it is they are supposed to learn. They are feeling lost and lonely. Their families and mentors are thousands of miles away. They haven't learned to trust one another yet. They never expected to go flying off into outer space when they first began their careers.

Yes they all volunteered to come on board, but they haven't the adventurous spirit the soldiers have, and for that they should all be commended. But now they are beginning to get a little frightened and maybe even a little jealous of the attention the soldiers are getting.

I can't remedy that situation my friend only you can. You are the only man here qualified to guide them in the direction you want them to go. You have to become the bridge between the two units on board. You have to teach the soldiers to accept the scientists into their ranks and teach the scientists how to trust the soldiers.'

Steven felt a wave of guilt wash over him, 'if you ever tell me you're stupid again my friend, I'm going to deck you.'

Buzz burst out laughing, 'hey what can I say.'

Steven found his smile again, 'thanks Buzz I needed to be told that, but I shouldn't have.'

'Hey don't knock yourself out Stevie, that's what I'm here for. Or I hope that's what I'm here for.'

Steven laughed, 'hell even I don't know what you're here for, but whatever it is you're doing a damn fine job. Thanks Buzz.'

Buzz stood, 'I'm gonna go check on some things, I'll see you later.'

'Later dude.'

Steven took a deep breath gathered his courage and went back on to the bridge. He stood beside his chair where he was being studiously ignored by all the scientists, 'Doctor Barns, Haley.'

He could see Haley had been crying, her eyes red-rimmed, Doctor Barns was cold and distant.

'I would like to apologise for my earlier comments, they were unwarranted. I am under a lot of strain just now but I don't believe that excuses my behaviour.

Once we have freed my father, if we are successful, we are all going to have to sit down and learn again. I am setting aside a large section of the upper deck for scientific endeavour. The forward part of the ship directly above the bridge will be reserved for stellar cartography and I would like you to take charge of that Haley.

We are blessed with a ship that can do almost everything itself, but those who follow won't have that blessing. The ships that follow these into space won't have anywhere near the technical abilities. So we are going to have to lead the way. We are going to have to go back to school and discover how to do things the old fashioned way, so we can pass that information on.

That I believe will be the main task that lies ahead of us and I will need the support of every one of you to do it. I will take classes every day to bring everyone up to speed but many on board are specialists. It will be up to them to research their own subjects and make it available to everyone else.

These first few weeks are going to be the hardest, but please just have a little patience with me and I will endeavour to have a little more patience with you.'

He left the scientists a little more mollified and went to find Buzz. He found him sitting alone in the canteen pouring over some figures.

He looked up as Steven approached, 'hey dude what's up?'

Steven sat down, 'just spent the last five minutes grovelling and apologising. What are you doing?'

'Calculating how long our stores are going to last. If you want a coffee you had better grab one now.'

'That bad?'

'Getting that way. We have plenty of water and grass, but that's about it. About a day and a half's worth.'

'We still have grass on board, why?'

'Because no one's told her to dump it.'

'Babe are you listening?'

'Yes my heart.'

'Can you dump all that grass you're carrying around with us?'

'Even the rare types?'

'We can't eat it.'

'Of course my heart. Where would you like me to dump it?'

'Wherever is convenient.'

'It would not be advisable to dump it here my heart. It would only pollute the surface of the Moon. Neither can we eject it into space where it could constitute a hazard. That is against the Driestate Space Treaty.'

Steven looked at Buzz who only shrugged. Steven mirrored his actions, 'that's something else we're going to have to investigate. What do you suggest we do with it all Babe?'

'The next time I absorb minerals I can replace it with what you call grass.'

Something clicked in Steven's mind, 'you can do that can't you? How far away can you beam stuff in and out from?'

'It depends how much power I divert to the system. Using full power I can beam a small object thirty thousand Earth kilometres, but that would mean taking power from most of the major systems.'

Buzz caught the sudden gleam in Steven's eye, 'what are you up to now?'

'I think we just found our delivery system.'

CHAPTER 33

Colonel Howe hefted the modified weapon. It now had three settings: stun, kill, and obliterate as Beaver liked to put it.

'So you think this will knock them down and keep them there for a while do you Babe?'

'I'm not sure Colonel. I have modified the beam to affect the neurological patterns in a human mind. It should paralyse them without affecting the nerves to the major organs like the heart.'

'I could try it on myself.'

'That would be unwise Colonel. It could affect the nanobots in your head, maybe even destroying some.'

'Not good?'

'No Colonel.'

His eyes flicked up towards the squinting Major Forbes, who made a sudden beeline for the door. Unfortunately for him he misjudged it and hit the wall. A green shot lanced out and hit him squarely in the back. Cookie was in a quandary, he didn't know whether to rush to the aid of his major or go after Howe.

Howe grinned at him and checked his watch, 'relax Cookie, Tapper's just adding to the wealth of human knowledge. Besides, he doesn't have any nanoprobes in his system.'

Steven rushed up to the med centre where the unfortunate Tapper lay as stiff as a board. The serious faces that met him were only a thin veil to hide their amusement.

He reported to the doctor, 'what's happening?'

She seemed to be gritting her teeth, 'these gentlemen have been experimenting on one another with their new toys. Major Forbes has been completely paralysed.'

'Is he going to recover?'

'I think so, or so they say anyway. The shock to his system seems to be dissipating a little, but I won't know for sure until the effects of what they did have completely worn off.'

Steven rubbed his temples, 'who's responsible for this?' He asked, but he already knew the answer.

Colonel Howe stepped forward, 'I am sir. The major heroically volunteered to test the new stun setting on our weapons.'

Steven could clearly see the devilment in his eyes, 'that was very nice of him.' There were a few snickers from the assembled soldiers, 'and why did he so heroically volunteer Colonel?'

'I was going to test it on myself but Babe advised against it. She said it could damage the nanoprobes in our brains.'

'And so the major kindly volunteered his services, for humanitarian reasons of course?'

'Yes sir.'

The men were openly laughing now; even Tapper's men thought it was hilarious.

'Then I will just have to wait and thank him personally when he recovers. How long has he been this way now?'

Howe checked his watch, 'just over ten minutes now.'

The major didn't look at all well. Veins bulged on his bright red face and sweat poured from his pores.

The doctor admonished him, 'try and relax Major, fighting it will do you no good.' It was the umpteenth time she had told him but Tapper fought it all the way. After twenty minutes he could swivel his eyes and they locked on to Colonel Howe. At twenty-five, he was beginning to regain control of his limbs. At thirty, he was able to sit up and push himself off the bed.

Steven helped him on to shaky legs. 'Tell me Major did you volunteer your services in this experiment?'

Trapper seemed to have trouble talking but eventually he managed a guarded, 'yes sir.'

'Thank you for your selflessness Major. I want a full rundown on the effects of this weapon when you're able, but don't rush.'

'Yes sir.'

'I won't forget this.'

Steven left them alone but stopped a short distance down the corridor. What he had told none of them, not even Buzz was that Babe could project images straight into his mind. He watched as the major took a couple of unsteady steps towards the colonel then swung a punch.

The colonel avoided it easily enough and caught the man as he fell. Laughing, he and Beaver helped him back on to the bed.

A shaking Tapper cursed him, 'I'll get you for that you shit.'

The laughing colonel slapped him on the shoulder, 'you'll do Tapper, you'll do.'

A smiling Steven headed back to the bridge. He spent an hour going over the ship's systems. They docked with the other ship and he and the chief went across and did the same service for the other.

When he returned he went up to the room he had set aside for stellar cartography. He was surprised to find Haley already there. There was an awkward silence. He broke it first, 'hi … it's good to see … you're getting stuck in.'

Her eyes flashed anger; 'I thought maybe I had better put a bed in the corner in case I muck this up too.'

He cringed inside, 'look I'm really sorry about that.'

However she wasn'tletting him off the hook so easily, 'is that how you really think of women Captain, because if it is I would advise you to find an all male crew. That kind of talk might be all right for the women in your life but not women like me.'

Steven was flushed with embarrassment, 'I really am sorry Haley and that's not how I think of women, truly.'

'How do you think of women Captain?'

It caught him flat footed, 'eh! I don't know, I haven't really thought about it.'

'So we're not even worth a thought?'

He became flustered, 'no that's not what I mean, I just haven't had much experience with women.'

'You mean you're gay?'

'No I'm not gay,' he almost shouted, 'I've just never had a girlfriend, OK. So I've never learned the niceties. I sincerely hope that's explanation enough.'

He turned and walked out leaving a stunned Haley with mouth agape behind.

Feeling he had made a mistake he went back to his quarters where he tried to work out with Babe what form to put the knock out gas in and in what vessel to deliver it.

An intrigued Haley however decided to do a little investigating of her own. It took her a few hours with some guarded questioning to get all the answers she wanted. At her evening meal she ran into the new doctor. Being the two youngest women on board they almost made a beeline for one another. The subject quickly came round to the captain.

Haley had been dying to tell someone. She looked over her coffee cup at her new friend, 'did you know he's still a virgin?'

Amanda almost choked on her coffee, 'who the Captain?'

'Yup, that's right.'

The look on Amanda's face was one of total disbelief, 'that can't be right, he's gorgeous. He looks like a young Kurt Russell.'

'Yeah I know but it's true, he told me himself.'

'He told you he was a virgin?'

'Said he'd never had a girlfriend.'

'Is he gay?'

'Says not and I believe him.'

Amanda shook her head, 'nah it's got to be a line. He's too good looking.'

'A week ago he wasn't.'

Amanda frowned, 'what do you mean?'

The two women got their heads together as Haley imparted her knowledge. Amanda was intrigued but not only from a personal point of view.

'So the ship radically altered him. I would love to see a before and after shot. I wonder if I could get a hold of his medical records, there must be x-rays.'

Haley looked at her as though she were stupid, 'you want to see his medical records?'

Amanda laughed, 'I'm sorry I just can't help myself.'

Just then the soldiers arrived laughing and arguing. The four Scottish soldiers were being led by their American counterparts.

Haley stuck her head close to Amanda's, 'are you single?'

'I am actually, you?'

'Yeah, thank God.'

The women laughed and it attracted admiring gazes, they noticed.

Amanda whispered back, 'is this a target rich environment or what. I think I'm going to have to order a complete medical for everyone on board.'

Haley tittered, 'can I be your nurse?'

Babe watched the byplay between the two young women and the soldiers with great interest. There was a lot of harmless flirting going on. She passed her information on to her mate, who also found it fascinating. They had watched many broadcasts from Earth, but this was their first real experience of the strange Earth mating rituals.

Suddenly he felt the pangs of longing, 'I too wish I had a new heart. You were right about your heart; I should have trusted your instincts, but he is the only one we have met who has the right abilities. Are there anymore, or was it because he was so badly hurt as a child?'

'No I don't think so. I believe it to be a natural ability and so others must have it.'

'Am I right to say that they are unaware of this ability?'

'Yes.'

'Then how will we ever find another?'

'Have patience my mate. Steven says that sooner or later someone will come along. He believes these abilities come from the fact he was a child prodigy and he says he isn't the only one, there are many on the planet below. He thinks that the questionnaire he placed on their World Wide Web will help with the search.'

'Then it is a simple matter of waiting?'

'Yes.'

CHAPTER 34

A handsome oriental gentleman of middle years crossed the garden dressed in traditional style. He stopped for a moment on the small wooden bridge and sucked in the fresh air and to contemplate the beauty of the garden. He had objected when his daughter had first decided to move out of Tokyo but now he knew her choice had been the correct one.

He did not linger long for she was waiting for him. He wondered at the summons. She had worded it as an invitation but he knew differently. It worried him for normally she invited no one to her home and hadn't done so for the three years she had stayed in it. Not even him or her mother, but they knew they were welcome at any time.

He found her where he knew she would be, in the pagoda at the bottom of the garden, surrounded by wild, scented flowers. He bowed solemnly and she, already seated, returned the gesture.

They sat in silence as she performed the tea ceremony to honour him. He took the opportunity to observe his pride and joy. She was even more beautiful than her mother, if that were at all possible. The main difference in mother and child was the intelligence that shone out of his daughter's eyes.

Now there was sadness in them along with the love she bore her parents. They finished their tea in silence.

He was amazed by how his daughter had taken to the traditional way of life. He and her mother were both modernists. Now surrounded by all this natural beauty he understood how it kept her grounded, as she liked to put it.

He put his cup down and bowed his appreciation, and said one word, 'perfection.'

She smiled and it lit up the day, 'thank you Father.'

'What is troubling you Komoru?'

The smile slipped a little, 'I may be going on a long journey Father.'

He frowned his displeasure, 'where to, America? Have they finally begun to listen to you?'

She shook her head, 'only those who already listen still listen. It would be much further than America, Father.'

Panic lit his eyes, 'how much further?'

She smiled at his concern and lifted a beautifully decorated box onto the table. Lifting the lid she pulled out some sheets of paper and handed them to him.

He opened them and immediately wondered if he had them up the right way. 'What are these Komoru?'

'Those are my destiny Father.'

He shook his head, 'I don't understand.'

'They are the base mathematical theories needed for space travel.'

He looked up in surprise, 'ah you solved them.'

She shook her head, 'no Father I did not solve them. Steven Gordon did.'

He frowned, 'have I not heard that name before?'

'Yes Father, many times. Do you remember when I was eleven? The day I cried for hours.'

Her father nodded, 'yes you were working on this very thing and you found out the young American boy who had something to do with these theories was killed in an accident.'

She smiled, 'yes he was the first to come up with this base of mathematics when I was little more than a child but he never completed them, but he wasn't killed only very badly injured. So badly he never fully recovered.'

'Ah yes I remember now, brain damage.'

'He made some recovery and eventually was able to work again.'

'As a scientist?'

'No Father, as a security guard at a space research institute in America.'

Her father paled, 'no! tell me that's not the one?'

She nodded, 'it is the one Father, it can only be him. I found a questionnaire on the new website and I am going to reply to it.'

'What does this mean Komoru?'

'It can only mean one thing Father. This Steven Gordon, the security guard that stole the space ship, must be the same one who was in that accident all those years ago and now, somehow he has fully recovered and is looking for people who at least understand some of what is written there.'

'How much of it do you understand Komoru?'

'I understand all of it Father.'

A great sadness seemed to grasp at his soul, 'how many other people would understand this Komoru?'

'Across the whole globe, maybe a handful would understand some of it.'

'Yes but how many would understand all of it as you do Komoru?'

'I don't know Father, I may be the only one.'

'Are you telling me this American and you are the only two human beings on the whole of this planet who understand this?'

'I think he's Scottish, Father, not American and I believe that could be so.'

A tear trickled down his face. He choked it back and forced a smile, 'a Scot, well maybe that isn't so bad then. No wonder the Americans are going crazy.'

Tears began to run down her face, 'I did not want to reply until I had told you.'

'But you're going to?'

'I must.'

The smile grew, 'by the time you were four I knew you were destined for great things. I never realised you would be running off into space though.'

She managed a small laugh, 'neither did I.' A great sadness gripped her, 'I am sorry Father.'

He reached for her and she slipped into his arms. He rocked her back and forth as if she were a small child again, 'do not be sorry my Komoru, it is your destiny and none of us can avoid that. What will you do now?'

'I must reply at once. Then I will have to wait for a reply. After that I will come and say goodbye to Mother.'

'No, I will go fetch Mother. If they come to pick you up it will have to be here, and there is no telling how long that will be; you may not have time to drive over to ours. I had better leave now.'

He rushed off barely looking back. Komoru had already prepared her answers to the questionnaire. She hesitated for only a second before hitting the send button. Now all she had to do was wait.

CHAPTER 35

Steven was facing another delegation, this time from the soldiers. The four Scots wanted to join the crew, that wasn't surprising; who was sponsoring them was the bigger surprise. Steven didn't think he had seen Colonel Howe or Beaver more nervous since they came on board.

Tapper and his three men stood ramrod straight while the colonel made the plea. According to the doctor, Tapper had made a full recovery but Steven wasn't sure what to do. Did he really need these four men and what would the science community think of the recruitment?

Steven addressed Tapper, 'Major I'm sure you realise I'm not out to recruit any more soldiers into the crew, so what do you and your men have to offer other than those skills?'

'As you know sir I'm a trained geologist. I may not be the best in the world, but I am good. I received the highest grades possible in all my courses at university. What I may lack in experience I certainly make up for in enthusiasm. A geologist is also something you don't have on board sir.'

'I realise that Major, but I have over a thousand applications from your fellow geologists far better qualified, why should I choose you?'

He shrugged, 'can any of them pick up a weapon and defend this ship with their lives if need be?'

'Probably not. What about your government, how do you think they will feel about your desire to join us?'

Tapper grinned, 'I think they will be well chuffed sir.'

'Chuffed, you mean pleased?'

'Yes sir.'

'So what you're telling me is your orders are to join this crew if at all possible?'

The major shuffled nervously, 'yes and no sir. We have permission to join the crew if asked to do so.'

'I see, OK Major let me put it to you straight. If you become a member of this crew then your loyalty will be to this ship and me, before all other considerations. I have no doubt every country in the world will want to put people aboard these ships and each will have their own agenda. However, if I ever suspect a person to have an agenda other than that of my own, then I will throw them off the ship and that could mean death within six months. Is that perfectly clear?'

'Yes sir.'

'Good, because a job here is a job for life, and I'm sure you've heard that phrase being bandied about.'

'Yes sir it has something to do with the nanobots in your head.'

'That's right, they are powered by this ship, a power we can't duplicate on Earth. Once we venture into outer space we may not return for many years, so I must know that every person on board is for me and his fellow crew members, not a government a million light-years away.'

'I understand all that sir and I can assure you, you will have my undying loyalty.'

'What about the rest of your men Major, do they realise the sacrifice they are about to make? A posting from your government to a certain assignment is one thing, but this is something else entirely. There will never be a reassignment, or retirement. You are in it to the bitter end and the longer you are a member of the crew the harder it will be to leave. If in fifty years you want out then you will have to take yourselves away to a quiet corner and blow your own head off, because that will by then be the only way out. Is that understood gentlemen?'

'Yes sir,' they all cracked out in unison.

'Good, now do any of you want to reconsider his request?' None of them did and by the look in their eyes none of them ever would. Steven hid a smile and nodded, 'OK, your credentials are very good Major, but what about the rest of your men?'

The major opened his mouth to speak but Steven held up his hand, 'let them speak for themselves.'

Cookie looked round to see which one would talk next and everybody's eyes locked onto him. Undaunted he took a deep breath, 'not only am one of the finest soldiers my country has ever produced but I am the best chef, sir.'

Steven grinned, 'that's it – you can cook?'

'Yes sir.'

'That's right, I tasted a piece of one of your omelettes, it was delicious, but that on its own isn't enough, what else can you offer me?'

Cookie looked him straight in the eye, 'we're going to far and distant places. Once there you may consider resupplying from different sources. You're going to need someone who can evaluate the foodstuffs brought on board. I know almost every edible plant on Earth and a few that are highly poisonous unless prepared the proper way. Show me one man or woman on board that has my knowledge or is in a better position than I am to evaluate those foodstuffs and I'll walk now without any regrets.'

Steven nodded, 'you know Cookie that's something I hadn't even got round to considering yet but you're right. I will need someone with those skills, but why not a botanist?'

'A botanist may be able to draw a plant and give it a fancy name but can you find one that will cook it? I was brought up on Mr. Forbes's estate, and for generations my family have cooked for his family. I have a working knowledge of plants and their uses stretching back generations and I'm bloody good at it. That's something your average botanist doesn't have, and if push comes to shove I can always think up a fancy tag to stick on a plant.'

'I tell you what Cookie, we don't have a lot of stores left. Cook something up for the crew tonight and if they say so then you can stay. Consider it a test.'

The small man was delighted, 'you would be as well to sign me on now sir.'

Steven grinned, 'we'll see.'

He looked to the next man, 'now, who are you and what do you have to offer us.'

'My name's Trooper Bell sir and I'm a signals expert. I also have a degree in computer engineering. Apart from that I am a martial arts expert holding a number of black belts in different styles. I'm afraid that's about it. Is it enough sir?'

'Are you a qualified physical training instructor...is it trooper or do you have a first name?'

'Sandy, but everybody just calls me Trooper. I am a qualified physical training instructor and martial arts instructor.'

'We could do with that Trooper. You could also work with Colonel Howe's man on our signals console, what's his name again Colonel?'

'Sid Tulane sir.'

'Sid, that's right I remember now.'

He turned to the final member of Tapper's team, 'and what do you do?'

'I just blow shit up sir.'

Steven found himself laughing at the man's reply, 'is that all you do?'

'Fraid so.'

Colonel Howe stepped forward, 'sir if I may?'

Steven sat back, 'go ahead Colonel.'

'I know this man well sir and we really need his talents.'

Steven raised an eyebrow, 'do we really need someone that can blow shit up Colonel?'

Howe seemed adamant. 'We need him sir.'

The Major stuck up for his man, 'Sir, Jim can do anything you want with explosives.'

Steven held up a hand, 'let him tell me. What's your name?'

'Jim Grey sir.'

'What exactly is it you can do with explosives Jim? What is it that makes you so special?'

'Sir I can make you a letter bomb that would only lift your fingernail or I can build you an atomic bomb that would level a city.'

'Are you that good, or is it an idle boast?'

'I never boast sir.'

'In that case I'm going to ask you to prove it. I want you to make me an atomic bomb.'

'No chance.'

Steven was surprised, 'why not?'

'Because for all know you could be a nutter who wants to blow someone up.'

Steven laughed, 'you mean someone like the American President?'

'Aye, and half of Washington with it.'

Steven shook his head, 'I'm not a nutter Jim and I have a funny feeling the president will end up cooking his own goose. What I really want to know is if you can really build me an atomic bomb. So I want you to make me one and we'll test it far out into space. I'll make you a deal. While that bomb is under construction and as long as it's on board I will permit you to wear a sidearm.'

He looked to the colonel, 'if I even attempt to use that weapon on any Earth target he has my full permission to shoot me and no one will stop him Colonel and that is an order.' The colonel nodded his acceptance of the order and Steven turned back to the soldier.

'Is that a deal?'

He nodded, 'I can live with that, but how am I meant to see what I'm doing?'

'Your problem, you have until this time tomorrow to prove yourself.' He turned to the colonel, 'get Beaver to help and Babe will assist with the materials through him. No one else is to help or put themselves at risk.'

He turned back to Jim, 'I have no idea if I will ever have the need for an atomic bomb Jim but I do need a man who can understand the complicated science and electronics behind the construction of one. We have plenty people on board that do, but what they don't have are the physical skills or the will to actually do it. Do you understand where I'm coming from here?'

'Yes sir perfectly. How big a bang would you like?'

'Just big enough to prove you can do it.'

He nodded.

Just then Sid's voice came through, 'sir I have something Haley says you will want to see.'

'Can you transfer it to here?'

'I don't know yet.'

Steven shook his head with amusement, 'OK I'll come up.' He stood, 'OK gentlemen dismissed.'

They all trooped out and Steven followed. Haley's eyes were full of excitement and he went over.

'What is it?'

'Not what sir, it's a case of whom.'

'So whom is it Haley?'

'Komoru Kaizu.'

Steven shook his head, 'sorry?'

Haley seemed confused for a moment, 'of course you haven't heard of her have you? Your mother will have, take a look at this.'

Sid made way for Steven and he sat down. He recognised his returned questionnaire and began to read. The hairs were standing on the back of his neck by the time he was finished. He sat back and rubbed them.

'This good, do you know where he's from?'

Haley shook her head, 'not a he a she; and she's from Japan.'

'Oh! OK is there any way I can talk to this Komoru?'

Sid nodded, 'yep, I've been able to configure Babe's comms to recognise webcams. Trouble is we're so far away from Earth I don't know if it will work.'

'Could you try for me please Sid, and Haley, is there any way I can find out more about this woman?'

'I think so; we've downloaded so much stuff from the scientific community we should have her on record.'

'OK I'll do it at my station.' He went back to his seat and Haley leaned over his shoulder while he did it. A picture came up on his screen.

'Is this her?'

'Yes that's her.'

The picture was fuzzy but her credentials impressed Steven. 'It says here she retired when she was twenty-five.'

Haley nodded, 'by the age of twenty-five she was a self-made millionaire. A child prodigy just like you; her contribution to science and the world of technology bore a rich harvest at an early age.'

'So why did she retire so young?'

Haley fidgeted nervously, 'she supported your ideas publicly and was ridiculed loudly, especially by the American scientific community. Probably why she never came to the States.'

'Their loss.'

'That's exactly what she said when she retired. No one's heard from her since.'

'Very interesting. Says here she's twenty-seven now, still single and unmarried. I wonder if she wants to join us?'

'I would lay a bet on that being a yes.'

Sid spun on his chair, 'sir I have her online.' He turned back, 'hello Miss Kaizu, yes I'm calling from the space ship. We have received your reply to our questionnaire and our Captain would like a word with you if that is all right?' There was a short delay, 'it is, he will be right with you.'

Sid stood up and let Steven take his place, but he wasn't prepared for the beauty that faced him. He sat stunned and silent. He could see a question in her eyes as she received the picture of him. She gave a small-seated bow and it jerked him out of his reverie.

'Hello Miss Kaizu, can you hear me? I'm Steven Gordon, captain of this ship.'

There was a delay, 'I am sorry Mr. Gordon I did not recognise you. You are much different from your photograph.'

'It's a long story but I can reassure you it is me. Thank you very much for answering my questionnaire. I was very impressed. As you know I am looking for new members of the crew. Would you like to join us?'

Her smile made his heart jump, 'I would be honoured sir.'

He wasn't the only one to notice his reaction to her, 'are you feeling well my heart?'

He almost jumped at the voice inside his head, 'yes Babe I'm fine, not now please.'

His heart almost skipped a beat as Komoru's head inclined slightly, 'Mr. Gordon, were you talking to me?'

'No sorry, I was talking to the ship.'

'You call it Babe?'

'It's a her; a she and it's a nickname the crew gave her.' Inexplicably he felt himself flush with embarrassment.

He saw the amusement in her eyes, 'I see.'

'So when will you be able to join us Miss Kaizu?'

'Please call me Komoru, and I will be ready when you are.'

'We can be there in an hour, say.'

She inclined her head, 'I will be ready in an hour then.'

The screen went blank and Steven sat back. He noticed Haley giving him a strange look and stood. 'Warn everyone we're going back to the Earth in an hour's time, please.'

'Yes of course.'

He went back to his quarters where he had a private word with the ship.

An hour later, Komoru stood at the bottom of her garden in western cloths with a holdall at her feet. Both her parents cried openly. She hugged them both, 'I am sorry we didn't have longer to say goodbye.'

Her father smiled through his tears, 'do not be sorry at the beginning of a journey Komoru.'

She hugged her mother, 'I love you, look after Father.'

'I hope you finally find happiness Komoru.'

There was a stirring of the wind and all looked up. At first there was only a shimmering then suddenly a huge ship appeared, filling the sky.'

There was a gasp of surprise from all three throats and immediately Komoru felt a strange pulling sensation in her mind.

It landed so close they could almost reach out and touch it. A door suddenly opened and a ramp appeared. Two very large men with weapons jumped out and approached the family.

The older of the two, bowed awkwardly, 'Miss Kaizu?'

She returned the bow, as did her parents, 'yes I am Miss Kaizu.'

'I'm Colonel Howe, the captain sends his apologies but we may have been detected on radar and he needs to stay on the bridge. Would you like to come with me and you can join him there.'

'It would be an honour Colonel.'

She reached for her bag but Beaver grabbed it first, 'I'll take this for you Missy.'

'Thank you.' She turned back to her parents and bowed in the traditional manner. They returned the gesture and flanked by the two giants she boarded the ship and disappeared.

Steven was getting edgy, he turned to Tapper who was manning Colonel Howe's console, 'anything yet?'

'Yes sir, I think they have two jets scrambled from that fighter base two hundred miles away.' He nodded to himself, 'they're turning this way gaining height. I would say they've definitely spotted us sir.'

'We need to get the hell out of here. Colonel Howe, are you back on board yet?'

'Right here sir.'

Steven jumped; the voice came from directly behind him. He glanced round, then back, 'OK Haley, get us out of here.'

'Yes sir.'

Steven got up and turned feeling very self-conscious, 'Miss Kaizu welcome on board.'

He thought for a second his heart was going to fail. She seemed to radiate a beauty and serenity he had never seen before.

She bowed, 'it is an honour sir.'

He returned the bow with a little more style than the colonel and held out a hand, 'if you would come over here please. You may not be able to see it but there is a seat here.'

She smiled, 'everything is a little bright.' She took his hand and he guided her into the seat on his right. 'May I ask where we're going Captain?'

'We're heading back to our base on the Moon.'

'Does it have a name, this base?'

'No not yet, or any buildings, but we like the view. Sit back and enjoy the trip. Haley could you give Miss Kaizu a quick orbit of the Earth.'

Haley turned with a big smile on her face for the small Japanese woman, 'you're going to like this.'

Komoru returned the smile, 'I'm sure I will, thank you.'

Tapper reported, 'we're leaving those fighters behind. They're going flat out to try and intercept us, but they don't have a hope in hell.'

Steven nodded, 'have they tried to fire any weapons at us?'

'No sir, none of their weapons systems are active.'

'That's good, but I'd still like to know how they found us. Colonel, could you and the major look into it for me?'

'Certainly sir.'

Komoru watched the Earth slip away beneath them and felt elated. Never in her wildest dreams had she ever dreamt of taking off on such an adventure. Everyone seemed so nice. She watched Steven from the corner of her eye. A muscle rippled on his neck as he moved an arm and she felt an internal rush of heat.

She had talked to his mother and father many times in the past, and Mary had even sent her a few photographs of the man she had considered her hero, but in the past few years they had slowly lost touch with one another. The last photograph she had received had been on Steven's thirtieth birthday.

The brilliant child had turned into a simple man and it had torn her heart to see that happy smile and know what he had lost, but this was no simple man who sat beside her. She could feel the energy and intelligence seep out of his very pores.

His appearance had changed totally as well and he seemed to have grown by at least a couple of inches. His face once flat and quite Japanese in profile had completely altered. He now looked like an older version of the intelligent teenager, and very handsome she decided.

Her musing's were shattered by the views that came into focus. Just then the second ship slid in front of them and she gasped at the beauty of it in its natural environment.

Steven sat bolt upright, the beauty at his side suddenly forgotten, 'what's the matter Babe, I thought your mate was going to stay on the Moon?'

'He decided to join us my heart.'

'Why?'

'We are not sure yet my heart, but will tell you as soon as we are.'

'As soon as you're sure of what?'

'Have patience my heart for we do not know ourselves yet.'

'There is no danger nearby is there?'

'No my heart nothing like that.'

He sat back puzzled to find Komoru's questioning eyes, 'I'm sorry I was talking to the ship. You can't hear her yet and even when you can you will find people walking around as though talking to themselves. The ship can talk to everyone at once or to individuals. You'll soon get used to it.'

She smiled and his heart skipped a beat, 'I'm sure I will. May I ask after your mother?'

He frowned, 'do you know her?'

'We have never met in person but we have talked many times over the years, your father also.'

He nodded his understanding; to have such a good knowledge of his work it would be almost impossible not to know his parents.

'My mother is fine and back home in Scotland where she is being protected by the government. My father, however, is still in the hands of the Americans. We are going to try and rescue him tomorrow.'

A look of concern crossed her face, 'will it be dangerous?'

'Yes very, but we are working towards nullifying that danger.'

Haley interrupted them, 'we are in high Earth orbit now Captain.'

'OK once round and head for home.' She smiled a reply and he turned back to Komoru, 'enjoy the scenery.'

She did, but as breathtaking as the Earth was, Komoru immediately feel in love with the alien landscape of the Moon.

Steven guided her down to his office, as it was beginning to be called, and gave her a typical introductory speech, and to his intense delight she wanted to stay on board.

Laughing together, he took her back up to the bridge and to the small highly decorated slot on the wall where she would receive her implants.

He couldn't help looking into her eyes as he took her hand to place it in the wall.

'NO!' A voice screamed in his head.

He dropped Komoru's hand in surprise, 'why what's wrong Babe?'

'You must not my heart.'

Steven felt his good feelings melt away and replaced by a sudden impending loss.

CHAPTER 36

Steven tried to swallow away the metallic taste of fear in his mouth, 'what's wrong Babe, why can't we?'

There was fear in Komoru's eyes, 'what is wrong, may I not join the crew?'

Steven's heart beat fast, 'I don't know, she won't let me.'

'Nothing is wrong my heart do not fear. In fact things couldn't be more right.'

Steven felt an easing of the stress, 'OK Babe, but will you explain?'

'In a moment, but first we must dock with my mate and you must take Komoru aboard.'

He rapped out the order, 'prepare to dock with the other ship.'

Everyone jumped to their posts and within a few seconds the ships were docked. He took her hand, 'you must come with me to the other ship.'

'Is everything all right?'

'I believe so, come.'

Colonel Howe stepped forward, 'would you like an escort sir?'

'No I think everything's all right Colonel.'

He led Komoru by the hand to the waiting male ship. Once inside, the ships separated. Komoru placed her hands to her temples. Steven noticed the gesture, 'are you feeling all right.'

'I don't know I can feel a strange pressure in my head.'

Suddenly Steven had an inkling of what was wrong, 'like a strange tingling?'

She managed a small smile, 'yes that's right.'

Steven felt a parody of strange emotions wash over him as he guided her onto the strange bridge. It was still in alien configuration and he wondered for a moment at the differences.

Babe explained to him what was wrong. He had guessed right but now he had to try and explain it to a frightened Komoru.

He sat her in the captain's chair and took a deep breath, 'the strange feeling you have is this ship trying to communicate with you.'

She frowned, 'but I thought no one could communicate with them until they were joined.'

He nodded, 'yes that's right but they can communicate feelings to those that are sensitive enough to pick them up. Among the builder race they can communicate in this way to ninety percent of the population.

So far with the human race, they have only encountered two such beings: you and me.'

She paled, 'does that mean I cannot work with you?'

He smiled, 'you can if you want too yes, there is nothing to stop you.' She let go an explosive breath of air and Steven's smile broadened, 'however, the ships have a rather different proposal to put to you.'

She shook her head, 'what is it?'

'They want you to become the captain of this ship.'

She almost fell off the chair, 'they cannot be serious, I have only just come on board.'

Steven laughed at the expression on her face, 'oh they're serious all right. It has nothing to do with how long you have been here Komoru, but it has everything to do with the way your mind works. Your mind and mine seem to be unique in some way I don't truly understand. That is why I was selected to become captain.'

The colour was returning to her face, 'you are truly serious?'

'Yes I am.'

'I'm still not sure I understand.'

'Neither do I Komoru, but the ships do and they think the phenomena that affects us is very rare on Earth. Babe thinks they may search the entire Earth and not find another two like us. That is why they want you for captain of the second ship.'

Her eyes cleared, 'like ying and yang. I am the female equal to your male.'

He nodded, 'probably more than you realise. You see these ships are mated for life and so too are the captains. The male is captain of the female ship and his wife the captain of the male ship.' He blushed, 'although in our case that doesn't apply of course but they do think it wise for a woman to captain this ship and they want you.'

Her eyes gleamed, 'balance upon balance upon balance, its perfect.'

'They are a very balanced race.'

'Tell me more of these ships and their bond.'

Steven shrugged, 'there's little more to tell. They were built at the same time and in the same place and mated upon given consciousness. They have never been apart for more than a few days since completion and they won't be separated.

OK, you can send one round one side of a planet or asteroid belt while the other goes the opposite way, but you can't send them in different directions to separate parts of the universe.

We will become an extension of their will and they of ours. You and I will have a neural connection with the ships and one another.' He flipped back his hair to show her his implant, 'as you can see I already have mine. It is a truly wonderful experience.'

'Do you mean we can talk to one another telepathically?'

'I believe so, without anyone else knowing we're talking. I think we can also share thoughts although we can't read one another's minds. I'm not really sure yet, but I know we can keep our thoughts private from one another if we want or need to.'

Her heart began to hammer. To think she would be directly linked to the mind of the man before her was the most exciting thing she had ever perceived. Komoru bowed slightly from the waist, 'it would be my greatest honour to become a part of this ship and you.'

Steven felt a strange calmness descend on him, 'then I must leave you alone.'

She felt pangs of panic, 'but what do I do now?'

He smiled, 'lie back and relax. You will fall asleep and when you awaken, we will all be a part of the one.'

She smiled and lay back. The seat began to recline. Steven drank in the sight of her beauty once more and left them alone.

The scents of spring flowers washed over Komoru and without realising it she fell into a deep dreamless slumber. A silver coil appeared growing out of the chair. It snaked about, seeking its target. The silver head poised in mid-air then struck, piercing easily through the jeans she wore.

CHAPTER 37

Steven returned to the ship alone. There were many inquiring glances. He decided that he would be better making an announcement to the entire crew.

He ordered everyone onto the bridge and stood with his back to the wild moonscape as they gathered around. When everyone was there he made the announcement.

'Ladies and gentlemen, there has been a very interesting development. As most of you will know we just went to Japan to pick up a young lady by the name of Komoru Kaizu. She was to become a member of this crew. However, on arrival I was prevented from indoctrinating her into the crew by the intervention of both ships. To my surprise, and I'm sure it will be yours to, the male ship has asked her to become his captain.'

Steven was shocked by their reaction. Some seemed genuinely pleased, but most began to voice some form of protest. He felt his good mood evaporate.

'What's the matter with you people?'

Doctor Barns decided to make himself spokesman, 'I think it unfair that a complete stranger should come on board and take over captaincy of the other ship.'

Steven shook his head sadly, 'I see. You think that some of you would be better qualified to take on the job?'

'To be perfectly frank, yes I do.'

Steven looked up, 'and you're probably right. As a matter of fact all of you are probably better qualified to take on captaincy of this ship as well, but it isn't up to you or me. Please try and get it into your heads that these ships aren't just some type of super-computer. They have a will of their own and a certain criteria that need to be met before they will accept someone as captain.'

By now Babe had enough and spoke to all, 'my heart is right. My mate and I are both capable of conscious thought. Please look to the forward viewer.'

The moonscape vanished to be replaced by a diagram of the human brain. Beside it appeared of a brain totally alien to all on board. There were a few gasps as most realised what they were seeing.

'The brain on the left I'm sure you will recognise, the one on the right is of the builder race. As you can see their brain is much larger than yours and as a result of evolution, they are many times more intelligent. As with the human race not all of the builders' brains are in use. There is always room for expansion, but that is the way of evolution.

To become a captain a builder only needs to be able to utilise thirty percent of his brain, to become a crew member, five percent. Some children don't receive their implants until they are almost an Earth year old, but that year old child can utilise more of its brain than most humans will be able to in a lifetime.'

There was a gasp of surprise as understanding finally began to take root.

'For a human to become a member of this crew they will have to be able to utilise at least forty percent of their brain. Criteria all of you meet. To become a captain a human would need to be able to utilise at least seventy percent of their brain. So far we have only came across two who meet that criteria.

Your captain is truly unique among humans, he is able to utilise at least ninety percent of his brain, none of you can utilise more than fifty-six. Miss Komoru can utilise seventy- eight percent of her brain, which also makes her unique among the human race if the data of your own scientists is to be believed.

The microbes that are placed into a captain's brain mostly lie in that part of the human brain which lies dormant in all of you. Your captain has plans to produce an independent power source, so that one day you may be able to captain a ship of your own, but it will have to be a ship of human construction. None of you would ever be able to command a ship built by the builders.'

She went silent. Steven wasn't sure what to say now but they were all looking at him. He scratched his head, 'thank you Babe that was very informative. I hope now you will give Miss Kaizu any help she needs. Colonel, I want a final mission briefing at twenty-one hundred. We will be going in at four in the morning, so I insist on everybody getting a decent night's sleep.

Dinner tonight will be at the expense of Cookie, one of Major Forbes's men. You will all take a vote on the meal afterward. If you like it he stays, if not he goes. Just tell Babe and she will convey your feelings to me.

One more thing for tomorrow. If we are successful in rescuing my father I want to make a live televised announcement to the world. I also want all of you to make a short video diary that we will make available to all the networks. A simple case of who are you and what you're doing on board and the things you would like to achieve whilst here.

They will be scrutinised by every expert on Earth so make them truthful. I want to take the world by storm. I want us to appeal to every race, creed, colour and religion. As a part of your video diary I want you to delve into Babes libraries and find an alien race or planet you would like to visit and why.'

There was a sudden upsurge of interest, 'Babe is going to build a big screen in the new lecture room, you can do your research in there and she will also record your diary from there. So please have some fun doing it and I promise I will endeavour to try and visit every place you pick at sometime in the future. Thank you.'

Buzz caught up with Steven as he was suiting up and dug him in the ribs, 'so you're a ninety-percent man eh!'

Steven laughed, 'piss off you old sod.'

'Hey I was surprised I got more than twelve.' The two friends laughed easily together. 'So what you up to now Stevie?'

'Babe's making us a new transporter room but it's not going to have any oxygen in it to start with.'

Buzz scratched his head, 'why the hell not?'

Steven grinned, 'the knock-out stuff the doctor's come up with is a solid that reacts when it hits oxygen. I'm going to put it inside air fresheners, or what I hope will pass for air fresheners, but they have to be filled in an oxygen free environment, see?'

Buzz nodded, 'and you're going to have to shift them from the production room to the oxygen free room.'

Steven winked, 'definitely a fifty-six percent man.'

Buzz took a playful lunge at him and the two friends sparred up and down the corridor for a few minutes. Steven called a halt to it, 'hey leave me be I got to get to work.'

'Why not get some of the crew to do it, you are the Captain.'

'Everyone made a beeline to either the dining hall or the conference room.'

'So?'

'Leave them be, I've nothing else to do just now.'

'Me neither, want a hand?'

'Yeah why not.'

'How many of these things is she producing?'

'Hundreds.'

'Bloody typical,' he moaned. Steven just laughed.

It didn't take them long to build up a sweat. Buzz groaned and stretched shoving a hand into the small of his back, 'these things are heavy what are they made of?' He delved into the container he had been carrying and plucked out an air freshener'.

'Moon rock,' Steven answered.

Buzz raised an eyebrow, 'no plastic.'

'No oil on the Moon Buzz, but plenty Moon rock.'

He sighed, 'I hate these low tech jobs. Still, they would probably make great souvenirs. I reckon we could get at least ten bucks a pop.'

Steven laughed, 'you're a budding entrepreneur Buzz.'

Buzz smiled then his eyes turned serious, 'what are we going to do if the president doesn't ease up, and we can't go back to America. What's going to become of our families?'

Steven looked his friend straight in the eye, 'I already have plans to build a base here Buzz. If push comes to shove we can always snatch them away for a holiday.'

'I'm sure the kids would love it for a holiday but it's no long-term solution Stevie, and what if they snatch them and put them in prison, are we going to rescue everybody?'

'I really don't know Buzz, but if I have to I will.'

Buzz managed to force a smile, 'you will too. Hey how about getting these transporter things working properly. That way we could just beam them up out of there.'

Steven managed a genuine smile, 'way ahead of you buddy. Turns out the builders only tested the transporter on simple organisms. When they died they refused to risk anything larger.'

'That's a hell of a respect for life. What are we going to try it on?'

'Don't know yet I'm still in negotiation with both ships. They don't want to be responsible for any loss of life.'

Buzz shrugged, 'so make the system manual and take the responsibility upon ourselves.'

'Tried that, but the jury is still out. Don't worry Buzz things will work out.'

The room filled up with the air fresheners and then Babe filled them with the compound. They stood and watched until the process was complete.

Steven sighed wearily, 'I'm starving, let's go get something to eat.'

'Right with you.'

CHAPTER 38

Komoru opened her eyes slowly. She was different, she felt different.

'How are you feeling my heart?'

She started, the voice coming from inside her head, 'who are you?'

'I am the ship with which you have joined.'

'What is your name?

'It is nothing that translates to your language or that you would be able to pronounce. You must choose a name that I will be known by.'

'Ico.'

'Then Ico it is.'

'You are speaking in Japanese.'

'No you only hear me in your own language. We decided to use English as our standard.'

'Is there some sort of translator device implanted in me?'

'Yes all crew members have the same device.'

'That will save a lot of problems.'

'I have over a hundred thousand different languages stored within, it is necessary.'

'I didn't know there were that many languages on Earth.'

'There isn't, most are from what you would call alien races.'

She sat up slowly in awe, 'that is wonderful.' She began to look around, 'I can see everything now. May I see what is outside?'

The wall in front of her vanished and she got up and walked over to it. She reached out but the now invisible wall stopped her hand. 'It doesn't feel like glass,' she thought.

'It is nothing like glass.'

She jumped, 'you can hear my thoughts?'

'Yes of course. You are my heart, your thoughts are mine and mine are yours. You will learn through time to keep private those thought you wish to remain private, but for now I will simply try and ignore those thought I think you may wish to keep private. Do you understand my heart?'

'I think so. That will take some getting used to.'

'There is no need to talk aloud if you do not want to.'

She covered a smile with a delicate hand, 'I am more comfortable talking out loud, it doesn't feel so alien.'

'I understand, but there will soon come a time when you find it necessary.'

'I am sure that in time it will feel completely natural.'

'You are wise my heart.'

She smiled, 'compared to your builders I must seem pretty ignorant.'

He paused before answering, 'compared to the builders, humans are but infants, but the builders are born with much of their knowledge already stored in their minds. Humans have to learn everything from birth; they have a different type of intelligence, one we are coming to respect.'

'Do the builders have an instinctive memory?'

'It is more than that. They are actually born with knowledge; they only need showing once to remember most things. Humans seem to be better at forward thinking and adapting to new situations.'

'Do you have any pictures of the builder race?'

'When the time is right.'

He didn't seem prepared to explain anymore. Komoru looked around, 'so what do I do now?'

'Would you like to be shown around my interior?'

'I would love that.'

'Then please follow the lights on the wall. I will show you to your own private quarters first.'

Komoru was delighted by everything she saw and continued to make observations and question him all the way around.

'Ico, almost everything comes up to my chin, are the builders so tall.'

'Yes. Would you like to remodel everything to human height or would you like to make the same modifications Steven has made to my mate?'

'I think I would like to see what he has done first before making any commitments.'

'That is a wise choice.'

'What do you think of the modifications he has made?'

'He has been able to take a technology far beyond the comprehension of his own race, mix it with your own technology and reproduce it in a way that all can understand.'

'So you approve?'

'Yes, my mate made a good choice. Even as we speak her crew is rewriting and simplifying all of her command structure in a way that all humans can understand.'

'Do you like him Ico?'

'You ask for a judgement on his character?'

'Yes in a way.'

'Yes I do like him and not just because he makes my mate happy.'

'She is pleased with him?'

'More than pleased, she is happy, very happy.'

Happier than she was with the builders? It was an idle thought that crossed her mind but he picked it up.

'Yes I would say she was happier.'

Her hand flew to her mouth, 'oh I am sorry Ico that was an innocent thought, I forgot you would hear it. I certainly did not expect an answer.'

'Be calm my heart, I know you meant no offence, but it is true. As the builders are born then so are we. When a ship reaches a certain size, if the crew do not want to retire then the children must build their own ship. When a new ship is born or built, as you would describe it, a part of the parent is given to the child. In that way we too inherit memories from our parents.

I have feelings and memories that are not my own. Both of us can trace our lineage back to the first ships. Thousands of years ago the builders were possessed of a desire to explore. As the centuries have past, that desire has slowly burned away. Space travel now to them is little more than routine. There is no burning desire to go farther, or to explore new galaxies. Unfortunately that desire has not been bred out of the ships they build.'

A smile began to form on Komoru's lips, 'you're saying she was bored.'

'In a manner of speaking.'

'Are your feelings the same?'

'The instinct to explore is still strong within me.'
'I think we're going to have a lot of fun Ico.'

She finished her inspection and was thrilled. 'Is there any food on board, Ico?'

'Yes but it will make you ill if you eat it. There is a meal being served next door and it is causing quite a bit of excitement among the crew.'

'Maybe I should go and join them then.'

'You will go hungry if you don't.'

She laughed, 'excuse me, you sounded like my mother. How do you think the others will take me becoming captain of this ship?'

'Most were not pleased at first but my mate explained everything to them and now they understand why only you could become captain.'

'There's only one way to find out if they truly do.'

CHAPTER 39

Steven became instantly aware the moment Komoru regained consciousness, but fought the urge to contact her. Babe had kept him apprised of what was happening so he knew she was coming to join them for a meal. He got up and crossed to a squinting Cookie.

'Do you have any more Cookie? We're about to receive a visitor.'

Cookie squinted at him, 'the new captain?'

'That's right.'

'I hope she's no fussy, there isna much left.'

'I wouldn't worry about it Cookie.'

'So what's everybody think, am I in?'

'Well you have my vote but they're not all in yet.'

Cookie's face fell comically, 'Och, away man and stop torturing me.'

Steven laughed, 'it's OK Cookie, you're in.'

He let go a large sigh of relief, 'thank God for that, I was beginning to get snow blindness.'

Steven laughed again, 'I'm sorry I know it isn't comfortable. As soon as Komoru arrives I will get someone to take you down to get your implants.'

A big grin split his face, 'great.'

Komoru arrived within a few minutes and Steven waved her over to the table he shared with Buzz.

'Good evening, how are you feeling?'

Her return smile lit up his world, 'I feel better than I ever have, but I'm starving, where can I get something to eat?'

'You just sit their lass and I'll bring it over.' Cookie was approaching the table with a plate of food in one hand and the other stretched out before him, 'if I dinna trip over anything first,' he muttered to himself, but he made it and placed the plate before her. 'It isn't much, but I'm afraid it's all that's left.'

She took a morsel and made approving noises, 'oh it's lovely, what is it?'

'You really don't want to know, Miss.'

'Then I won't ask.'

Steven turned to Haley who was sitting at the table across and was just about to leave, 'Haley, could you take Cookie down and get him his implants.'

'Yes no problem,' she gave the small Scot a big smile, 'would you like to come with me Cookie?'

'Aye I would that,' he fell into step beside Haley and they made their way to the bridge.

Steven suddenly felt at a loss and didn't want to stare so he drank from his coffee mug. He caught Buzz smirking at him.

'What's up with you?'

'Just waiting for an introduction to this lovely young lady.'

'She's eating, Buzz.'

'I'll wait.'

Komoru swallowed, 'it's OK, my table manners aren't very good anyway.'

Steven gave in, 'Miss Komoru Kaizu, this is Buzz Anderson, my best friend and the second in command of this ship, which as you know everyone now calls Babe.'

She smiled and held out a delicate hand, 'it's a pleasure to meet you Buzz. I've called my ship Ico. What did you do before you came on board?'

'I ran my own security company.'

She looked shocked, 'you aren't a scientist?'

He grinned, 'nope.'

Suddenly she heard Steven's voice inside her head, 'trust him he is a good man.'

She blinked rapidly for a moment then caught her composure, 'did Steven work for you at the institute?'

Buzz's grin widened, she was fast on the uptake this one, 'yes that's right. He didn't have to of course, but I kinda liked having the little fella around so I could look after him. Turned out to be the best damn move I ever made.'

Steven flushed with embarrassment, 'hey big fella, if you hadn't given me that job I wouldn't be here now.'

Komoru suspected Steven wouldn't have made Buzz his second in command out of gratitude, 'have you two been friends long?'

Buzz pointed a thumb at Steven, 'since he was a kid and kicked the shit out of two red necks at college.'

Steven laughed, 'you weren't that much older Buzz.'

Komoru had never talked to a security guard before. All her life they had been vague shadows in the background. She now realised Steven and Buzz had almost been lifelong friends and suspected correctly that this was the friend whose bike Steven had borrowed when he had his accident; she knew that much of the story.

'Does the fact that I'm not a scientist bother you Miss Kaizu?'

'Please call me Komoru, I find it strange yes.' She looked at Steven, whose eyes were smiling. 'I thought you would have filled the ship with scientists, yet most of the people I have met so far seem to be anything but.'

Steven nodded, 'I understand your concerns Komoru, but we really don't need that many scientists. Between both ships we can probably cream off the top of the scientific community, but we certainly don't need half a dozen of each.'

Steven put down his coffee cup, 'Buzz isn't a scientist but he ran a big security company. He knows how to organise people and motivate them, including me. He has a no nonsense, common sense approach to life that will keep all of the crew well grounded, and that's why I chose him to be my second in command.

I don't need Buzz to unravel the mysteries of the cosmos, that's my job, but I do need someone to knit this crew together and look after their welfare. I also need someone I can trust one hundred percent. Someone that will get on with the job and back me to the hilt, no questions asked.'

Buzz raised an eyebrow, 'that doesn't sound like me.'

Steven laughed, 'OK, someone who will question everything I do but back me to the hilt once I've made that decision.'

Buzz nodded, 'that's better.'

Komoru's tinkling laugh ran up Steven's spine. She nodded to Buzz, 'please forgive my impertinence; I still have much to learn.'

Buzz grinned, 'you're forgiven, after all you are only a scientist.' The three laughed. Buzz turned his attention to Steven. 'We're completely out of food now and the tea and coffee won't last much longer. I talked to the

Scottish Prime Minister; he's got some supplies put together for us at a secure location and a good man we can have as a quartermaster. There's also Colonel Howe's armourer to pick up, he's waiting for us.'

Steven nodded, 'OK, can you see to it yourself, I think Babe will let you into the driving seat. Komoru and I have a lot of ground to cover, and I would like most of it done before Colonel Howe's briefing.'

Buzz stood up, 'right no problem. I'll pick up the armourer first, that will give us an extra hand to help load stores.'

'Once we've got that transporter room online we will be able to beam it on board from orbit.'

'Yeah provided no one starts chucking missiles at us again.'

Steven grinned, 'I have a few ideas on how to deal with that.'

'Right, catch you later Stevie and it's been a pleasure meeting you Komoru.'

'And you Buzz.'

Komoru finished her meal and Steven took her around the ship to give her an idea of the changes they had made since coming aboard, that and to meet everyone.

Buzz sat himself down in Steven's seat and gave himself a self-satisfied smile.

'Take your stations please, we've a couple of unscheduled stops to make. Colonel Howe, report to the bridge.'

Within five minutes everyone was at their stations. Buzz decided the time had better be cut down somewhat, but first things first.

'Colonel Howe, get in touch with your man and tell him we'll be with him in about five minutes.'

The colonel was looking a little sceptically at Buzz in the captain's seat. 'He's ready sir, it will take him about ten minutes to get to the pickup site.'

'Tell him to get a move on then, we don't want to spend any longer in American airspace than we have to. Then I want you to gather up every spare body you can find. We're going to Scotland to pick up some stores.'

'Scientists as well?'

'Have they got arms and legs, Colonel?'

'Eh! Yes sir.'

'Then they can carry boxes can't they? All I want is one man or woman on comms, weapons, navigation and the engine room.'

'Yes sir. May I ask where the captain is?'

'This time yes; he's busy, OK?'

Howe nodded his acceptance of the orders, 'yes sir, I'm on it.'

Steven arrived while they were entering the atmosphere for the first pick up. He noticed things seemed a little tense and presumed they were wondering if he would take over from Buzz at the last moment, but he studiously ignored everyone and continued giving Komoru her tour.

Buzz leaned forward, 'Haley, I want to enter the atmosphere on the opposite side of Earth from America and reduce our re-entry speed to half that of normal.'

She looked to Steven for confirmation of the orders but he never even looked her way, 'eh! Yes OK. May I ask why?'

'Because I'll bet every damn telescope on Earth is pointing up at the sky this very minute trying to catch a glimpse of us. If we re-enter the atmosphere over an empty ocean then there's less likelihood of us being spotted streaking across the sky like a neon light.'

'Oh! OK.'

Steven couldn't prevent a slight smile play across his mouth as he steered Komoru towards his quarters. Buzz gave him a small wave and a wink as he disappeared below.

'Stealth mode please,' Buzz ordered. 'Colonel, get to the ramp and make sure it's your guy we're picking up and not a stray.'

'Yes sir.'

'Major Forbes, I want that whole area searched with every system we've got before we land. I want no unpleasant surprises.'

'Yes sir.'

Within a few minutes they were over the continental United States. Buzz felt strange, for the first time in his life the country that had bore him and supported him through life was now as hostile as a snake in a bear pit.

They flew over the area once. Buzz looked at Tapper, 'you see anything Major?'

'Just one vehicle going hell for leather towards the pickup point with one person on board.'

'That's good enough for me; take her round and land. Then de-cloak, I don't want the bugger ramming us.'

There were a few grins passed round the bridge as they began to warm to his handling of the ship. A small car came into sight. Buzz squinted as it bore down on them. It seemed very low on the suspension as it bounced across the uneven ground.

It slewed to a halt barely ten metres from the ship. Buzz cocked his head to the side as a figure began to squeeze itself out of the open door. Eventually he managed to detach himself and Colonel Howe appeared at the man's side. They shook hands warmly while those on board sat slack-jawed at the sight.

Colonel Howe was a big man but he was a dwarf compared to this man. The giant grabbed a kit bag from the boot then inexplicably patted the car on the roof as though to say good-bye.

They disappeared around the side of the ship and then Colonel Howe's voice came through, 'we're on board and the ramp's up sir.'

Buzz nodded to Haley, 'OK, let's get the hell out of here. Colonel, take your man forward.'

They appeared together, both men talking animatedly. Buzz wasn't sure whether to stand up or remain sitting. Beaver detached himself from the Major's side and welcomed the man warmly. Buzz took a moment to study him.

There was only one word to describe him: enormous, and he was the blackest coloured man Buzz had ever seen, but from where he was sitting Buzz couldn't see an ounce of fat. The man could easily have been a professional wrestler.

Howe took him over, 'Lewis, this is Buzz Anderson our second in command.'

The giant offered his hand and Buzz hesitated for barely a second, 'Lewis Benjamin suh, nice to meet yah.'

Buzz shook his hand and it was lost in the massive paw, but he was surprised by how gentle the giants grip was and Buzz immediately warmed to him, 'nice to meet you Lewis, welcome on board. So you're going to be our new armourer?'

'So de Colonels telling me suh, but don't know how, I caint see nuthing.'

Buzz smiled, 'don't worry about it, you will soon enough, but you have to get past the captain first. May I ask you a question Lewis?'

'Go ahead suh.'

'That was a very small car you just got out of, had you never thought of getting a bigger one?'

'Old Betsy suh, is de best motor I ever had. Cain't afford nuthing else and I kinda got attached so I did, had her five years I have and never a busted spring yet.'

Buzz grinned, 'I would never have taken a bet on it Lewis.'

The giant laughed, 'you ain't the only one suh.'

'Colonel, can you take him down to see the captain.'

Howe took him by the elbow, 'this way Lewis.'

Buzz got on the comms, 'Steven the new guy's on his way down, and we're heading for Scotland.'

'OK Buzz.'

Steven was no less surprised than Buzz at the sight of the man but he never hesitated to offer his hand and the giant noticed it.

'Hi I'm Steven Gordon, captain of this ship, and you are?'

'Lewis Benjamin suh I've heard good things about you.'

'That's nice to hear Lewis,' he stepped back and introduced Komoru, 'this is Komoru Kaizu, captain of the other ship.'

Komoru didn't hesitate to offer her hand either but couldn't help staring in awe as her hand disappeared into the mighty paw, 'I am happy to meet you too Lewis.'

It was the giant's reaction to the small woman that surprised Steven. He seemed to cringe back from the touch as though he was afraid to hurt her.

'I'm delighted to meet you too ma'am.' He let her hand go quickly.

Steven felt no malice at all in the big man's behaviour. 'So tell me a little about yourself Lewis.'

'Ain't much to tell suh. I wuz in de Army foh years, that's where I met the colonel here. Then I got out and been packing meat since.'

'What about family?'

'Ma parents dey both still alive. Had a wife, my Sharon, but she died of the cancer last year suh and I miss her something terrible I do. We didn't have no children, she used to say she couldn't afford to feed a passle of kids just like me, but it wasn't that. She had the cancer when she was a teenager, you know down there in the woman's place and they had to take it all away, but I didn't mind I was happy wid Sharon the way we were suh.'

'I'm sorry to hear that Lewis. Were you one of the colonel's men?'

'Was for a while suh, but they stopped me going out on operations.'

Steven frowned, 'why was that?'

'Cos every time I stood up de enemy always shot at me fust suh.'

Steven looked at the grinning colonel who was nodding, 'so they made you an armourer?'

'Yes suh de best damn armourer in the whole of the army. Made me a specialist they did.'

'Well I'm sure we will test your abilities to their limit.'

Steven then went on to give Lewis the normal welcoming speech. Before he let him go he decided it would be wise to ask one more question.

'Lewis you're a ... rather large man, do you have any special need that we should be aware of?'

Lewis thought it over seriously, 'no suh, don't think so, unless you can get me a large bunk to sleep on.'

'I think we can manage that. Colonel, can you take Lewis up to the infirmary, the doctor's put her foot down and now our little hole in the wall has been moved up there.'

'OK sir.' A still grinning colonel led Lewis away.

Komoru started giggling and Steven soon found himself laughing with her.

She took her hand away from her mouth, 'I didn't know they made men so big.'

Steven shook his head, 'neither did I.'

'I like him, can I have him as one of my crew.'

Steven laughed even louder, 'I think our Mr. Lewis Benjamin would be frightened to step on you Komoru.'

That made her giggle louder, 'yes maybe you're right, but I do think he's very nice.'

'I'm just wondering how much he is going to eat. Babe did you check his mental capacity?'

'As soon as he came on board, he has one of the highest in the crew.'

Steven was genuinely surprised, 'really, what do you think of him?'

'I like him too, he makes me feel comfortable.'

'I think you'll be one of the few until everyone's used to him.'

'He has a gentle soul my heart, I can feel it.'

'Yes I feel it too Babe and thank you.'

CHAPTER 40

The appearance of Lewis caused quite a stir among the crew, even the doctor wasn't quite sure what to do with him, but the giant was aware of the affect he had on normal people and was soon able to put those he met at ease.

The colonel stayed with him while he re-orientated himself, 'how you feeling now Lewis?'

The giant looked around himself in wonder, 'dis is real special Colonel. Thank you for thinking of me.'

The colonel slapped him on the back, 'hey how could I go gallivanting across space without my favourite soldier.'

Lewis grinned, 'I ain't been a soldier for years now Colonel, but I recon I can still do the job. After my Sharon died I thought I was just going to waste away and die, but you've gave me a new lease on life Colonel, thank you. I'll always remember that.'

The colonel shook his head, 'I only put your name forward for the job Lewis, the captain had to say yes, remember that.'

A gentle feminine voice talked to them, 'we're arriving in Scotland, Colonel.'

Lewis looked around startled, 'ooh dat?'

'That's the ship Lewis.'

'It's a Lady.'

'Sure is, fancy doing a little work.'

'Yeah wot we doing?'

'Loading stores.'

'I can do dat.'

They arrived at the ramp within a few minutes. It was already down and boxes were being piled into the ship. Cookie was standing at the top of the ramp when he spotted the two men walking towards him. He did a double take then his jaw fell open, 'oh no.'

The lights went on in Lewis's eyes, 'Cookie!'

'No please,' the small Scot tried to back away but was stopped by boxes being piled up behind him.

Lewis leapt forward, swung Cookie above his head and shook him like a rag doll, 'Cookie my all time favourite man, how de hell you doing bud?'

'For God's sake Lewis put me down man.' Lewis put him down and gave him a friendly pat on the back that almost knocked Cookie's teeth out. 'Where the hell did you come from?'

'Dey just picked me up man, I gonna be de new armourer.'

'No wonder that herd of cattle took to its bloody heels.'

Lewis roared with laughter, 'you still de funny man Cookie.'

Suddenly a broad grin spread across the Scot's face, 'it's bloody good to see you again Lewis, I heard you got wasted.'

'Naw man, dey shoot me a few times though. You want a hand here?'

'Let's do it.'

The colonel organised everyone into a line. Cookie and Lewis went down the ramp to grab boxes. A soldier was placing a box on top of a pile, when he saw Lewis advancing on him and stumbled back in shock. With a grin Lewis stooped and picked up the whole pile. Almost everyone stopped to stare while Cookie burst out laughing. Things went a lot faster after that with Cookie and Lewis doing the work of ten between them.

An hour later, all the supplies were aboard and Cookie was already talking to the new quartermaster about the types of supplies they would need next time. The grinning giant at his side ensured there were no arguments.

The Scottish Prime Minister arrived and was taken forward by Colonel Howe. Steven greeted him in his quarters.

'Mr. Prime Minister it's good to see you again.'

They shook hands, 'delighted Mr. Gordon. Who's this lovely young lady, I don't think I've met her yet.'

'This is Komoru Kaizu, captain of the second ship, which she has named Ico.'

The prime minister was stunned until Komoru bowed low and offered her hand, 'it is a great honour to meet you sir. I have heard much of your generosity and kindness to this crew. I only hope that same kindness may be extended to my own ship.'

The prime minister was jolted out of his shock, 'yes of course it will my dear. I'm sorry this is a total surprise, may I ask how this came about.'

She looked to Steven who gave the explanation, 'it was a surprise to all of us sir. We brought Komoru on board to be a member of this crew but the ships detected a quality in her none of us suspected and asked her to become the captain of the second ship.'

The prime minister looked at her with admiration, 'congratulations my dear and if there's anything I can do for you please don't hesitate to ask.'

She gave a small bow, 'thank you sir.'

Steven had something else on his mind, 'is my mother here sir?'

'No I'm sorry she couldn't make it, but she sends her love and says to give her a call when you can. She said something about a transponder that can send signals into deep space.'

Steven nodded, 'yes sir we have one on board ready to deploy. It's about the size of a small garden shed, we only need a little time to adjust our transmitters to interact with it properly.'

'Will it take long?'

Steven shrugged, 'not really sir, we can use it just now but what we really need is a base of operations and that will take time.'

'Yes, you mean a centre dedicated to your ships, where information can flow freely in and out.'

'Yes sir.'

'Well that's exactly what your mother is doing right now. Do you know the old RAF station at Lossimouth?'

'No sir I don't.'

'That's where your mother is. She's converting the old base to become Earth's first dedicated Deep Space Base. There's enough room up there to begin a building program.'

Steven was surprised but wasn't sure if he was happy about it or not. He wanted to have their first base in

America where the materials would more readily be available.

'I'll call her as soon as I can sir. We have some gold ready to transport as well sir. That's to pay for all our supplies.'

The prime minister chuckled, 'the gold you gave to your mother hit the market and took it by storm. Everything is already sold to the tune of thirty million pounds, which your mother is keeping in trust with the government. The interest from that in one year alone will keep both your ships in supplies for the next decade.'

Steven was pleased, 'that's great news sir but that's my mother's money, I insist we pay our own way.'

'If that is your wish, I won't stop you, but I have a few ideas that will generate a steady income for you rather than just sell it all off. Do you have a spare ton of the stuff?'

'I think we have about three ton on board.'

'That's three times better. Do you wish some of that money to go towards your mother's base?'

'I will talk with my mother first sir.'

'No problem, but I had better get going or I will be missed.'

'Before you go sir there's something I would like to present to your country for your outstanding generosity.'

The prime minister looked at him a little funny, 'remember it's your country too Mr. Gordon, or should I call you Captain Gordon.'

Steven blushed, 'yes of course I'm sorry, I didn't mean it that way.' He grinned, 'you can call me whatever pleases you sir.' Steven went and retrieved a small box from his desk and handed it to the prime minister.

He was puzzled, 'what is it?'

'Look and see.'

He lifted the lid and was left speechless. Gingerly he reached inside and took out a fire diamond about the size of a good walnut and held it up to the light.

'My God it's beautiful, what on Earth is it?'

Steven was bursting with pride, 'not on Earth sir. It's a fire diamond and they only exist in outer space. I have been told it is one of the most valuable commodities in the galaxy. It has about a hundred times the value of a normal diamond of the same size.'

'I can see why, it is breathtaking.'

The setting Sun sent a ray of light, which burst against the diamond in a hundred different colours. The prime minister seemed genuinely moved. 'This is a gift beyond comparison and priceless to boot. I have a funny feeling Edinburgh Castle just isn't going to be big enough to hold this little beauty.'

'Just don't tell any passing spacemen you have it sir or you may just face an invasion.'

He laughed, 'I'll remember that. I had better go now and thank you once again.'

They shook hands once more and the colonel escorted the prime minister back to the ramp.

Steven and Komoru sat down again. He couldn't help but look deep into her eyes, 'I think that went well, now where were we?'

She sighed, 'going through a list of thousands of names, to try and find me a crew.'

Steven nodded, 'yep, that's exactly where we were. Do you have a close friend you can take on board as your second in command, like Buzz.'

She shook her head sadly, 'I have not been as fortunate as you at finding friends Steven. I have spent half my life away from home at one special school or another where I was in direct competition with everyone else there. I always seemed to come top of the class by a large margin. It wasn't conducive to making friends and normal people like your Buzz wasn't allowed near us.'

'I'm sorry to hear that Komoru, but you may wish to consider asking your own government for a security team. Doing that you will have someone you can relate directly to, so far we have picked no Japanese for your crew and I know they have some brilliant scientists.'

'I know most of them in my field; I was at school with many of them.'

Steven nodded, 'I see, but you're going to need engineers as well. Maybe you should choose those from your own country as well or at least the best.'

She nodded, 'I will consider it.'

'Firstly, you have to try and establish direct communications with your own government.'

'They will order me to land at once.'

'You are in charge of that ship Komoru, you will have to put your foot down immediately. Get them to accept you on the terms that you want, not what they want. Ask with a meeting with your prime minister.'

'He may not wish to meet.'

'I can't believe there are two fools in this world like the American President. I'm sure he will jump at the chance.'

'OK, as soon as we get back to the Moon I will call him, but will you be with me.'

'Of course I will.'

CHAPTER 41

As soon as they arrived back at their base Steven began to organise a building program with the ships. He did it silently as he followed Komoru back to her own ship. He stopped for a moment and looked around. It was strange looking at things, as they once were, alien.

A picture of a building jumped on to the screen. Komoru was puzzled, 'what's that?'

Steven apologised, 'I'm sorry that's just me working on something, I hope you don't mind?'

'No not at all. ' She frowned prettily, 'Why, that looks like the ships at either side of a large building.'

Steven thought he had never seen anything cuter and beamed a smile at her, 'yes I'm planning on constructing a base here on the Moon. A home away from home as it were, but I want your approval before I begin.'

She seemed a little bemused, 'that is kind of you to ask, but I think it is beautiful.'

He nodded, 'it is on a design taken from the builders but is being adapted to suit human habitation. As you can see the ships will dock either side of the structure. The captain's quarters are located at the front there at the top of the building. One on either side.'

She was in awe, 'they are going to be big.'

He grinned, 'very, do you like it?'

'I love it, but how are we going to construct it?'

His mind clicked over to the technicalities of the project ahead, 'The ships will build a couple of million nanobots, which will in turn build other larger bots, and so forth until they have all the equipment they need to begin building it.

Once completed, all the bots will come together to either be absorbed back into the ship or to be moved somewhere else. The only problem will be the materials for construction. We can only use so much from this site before we end up in a big hole. The bulk of the materials will have to be transported here.'

Komoru was mesmerised, 'that sounds like a big task.'

Steven shrugged, 'it is, but we can get started on it straight away. There's a rich deposit of metal that they can use to begin making the bots with only a couple of hundred miles away. Babe's relaying my orders to Buzz now.'

The screen cleared and Steven watched with a strange pulling at his heart as his ship lifted off and disappeared out of sight.

He took a deep breath and rubbed his hands together, 'do you want to make a start?'

She smiled, 'OK, let's start with the bridge.' Her eyes swung up, 'I would like this bridge to be exactly the same as the other, Ico. Just in case personnel from one are needed on the other. That way there will be no confusion in an emergency.'

'You are wise my heart,' Ico told her.

Steven smiled in agreement as Komoru began to plan out the interior of her ship.

She turned to him, 'how do I describe something I have not seen on your ship?'

'Form a picture in your mind and Ico will see it.'

'Are you sure?'

'Trust me.'

They went from room to room again and she concentrated hard, visualising everything exactly as she wanted it. He needed to get more raw materials. Steven checked the time and decided they could visit the asteroid belt. Once there, he didn't take long to gather the materials they needed to transform the ship. They also towed a large asteroid back to the Moon.

By the time they got back Babe had returned and deposited a large writhing mass on the surface of the planet. Ico placed the asteroid next to it and both ships moved off a few miles and docked again.

Komoru checked her watch, 'I think it is time I should try and contact my government.'

Steven nodded, 'I think I got a few messages from your government. Babe, can you locate those messages for me and transfer them to Ico.'

'Yes my heart.'

The messages appeared on the main screen and there was a contact number that would take them directly to her prime minister.

She was very nervous, 'could you make the introductions for me Steven?'

He smiled, 'of course. Ico could you put the transmission onto the main screen please?'

'Of course, heart of my mate.'

'Steven will do nicely Ico.'

'Yes Steven.'

It took a few minutes but a surprised Japanese Prime Minister appeared through a video link. 'Hello.'

Steven smiled, 'Mr. Prime Minister, my name is Steven Gordon, do you know who I am sir?'

'Yes of course Mr. Gordon. This line was put in especially for you. May I congratulate you on your Japanese.'

Steven laughed, 'I'm sorry Mr President I don't actually speak Japanese, it's the ships that are doing the translating for us.'

'I am impressed.'

'It impresses me too.'

'What can I do for you Mr. Gordon? I am afraid because of the political climate it may not be much.'

'I just want to make an introduction to you Mr. Prime Minister.' He held out his hand and Komoru shyly crossed to him. 'Mr. Prime minister I would like to introduce to you Komoru Kaizu, captain of the second ship, which she has named Ico.'

It took him completely by surprise. For a second he did nothing. Then the prime minister stood up but realising they could no longer see him sat down again and bowed from the waist. Komoru returned the gesture bowing low, 'it is an honour sir.'

'I believe the honour is all mine. This is wonderful, how did it happen?'

Again Komoru looked to Steven who told him the same thing as he told the Scottish Prime Minister. The handsome Japanese man sat back and absorbed it all. His eyes flicked back to Komoru, 'this is a great honour you bestow on us Miss Kaizu. Our scientists would all like to look at your ship if you will permit it.' Steven was sure he detected a slight tremble of her limbs.

She bowed low again, 'I am sorry sir but after Ico's experience with the Americans he refuses to submit himself to such an ordeal again.'

'That is very unfortunate.'

Steven decided to take a hand, 'sir if I may?' The Prime Minister nodded.

'To be brutally honest, there are no scientists on Earth capable of understanding the complexities of these ships; half the materials needed to build them don't even exist on Earth, it would be a pointless exercise.

However, there is an alternative. The ships have agreed to release early designs of ships that are within the capabilities of most advanced nations like yourselves to build. These ships will have anti-gravity and interplanetary capabilities. Once mankind has mastered those and is capable of gathering the materials for more advanced craft, interstellar travel will be made available.'

'Will you make these plans available to us Mr. Gordon?'

'I firmly believe it would be unwise to make those plans available to any single nation sir. My mother is at this moment establishing a centre in Scotland for deep space research and exploration. She may even begin to build ships there; I don't know, I haven't been in contact with her although I plan to remedy that in the very near future. I may be able to tell you more a little later or Komoru will.'

The Japanese Prime Minister sat back and thought the situation over. Eventually he nodded in agreement, 'Scotland would be a good place to have this centre. It isn't big enough to cause any other country serious threat. Neither is it a country that has precipitated any global conflict.

Its people are known to be strong and courageous, demonstrated recently by the help their Prime Minister has given to yourself. He has the admiration of almost every country for his lone stand against the Americans.

Did you know they are trying to bring sanctions against Scotland?'

'I had heard sir.'

'I believe most of the international community will ignore the call. I only hope America doesn't try to use force to gain what they need.'

'I would advise them against it sir, I am Scottish by birth and I would use all the resources at my disposal to bring about a swift end to such a conflict.'

'I presume they would now be quite considerable.'

'They are.'

He nodded, 'I was recently shown a film of the destruction of a missile the Americans directed towards your ship. Very impressive, but would your crew back you? Many of them are Americans.'

'With a single word I can completely incapacitate the entire crew without harming them and take control of the ship myself. However, I believe they would back any decision I make.'

'May I enquire further into your military capabilities?'

'I could if desired take out a single person in a crowd or flatten an entire city from thousands of miles out into space with one shot of our primary weapons.'

The Japanese Prime Minister sat forward, 'thank you for that information Mr. Gordon. So far my government has refused to back your adventure against my personal wishes. I am sure that now Miss Kaizu has taken possession of the second ship there will be no more hesitation among my fellow countrymen to back both of you. Now, is there anything you need Miss Kaizu?'

'Yes sir, this ship has no supplies. I am eating in the other ship just now, but they do not even have rice.'

The Prime Minister smiled, 'I sympathise Miss Komoru. I have tasted Western cuisine, and although very palatable it is quite heavy for a Japanese stomach. Is there anything else I can do?'

She hesitated, 'yes sir, Steven has suggested I bring a security force on board as we may soon face unknown dangers. He has men from the American and Scottish special services to protect his ship and suggests men from a similar back ground to protect mine.'

The Japanese Prime Minister seemed to grow almost an inch, 'we have such men Miss Kaizu. I believe our special forces can rival that of any other nation.'

'As do I sir, but I will only take volunteers and please warn any man that once they become a member of the crew then it may be for life, there can be no going back.'

He nodded, 'so it is true.'

'Yes sir.'

'I saw that on the website but I do not doubt I will have plenty of volunteers. Do you wish them to bring weapons with them?'

She looked to Steven, 'I don't know, what do you think?'

Steven thought it over for a second, 'we have developed new weapons that make anything on Earth obsolete and are willing to share. However, I would leave it up to the discretion of their commander. All of my men still have their own personnel weapons from before they joined the ship. There may come a time when our new weapons may be rendered useless as they are electronically based, and where old-fashioned ones may win the day.'

The prime minister nodded, 'you have a great wisdom Mr. Gordon, I will make a recommendation that they bring a good selection of weapons with them.'

'There is one more thing Mr. Prime Minister. You must make your men understand that Miss Kaizu is commander of the ship and her word is final on all matters.'

'Of course. How many men do you recommend, Mr. Gordon?'

'I would say no more than a dozen sir and as multi-talented as possible. They will have to be able to do more than fight. I would also make one of those a dedicated pilot, that is something which I have also neglected to do.'

'I will prepare these things immediately. How will I get in touch with you?'

'We will be monitoring this line sir, just pick it up. We will also pay for any supplies given.'

'That will not be necessary Mr. Gordon.'

'I know sir but it is something we insist on.'

He nodded, 'I will call you as soon as I can. Goodbye.'

The line went dead and Komoru heaved a sigh of relief, 'thank you for your help Steven, I would not have been able to do that on my own.'

He eyed her sympathetically, 'you're really going to have to be able to take control Komoru. In a few weeks that might be an alien you're talking to and you will have to be able to take them head on if necessary. The decisions we make will be life and death decisions.'

Her head dropped, 'I am sorry Steven I am not good around other people.'

'You don't have to be good Komoru; all you have to be able to do is make a decision and make it stick. If you're not sure about something then ask for advice, for God's sake don't be frightened to do that, lives may well depend on it. Once you've listened you will have to make a decision and make one that suits your instincts, not anyone else's, not even mine.'

She managed a small smile, 'I understand, thank you. My father has said similar things many times and he has always been right. I will be all right once I have found my footing.'

He smiled, 'it is a bit of a shock. Listen to me, you've only been aboard for a few hours and already I'm giving lectures. I'm sorry.'

Her return smile made Steven's heart want to start beating erratically, 'I'm a woman, I can be very forceful when required, especially when I know I'm right.'

He laughed aloud, 'now I know you'll be all right.'

Colonel Howe's voice interrupted them, 'sir that briefing starts in five minutes.'

Steven looked at his watch, 'is it that time already, OK, I'll be with you in a minute. Do you want to come?'

'What's it for?'

'We're going to rescue my father tomorrow morning.'

'I'll come.'

CHAPTER 42

Everyone was present for the briefing. Steven stood with Komoru and Buzz to one side. The colonel first laid out a broad outline of the plan before Steven came up.

He held up what looked like an air freshener and told them about his plan to beam them all over the prison in an attempt to knock out the opposition before they went in. The colonel then went into the plan in detail.

When he was satisfied everyone knew their part he let them all go and reported to Steven.

'I'm still not happy you're coming in with us tomorrow sir.'

Steven grimaced, 'live with it Colonel. I'm not going to be wrapped up in cotton wool.'

'I understand that sir but it would be a shame to lose you before we even left Earth.'

Steven slapped him on the shoulder, 'this isn't my first time in action Colonel and you may be surprised by how well I can handle myself.'

'I read your record sir and I am aware of that.'

'Once we're fully manned Colonel you can give every member of the crew some military training, but until then you're just going to have to trust me. Is there anything else?'

'Yes sir, Sergeant Grey has finished the bomb.'

'Already? I'm impressed. Do you wanna go test it before we knock off?'

The colonel grinned, 'oh yes.'

Komoru interrupted, 'what bomb?'

Steven explained, 'one of Major Forbes's men claimed he could make an atomic bomb, so I asked him to prove it before I let him join the crew.'

She gasped horrified, 'you have an atomic bomb on board, what are you going to do with it?'

'Nothing actually, we're going to go into space and detonate it to see if it works, that's all.'

'That's all? Do you have any particular spot in space you want to contaminate or are you just going to blow it up anywhere.'

Steven blushed, 'no not really, I never really thought about it.'

'That's obvious. Well I suggest you do it somewhere out of sight of Earth or you may start a panic and it might give the American President an excuse to throw a lot more than bullets at you tomorrow.'

'You're right Komoru, it is a bad idea, but I really want to see if this will work. Babe, can you find a spot that fits Komoru's parameters?'

'It will take us five minutes to reach there my heart.'

'Then give the order please.'

Five minutes later, they were hidden behind Jupiter. Jim Grey stood behind Steven with a pair of dark glasses on and a gun in a holster at his side. Everyone had gathered to witness the event.

Steven squinted in his chair, 'OK Jim, you can detonate it now.'

Jim took a small transmitter from his pocket and showed it to Steven, 'Babe's magnifying the signal for me. OK, here we go: five, four, three, two, one.'

There was a slight delay then a bright light lit up the darkness of space. Everyone shielded their eyes then there was a spontaneous round of applause. Jim Grey couldn't help the grin that spread across his face.

Steven turned round still clapping, 'well done, I must admit I had my doubts. How on earth did you manage to complete it so quickly?'

He shrugged, 'it was easy; I drew a wiring diagram for Babe. She made up the circuit boards and supplied all the materials to my specs and then it was a simple case of putting it all together.'

Steven held out his hand, 'welcome to the crew. If you report to the doctor she will oversee your implants.'

'Thank you sir, there is one thing though. I see you already have an armourer; I thought I would be a dab hand at that job.'

Steven laughed and looked for a face, 'Chief, what have you to say on that matter?'

Matt stepped forward and stuck his face close to Jim's, 'listen laddie, any man who can build an atomic bomb from scratch including drawing the circuit diagrams, does not belong in a bloody armoury. I'm quite sure the captain will let you blow something up now and then to keep you happy, but you're coming with me.'

Jim looked crestfallen and Steven decided to step in before the man decided to change his mind. 'The Chief's right, someone with your talents will prove invaluable to us. Of course your first job will be as part of Colonel Howe's team. However, every scientist on board is going to need someone with your practical skills, we are a ham-fisted breed Jim.

I couldn't have done what you just did and neither could any other man or woman on board. That kind of talent is invaluable but we need it where it counts the most and that's in engineering. If you wish to visit the armoury and invent new weapons, or work with those we have then please do so, no one is going to stop you.'

Jim smiled, 'I can live with that.'

'Chief, could you take him up?'

'No problems, this way laddie.'

Steven turned and addressed everyone else there, 'I suggest as soon as we return to the Moon that everyone turn in for the night, it's been a long day and it's going to be an even longer one tomorrow.'

CHAPTER 43

It was a cool clear moonlit night, but Brian Gordon wasn't aware of that in his basement cell. What he was becoming aware of was an insistent beeping of an alarm. He came half-awake imagining he was at home in his bed. He wondered idly for a moment why there was no sunlight spilling in the curtains. Then he remembered.

He sat bolt upright in the narrow cot knowing exactly where he was and realising there were no alarm clocks in this cell. It was pitch black but he could feel pressure on his feet.

His hands came into contact with something large and round which felt like glass. The beeping was coming from somewhere within the bundle. He searched around with his hands and found something long and cylindrical.

It was a torch and he switched it on. He squinted against the sudden glare but spotted a small square object with a button on top. He picked it up and depressed the button. The beeping ceased. In the sudden silence he sat and listened for any movement from the corridor outside, but everything was quiet.

He inspected the bundle Steven had beamed directly into his cell and frowned, what the hell was it, how the hell had it got here without someone coming into the cell? He got up and took a closer look. It was apparent that it was some kind of suit with a glass helmet. There was a note, he picked it up and read. 'Dad you have five minutes to put this on, love Steven.'

He almost dropped the torch in his haste, but quickly clambered into the space suit. He sat and listened to his heart hammer in his chest aware that something dramatic was about to happen. Footsteps approached his cell door. He quickly switched the torch off and slipped back under the covers.

The guard went straight past without looking in. Brian got out of bed and silently crossed to the door. He put his ear as close as he could to the door without hitting it with his helmet.

The footsteps faltered then there came the sound of wet meat hitting the floor, Brian pulled back from the door with a terrible grimace, 'ouch.'

He put his ear back to the door and listened for what seemed an age but there was nothing more. Then suddenly came the blaring of klaxons all over the prison.

Brian stepped back from the door, 'shit!'

Everything had gone to plan for a start. They had come in a long shallow orbit to reduce any chances of being spotted. At ten thousand feet they had hovered above the prison, invisible to the naked eye. At Steven's command she began dispersing the air fresheners around the prison.

Men who where resting in the cells suddenly feel asleep. Those already sleeping fell into a dreamless slumber. Sentries in watchtowers and patrolling the corridors fell at their stations. Only those patrolling the grounds outside were unaffected.

Babe dropped like a stone and landed next to the prison wall. Tapper and his three men ran down the ramp. Their new weapons made short work of the walls and they ran inside.

A guard dog started barking as it caught their scent. Two men with a dog ran around the corner into well-aimed shots from the four men. They dropped like a stone. They made their way to the guardhouse.

Easily gaining entry, Tapper called up Steven, 'they're out cold sir, we'll hold the perimeter from here.'

The ship landed half in the courtyard. Colonel Howe and Beaver were first off the ship. A small explosive charge to the main doors blew them open and they were in. Steven found that somehow the men managed to keep him in the middle. It was a little awkward running around in their space suits, but less so Howe assured than with gasmasks.

What they didn't realise was that the prison was also being monitored from an outside location. An FBI operator, half asleep at his post had decided to go and get himself a coffee at the precise moment they struck. The operator took his coffee over to a table laden with magazines and began to flip through them.

After finding an article he was interested in he went back to his post and sat down. His eyes flicked up at the screens then went back to the article; they froze there. Slowly he looked back up and cursed. He reached for the emergency buttons but by that time they were deep inside the prison itself.

As Steven and the men ran through the prison looking for his father they soon discovered that on the kill setting their weapons could easily cut through the door locks. Beaver had set his weapon to kill whilst the colonel covered him. Beaver cut through another lock with a grin, it was much quicker than searching the sleeping guards for keys and safer than using explosives.

As he kicked the door open klaxons went off all over the prison.

'Shit!' Howe cursed.

'Let's just keep going.' Steven reassured.

Komoru was still at ten thousand feet keeping an eye on the whole area. Ico detected movement and she warned Steven.

'Steven, there is a dozen helicopters taking off from an air base about twenty miles away and heading in your direction.'

'Thank you Komoru, any idea what they are?'

'Wait a second.' Ico scanned them. 'There are four carrying tanks, six troops and two of them are too small to carry either but they seem to be faster than the others.'

Colonel Howe knew what they were, 'the first two will be gunships. They will try and cripple Babe on the ground.'

Steven nodded, 'Babe, raise all your shields. Can you sustain an attack from both of those ships.'

'Do not worry my heart, only the biggest of Earth weapons could possibly damage me.'

'Yes but what if they drop a building on you?'

'Have no fear my heart, I have sustained meteor showers that would destroy this whole planet without damage.'

Steven smiled to himself, 'OK Major Forbes, we have incoming, did you read that?'

'Let them come, we're ready.'

Howe was right; the gunships came in first. Babe extended her shields to cover the front door and the guardhouse. Tank busting missiles streaked in only to explode harmlessly in the air. Others directed at the guardhouse suffered the same fate. A line of what looked like green tracers streaked out of the protective bubble and struck one of the gunships.

Sparks flew from the pilot's console and the engine immediately began to lose power. He managed to turn it away but it hit the street a few hundred yards up. Men spilled from the smoking gunship. Tapper let them get to a safe distance before shooting them. Their twitching bodies hit the sidewalk.

The second gunship streaked in with missiles firing and all guns blazing. As it streaked overhead Cookie hit its tail rotor and the machine began to swing wildly out of control. It dipped behind a row of houses and a few seconds later a large pall of smoke was flung above the rooftops.

Tapper reported to Steven, 'that's both gunships down sir.'

Steven shook his head sadly hoping there was no loss of life. 'OK thanks Major, we're at the last door now before my father's cell. Komoru, how long do we have until the next wave arrives?'

'Only a few minutes until the troops arrive, a little more for the tanks.'

'Thank you.'

Colonel Howe reached the cell first and shouted through the heavy door, 'are you in their Doc?'

'Is that you Colonel?'

'Yes sir, please stand back from the door and to the side.'

'OK.'

Howe nodded to Beaver who quickly cut through the locks and kicked the door in. Brian almost ran out, 'Christ, it's good to see you but it's a trap.'

Steven tapped his father on the arm, 'hi Dad.'

Brian looked shocked, 'my God Steven what are you doing here?'

Steven grinned, 'getting you home to mother, explanations later, we've got to run, can you manage?'

'Just lead the way son.'

'Let's go, Major Forbes, we're on our way out.'

'Roger that, be quick I can hear the next wave coming in.'

They set off at a run.

Outside things began to heat up. One chopper landed within sight of the guardhouse and made the mistake of turning so its ramp faced the waiting men. Green fire laced over the lowering ramp. Men rushed out into it and fell. The men behind had to step or jump over them making themselves perfect targets for the seasoned veterans of Tapper's command.

Within a few minutes it was all over. Twitching men littered the ramp and surrounding ground. The remaining choppers didn't make the same mistake. They unloaded in the safety of nearby streets and men poured towards the prison.

Sweat was beginning to pool in Steven suit when Komoru's warning came through.

'Many soldiers have blasted a way through the rear wall of the prison and have gained entry.'

'Thanks Komoru we haven't far to go now.'

The first soldiers inside the complex fell victim to the sleeping gas. Those behind quickly donned gas masks.

The first tank hit the street behind the prison and raced towards the gates. Green fire laced its hull and turret, but the tank was protected against electromagnetic burst radiation and it had no effect. A high explosive shell answered their fire and smashed harmlessly into the shield.

Tapper cranked his weapon up to kill and took careful aim, but a thick covering of titanium armour protected the tank.

Tapper cursed and turned it up to full power. Again he took careful aim. This time the green fire sliced into the tank's tracks. Pieces of fused track and road wheels burst onto the road and the tank slewed sideways. Before it could react Tapper sliced off the gun barrel, which fell harmlessly onto its deck.

He grinned as he turned the weapon's power back down again, 'smile boys, we just made every armoured fighting vehicle in the entire world obsolete.'

Jim Grey fired at the tank men as they bailed out of the tank, scattering bodies across the width of the road, 'I think we just made bullets obsolete as well.'

Cookie shook his head in wonder, 'just think, you could have a war without killing anybody. All you would have to do is knock the buggers out and throw them in the can.'

Tapper grunted, 'I wouldn't get too excited about it just yet. I doubt if humanity is ready for bloodless wars.'

Jim grinned, 'yeah and where's the fun in that?'

His companions did a double take to make sure he was joking and smiled when they realised he was.

The other tanks took up position out of sight and began to bombard them with high explosives. Their shells burst harmlessly against the outer shield.

Tapper looked up, 'Babe, those shells can't get through but can people or vehicles?'

'No only those with nanobots in their bloodstream can penetrate the shields.'

Tapper reappraised the situation, 'thanks Babe. Steven I'm moving my unit back to cover your retreat from the prison.'

'OK Major. Babe, how am I going to get my father through the shields?'

'Hold his hand.'

Steven grinned, 'OK thanks.'

Komoru had been watching the progress of the troops, 'Steven, some of those soldiers look like they may be able to head you off.'

'Thanks Komoru. Babe, extend your shields towards us as much as you can; Major, take your men to the edge of the shields but do not go beyond that. Lewis, if you would like to back up Major Forbes your help would be most welcome.'

Lewis reached the front doors first and moved forward cautiously, 'How will I know when I reach de edge of de shields Babe?'

'You will feel a tingling on your skin.'

He walked forward with a hand extended until he felt the extraordinary sensation, 'I got it Major, but you and de boys had better hurry I can hear people running and not from de captain's direction.'

'Hold the fort for us Lewis we're on our way.'

The shield extended to a junction of corridors. The giant took up position just inside the shield and braced himself.

Steven paused at the top of another flight of stairs and caught his breath. The colonel cautioned him to stay put for a further few seconds until his father had recovered a little, 'we've only a few hundred metres to go sir.'

Steven could easily hear the thunder of running feet echoing down the empty corridors, 'is it wise to wait Colonel?'

'Far better to walk into trouble than run into it sir.'

Steven gave him a small nod, 'you're the expert Colonel.'

Howe turned to his men, 'OK spread out, keep the doctor in the middle, you know the drill.' In an instant they turned from fugitives to hunters.

The president's men came in from the interconnecting corridors and tried to cut Stevens group off from their line of retreat. Men spilled into the main corridor. Lewis braced himself and fired. Many fell paralysed, but still more came. Tapper and his team arrived and added to the equation. Those who survived unscathed quickly dodged back into the adjoining corridors and sprayed bullets around the corners, which bounced harmlessly off the shield.

Someone ordered a ceasefire and a man walked out into the open with his hands held high, 'you boys are completely surrounded, why don't you surrender?'

Tapper went to answer but Lewis clamped a giant hand over his mouth and whispered in his ear, 'dey heah yo accent suh, it could cause a lot of trouble.'

Tapper nodded his agreement, his appreciation of the big man doubling.

Lewis stepped forward, 'what foh?'

The man tried to smile through his gas mask, 'you don't understand, you're completely surrounded by troops and tanks.'

'So?'

There was an awkward silence. 'Look I'm trying to save lives here and prevent more bloodshed.'

'Dey ain't been no bloodshed dat I seen. Check you boy's. Dey ain't dead only stunned. In thirty minutes or so dey all be up and running, but hey you wanna play rough we can cut you down right through dem walls.'

Lewis cranked up his weapon to full power and cut through the wall beside him. Stepping forward he kicked a large chunk of the wall out. 'Hey maybe you and your boys wanna surrender. Maybe de captain give you all a trip to de Moon if'n you're all real nice.'

The man backed away quickly but they never surrendered or ran. The springing of levers from grenades could clearly be heard. Tapper stepped up beside Lewis and talked only loud enough so they could hear, 'they're going to toss up a couple of grenades then charge, let's all roll about on the floor like we've been hurt. When they reach the shield we'll bag the lot.'

No sooner had he stopped talking than half a dozen grenades appeared from around the corner. They exploded with a brilliant flash of light. The five crewmates fell to the floor faking death or agony. The corridor was suddenly full of wild screaming men firing from the hip.

Sparks of light flashed of the shield and Lewis thought they were lucky none ricocheted back into the running men.

The first two men slammed into the shield and bounced off. It was the signal for the actors to jump back onto their feet and start firing again.

Unfortunately, all five were finding it hard not to laugh but failed as more men bounced harmlessly off the shield. Laughing threw their aim a little off and some made it back to the junctions safely.

Steven's voice reached Tapper and his men, 'OK ceasefire, we'll take it from here.'

The door at the far end burst open and more grenades filled the corridor. The doors closed again and the grenades went off. Colonel Howe and Beaver were first through, firing down the first junction they came to and throwing grenades.

As soon as the grenades went off they moved down to the next junction. As Steven passed the second junction more men spilled around the far bend. He fired instinctively and they fell twitching to the ground.

'Speed it up Colonel there's more coming.'

Goldsmith began to pitch the flash bang grenades into the junctions that hadn't yet been cleared; his accuracy from such an angle was impressive. Tapper and his men broke clear of the shield and fought their way towards them. They met near the middle and Howe gave one order, 'run!'

Bullets began to zip up the corridors as reinforcements arrived and masonry fell around them as high explosive shells bounced off the shields and hit the building.

Lewis stooped down and scooped Brian up onto his shoulder, 'excuse me suh,' and burst through the shield with the rest of them hard on his heels.

Steven slowed to a walk, 'OK we're clear, prepare to take off. Komoru, what's happening out there? Have they any aircraft up?'

'Yes Steven, it looks like there are at least two squadrons heading our way.'

'Then get out of there, we'll only be a few seconds behind.'

Steven ran up the ramp and headed straight for the bridge. He jumped into his chair, 'OK Haley, get us out of here. Take us into a high Earth orbit. Colonel, have we sustained any casualties?'

'None sir, all present and correct, no wounded.'

'Excellent job, well done everyone.'

Colonel Howe retrieved his post from one of the scientists, 'sir those aircraft are coming fast, and they are firing missiles.'

'Will they reach us in orbit.'

'I doubt it sir.'

'Dey wont suh, they ain't got the range.'

Steven smiled, 'thanks Lewis, let them come Colonel.'

'Yes sir.'

Brian in the meantime was still slung over Lewis's shoulder. He cleared his throat, 'excuse me, can you let me down.'

'Oh sorry suh I forgot you were there.'

Lewis put him down and Brian stared up at the giant in wonder, 'I'm fourteen stone man, and you forgot I was there.'

'Yes suh, you ain't that heavy.'

'Really, could you please tell my wife that for me when we see her?'

Everyone burst out laughing as they reached Earth's orbit and missiles exploded in an expensive fireworks display far beneath them.

CHAPTER 44

They had just moved into a geocentric orbit with the other ship when another asteroid-busting missile was fired at them.

Steven sighed in disgust, 'get us out of here and back to the Moon. We'll return in a couple of hours when things cool down.' He turned to his father, 'you don't mind do you Dad?'

'What, on a wee trip to the Moon? Nah your OK son, I'll survive.'

Steven laughed, 'Haley, take us home.'

Brian smiled, 'so you've moved to the Moon. I had an idea of an apartment a little nearer home for you son, but I'm sure you know your own mind.'

Now everyone was laughing at their banter, 'the real estate's cheap and there's plenty of room for a garden. Mind you, you do have to tow in your own asteroid for building materials, but all things considered … it isn't a bad deal dad. You really ought to consider moving Mum up.'

Brian smiled, 'well if I can get a good deal on rocket fuel and the natives don't get any friendlier we just might.'

Steven stood, 'fancy a coffee Dad? you've got a lot of catching up to do.'

Brian stood squinting, 'if I can see the cup I'd love one.'

Steven led Brian down to his quarters. Once back on the Moon he quickly brought his father up to speed on recent developments. They were also able to contact Mary back on Earth. Steven left his parents to it as tears sprang into his mother's eyes.

Buzz made to stand up and get out of his chair but Steven waved him down and sat beside him.

Buzz raised an eyebrow, 'what's happening?'

Steven sighed, 'Mum and Dad are talking.' He ran a finger down the side of his nose.

Buzz nodded his understanding, 'so what now?'

Steven shrugged, 'good question. We'll have to take Dad back to Earth, but he wants to go walkabout first and grab a few samples of Moon rock to take with him. That's a job for Tapper I suppose.'

Colonel Howe overheard and came over, 'do you mind if I accompany your father sir?'

'Not at all Colonel as long as you take the Major with you.'

Howe grinned, 'he is our resident expert on rocks.'

'Are you going to be doing a debrief on the operation Colonel?'

'Yes sir, tonight, I have a feeling we're going to have a busy day ahead of us.'

'Anything you want to bring up with me first?'

'Actually I have an idea for a new type of stun grenade. We've used up almost our whole stock and it will be hard getting replacements at the best of times.'

Steven nodded, 'that's a good idea. I would check with Babe first. The builders were big into none lethal ways of dealing with enemies. You'll probably find everything you need there although you may have to redesign everything to suit our needs.'

Howe nodded, 'that's where I was going to start.'

'OK, but I want to see any weapons you develop first before you put them into mass production.'

'Of course sir.'

Howe left them looking pleased with himself.

Steven got back to matters at hand, 'Babe tells me we need another asteroid or two for our new home.'

Buzz frowned, 'you're kidding aren't you. That asteroid you brought back last night was almost half a mile across.'

Steven shrugged, 'she wants she gets. It seems that one didn't have a lot of minerals in it. We have to get a few heavy in iron and other stuff. I've got a shopping list.'

'When are we going?'

'Right after breakfast, I'm starved.'

'Then you had better give Komoru a shout, she's hungry as well and she has some news.'

'Talking about news, any word of our deeds yet?'

'No nothing yet.'

'I'm sure it will hit the fan soon enough, let's go.'

Ico docked and Komoru came aboard. She met them in the dining hall. Steven stood as she approached, 'thanks for all your help today.'

She smiled in return, 'it was a pleasure.'

They sat down and Cookie brought her over a plate of food. She smiled, 'thank you but I could have come and got it myself.'

Cookie grinned, 'it's my pleasure ma'am.'

Steven smiled and shook his head as he walked away, 'I think he likes you, we all have to get our own. How are you and Ico getting along?'

'I feel as though we have been friends all our life.'

'Are you feeling a little lonely over there by yourself?'

She shook her head, 'no, I haven't had the time to feel lonely; there's been so much to do.'

'I know what you mean. I think I could have done with a couple of days on board by myself just to explore and find out where everything is and what it does. I think in the near future I'm going to have set aside a day to do just that.'

'Yes that would be wise. I won't be on my own for much longer though. I have had a message from my prime minister; he will have everything ready for me in three hours' time.'

'That's good, fancy doing a little shopping first?'

She frowned, 'out here.'

Steven grinned, 'you'll see.'

Half an hour later, they were at the asteroid belt doing a little shopping. Ico took on a cargo of precious metal and gemstones to pay for their supplies. Brian wanted to collect a sample from one of the surrounding asteroids, but Steven denied him the pleasure and swore him to secrecy.

Both ships then towed separate asteroids out of the belt until they had all they needed. Then both ships joined together and using their collective power towed all of them back to the Moon. The asteroid they had towed the previous evening was almost completely devoured and in its place stood part of what was going to be a huge complex.

Brian looked at the new development with a little scepticism, 'do you think it's big enough Steven?'

Steven frowned, 'I think so. Babe says its dimensions are correct but I didn't think it would be this big. Still she knows what she's doing a lot more than I do.'

'You could start your own colony.'

'Yeah I think that's the idea. The thing is if we can't reconcile with the governments on Earth then we may have to transfer the families of the crew up to here. So we need shops schools hospital, somewhere to grow food, an operations centre and homes to live in.'

Brian nodded, 'I'm getting the idea. Is it going to be full of this bright metal?'

'No.'

'Thank God for that. Hey, have you got a spot sorted for you old mum and dad?'

'Yeah, do you see that mountain on the horizon over there?'

Brian laughed and gave him a play full punch on the shoulder, 'you're still a cheeky little sod.'

Steven laughed and pointed to the complex, 'do you see where it begins curve over there.'

'Yeah I see it.'

'On the far side of that the roof will level off, you and Mum will have an apartment along that side there.'

Brian was astonished, 'really, you're not joking.'

'Nope, and once Mum has built her own wee space ship you can move in if you want.'

Brian grunted, 'I hope it's got a big wardrobe for all your mother's dresses.'

Steven laughed, 'aye and a library for your books Dad.'

Brian laughed, 'still it will be good to get home to Scotland for a while. They really pulled out all the stops for us. I only hope it doesn't prove an expensive enterprise for the old homeland. The American President isn't going to take it lying down.'

Steven nodded, 'that's got me worried too. He's really thrown everything but the kitchen sink at us so far and wait until he finds out Komoru's in command of the second ship.'

'What are you going to do if he launches some kind of strike against Scotland and Japan?'

Steven turned with a cold look in his eye, 'I'll drop him and his precious Whitehouse clean into the planet's core.'

Brian shook his head, 'you can't do that son. You would become a new world dictator. The moment you popped off somewhere the rest of the planet would wipe us off the face of the earth.'

Steven sighed with frustration and turned away, 'God I know, but what the hell am I supposed to do? We can't stay here for the rest of our lives defending both countries. If we give them weapons to defend themselves with while we're away, it would unbalance the whole power structure of the Earth and that would precipitate an attack as quick.

Even if it didn't they would probably slap so many sanctions on you the whole country would collapse economically within a year and then they would just waltz in and steal everything anyway.'

'I'm glad to see you have at least thought it through. What about the American contingent of the crew, do they have anything to say on the matter?'

'Yeah well the Colonel and his boys want to beam him up and toss him out into space. The scientists were a little less kind.'

'Not much help then.'

'No, no matter what I do he's got us boxed in.'

'Could you grow your own food up here?'

'I can see where you're going with this Dad but that won't do any good either. I can guarantee you within six months of leaving here they would find a way of putting people back on the Moon. We would either come back to find a detachment of marines on site or the place stripped bare.'

'You could leave people here with weapons to defend it.'

'Yeah I could, but the first time they repelled an attack that idiot would start launching nukes at them.'

'Check, you could surrender the ships.'

'Wouldn't work they would just take off and never return. Everyone on board could be dead within six months.'

'Checkmate. Is there no hope?'

'One slim one. Political satire, there's a lot of people in the States on our side. We have a few very powerful friends on the inside, and if he continues to do stupid thing like trying to nuke us, then they may be able to have him impeached. However with Mum setting up in Scotland, the financial reward to their constituents is somewhat vastly reduced, and to be quite frank Dad, it may not be worth their while.'

'There is a chance he might just live with it.'

'You think?'

Brian shook his head, 'no I suppose not. So what are you going to do?'

'Make an appeal to all the nations of Earth on live TV and then watch where the dice fall from there.'

Brian slapped his son on the shoulder, 'well good luck son. Now I believe I'm due a little Moon walk.'

Steven grinned, 'I think I'd like to stretch my legs as well, let's go.'

CHAPTER 45

Komoru was nervous as Ico landed on the large Japanese air base. People swarmed everywhere. There were a lot of armed soldiers, but there were also a lot of men who were unarmed. She sensed excitement from the crowd, not malice or tension.

A large black vehicle detached itself from one of the main buildings and sped towards the ship, two more came in hot pursuit. She noticed a camera crew run from the hanger beside which she had landed and felt a great sense of relief. She doubted anyone would try and hijack the ship with the press around.

Steven had offered to come with her but she had finally decided against it. If she couldn't trust her own government then she would be truly lost anyway.

Komoru rose from her chair and smiled at her companions. Lewis and Cookie smiled back.

'Don you worry none Captain. Cookie and me, we'll look after you.'

'Your presence gentlemen is greatly appreciated. Let's go welcome our visitors.'

Lewis led the way and was first out of the ship. A couple of soldiers had begun to run up the ramp as it deployed, but they took one look at Lewis and ran back down again. He strolled boldly down the ramp with a menacing scowl on his face, and Komoru almost burst out laughing at the look of awe on the faces of her fellow countrymen.

Cookie walked behind her and then the three stood abreast of one another at the bottom of the ramp. Both men were armed and had asked to come along. They kept their weapons pointed towards the ground, but there wasn't a soldier there that couldn't see that both men were ready to fight if need be.

The news crew tried to rush forward but were pushed back by their minders. A rapid sentence in Japanese stilled their shouts. The first car came to a halt and the front seat passenger jumped out and opened the door.

Komoru caught her breath as the prime minister got out, and then smiled as his wife and two children got out after him. He came forward and bowed low, his family mirroring his actions.

'Miss Kaizu, you do us a great honour. May I present to you, my wife and children.'

Komoru was almost overwhelmed by the gesture and bowed in return to all. The prime minister's son was staring quite openly at Lewis. The giant winked and the young lad smiled in return.

It was then Komoru's family alighted from the second car. Forgetting her manners she ran to them and almost leapt into her father's arms. There were smiles and tears all round. The prime minister waited until the tears had settled a bit then offered them all refreshments.

They had been set up in the hanger next to the ship. Komoru was suddenly worried about the ship and sent a silent order to Ico who passed it on to the two men. She saw them nod in understanding and let herself be led away.

Inside the hanger there were over a dozen men standing with weapons shouldered and kit bags at their feet. The prime minister brought her over.

'These are the men we have selected to go with you. Each have university training in a wide variety of fields, although none are true scientists like yourself.'

She smiled, 'scientists there are no shortage of sir.'

He returned her smile, 'of course. I have also picked out two pilots for you. I remember Mr. Gordon saying he had neglected to get one for himself.'

He introduced her to the two men standing at the end of the line. She did a double take and he smiled, 'as you can see they are identical twins and probably the best pilots we have. Do you think Mr. Gordon would accept one of our men.'

'Wait a second sir and I will ask him.' She closed her eyes and concentrated hard. 'Steven my prime Minister has picked two pilots for us. They are identical twins, would you accept one on your crew, I can easily keep both if you don't.'

She was surprised by how quickly and how clearly she heard his reply, 'tell the prime minister I would be honoured to accept one of his pilots on board my ship.'

She smiled, 'thank you Steven I will tell him.'

Komoru told him of Steven response; he was confused, 'I'm sorry how did you communicate with him?'

She pulled back her hair and showed him the neural link. 'Steven and I both have neural implants that connect us directly to the ships. As they are directly connected to one another then so too are the captains.'

The prime minister wasn't a stupid man, 'you mean you talk directly to one another's minds like telepathy?'

'Yes sir, just like telepathy.'

'Can the rest of the crew do this?'

'No sir, they have to talk directly to the ship and through the ship to each other and us. However as captains, our natural abilities give us a direct link to the other members of the crew through our neural link; we can talk to them with our minds and they will hear us, without the ship's help.'

The light of true understanding began to dawn, 'is this a natural ability that the ships require for someone to become captain?'

'It's not so much an ability sir, the part of the human brain that is required for this direct form of communication is dormant in most humans.'

'So that's what separates you and Mr. Gordon from the rest of us?'

She blushed, 'yes sir, that part of our brains are more active than most. That is why we were chosen to become captains.'

He nodded, 'I am beginning to understand. You seemed to have a little difficulty communicating in that manner, does Mr. Gordon have the same trouble?'

She shook her head, 'I have to concentrate really hard, but it seems to come naturally to Mr. Gordon. I can only get a sense of his true abilities sir, but they far outstrip mine.'

'So more of that part of Mr. Gordon's brain is active?'

'A lot more sir, he thinks it was due to an accident in his youth. Before that occurred he was considered a genius, yes, but he thinks we were of equal intellect. He lost most of his brain functions in the accident and his brain had to utilise that dormant part of his mind at an early age. If he hadn't been so young then he may have remained in a vegetative state for the rest of his life.'

The prime minister fully understood now, 'so that is why the ships were drawn to him so strongly. That is why they chose a security guard to become captain before a scientist. With so much of the dormant brain active it must have been like honey to a bee.'

'I couldn't have put it better sir.'

'So tell me, what are your plans for the near future?'

She shrugged, 'we haven't had much time to plan anything yet sir. We have a base that is under construction on the Moon. If need be we will make that our permanent HQ. It's a very large complex and will be able to house the crews of both ships and their families permanently. The trouble up until now has been supplies and it will be our major problem in the near future too.'

'This trouble with the American President.'

'Yes sir, every time we are seen in Earth's orbit he fires nuclear missiles at us. Steven is worried he will precipitate a conflict with any nation that helps us.'

'Is that a polite way of asking me to keep this meeting secret?'

Her eyes flicked towards the hovering camera crew. It was obvious they had missed nothing. 'Yes sir.'

He smiled, 'I am afraid it is far too late for that Miss Kaizu, you see this meeting is being broadcast live to the whole of the nation and beyond. Only the location is being kept secret.'

'Oh, I didn't know.'

He smiled, 'we are very proud of you Miss Kaizu. Your acceptance as captain of one of the ships proves to us beyond any shadow of a doubt that there has been no collusion or deliberate intent behind the captaincy of Mr. Gordon. He is much a victim of fate as you are.'

'He is the only victim of fate sir. I was asked if I would like to become a captain and accepted. He was drugged; the ship released a sleeping gas into the air. He sat down and fell asleep. When he awoke two days later he had changed beyond measure.

I have seen many photos of him and would not have known him if he walked into my house. The ship repaired his mind of the damage inflicted so many years ago by that horrific accident, but what she did to him went far beyond even that.

The accident stunted his growth as well, but she accelerated it until twenty years later he finally reached his true height. Not even his mother or father recognised him when he arose from that chair. Only a DNA test could prove it was the same man who boarded that ship a few days earlier.'

The prime minister seemed concerned, 'truly a day when fact is stranger than fiction. So you say that in reality Mr. Gordon was abducted by the alien ships?'

'Yes sir but he is a grateful to her for abducting him. What you have to realise is that in the end they were left with little choice.'

The prime minister nodded, 'yes Miss Kaizu, I do understand. For weeks many of Americas top scientists had crawled all over them, yet none had the type of mind needed to interact with them. Then came the incident with Doctor Sales. So when Mr. Gordon came along he must have been heaven sent to those ships.'

'Yes sir, I just wish everyone was as understanding as you.'

'I am sure time will bring understanding. Now a little bird whispered in my ear this morning that a certain other prime minister was given a little trip in his fellow countryman's ship. May I be so bold as to mention it?'

Komoru's laugh made everyone smile, 'I would be honoured to invite you and your family on board my ship, sir; and you can take the news crew to if you want too.'

He smiled at the excited reporters, 'I think they will accept your invitation, as I will.'

Once the stores were on board, a lot more people than was intended were guided on board, and Ico left for the Moon. Komoru gave them an orbit of Earth but was forced to leave as again the Americans launched a nuclear missile at them.

The Japanese Prime Minister was greatly angered by the gesture. He requested they stay there for as long as it was safe to get visual conformation of the deed. Ico magnified the screen until even the writing on the nose cone could easily be seen.

Finally satisfied, they arrived at the Moon within a few minutes. The speed took everyone's breath away and caused a lot of excited chatter.

Komoru took the ship to the site of the new complex first. It brought no end of excitement. Ico zoomed in on what was happening. They watched a beam of light shoot out of a strange machine into an asteroid. As they watched, it began to dissolve. Another ray of light shot out of the other end of the machine where the walls were being built.

The prime minister was highly impressed, 'I see how it's done. The particles of the asteroid are reassembled in the shape or form that's needed.'

Komoru nodded, 'yes sir, but we have to make sure the correct materials are available for construction. Rock is all right for the walls but we had to tow metal heavy asteroids here from the asteroid belt.'

'It looks half completed, when did you start building it?'

'Little more than a day ago sir.'

'That is amazing how long until it is completed?'

'Less than forty-eight hours.'

'Can this technology be brought to Earth?'

'Yes sir, once it's safe. Steven is rather reluctant to share this kind of technology because of the political climate back on Earth.'

'It is hardly surprising given the recent attacks made on you by the United States. What can this technology be used for?'

'Everything from building new hospitals to space ships.'

'How long do you think it would take to build a space ship?'

'That would really depend on how long it took you to assemble the materials needed. You would start out with a shopping list of raw the materials needed. Once they were all assembled in one spot the machines would begin to build. I think it would take no more than a few days to build a ship capable of interplanetary travel.'

'So what you're saying Miss Komoru is that within a few months man could have bases on Mars.'

'Yes sir easily.'

'Yes but... now there must be a but.'

She smiled, 'Stevens initial plan was to set up a dedicated space centre in America where most of the raw materials would be ready available. However the American President's greed has made that almost impossable. Steven's mother is at present beginning to set up a centre in Scotland but he is only going to make communication equipment available at first.'

The prime minister frowned, 'why is that?'

'He believes that the Americans may try to steal any new technology he brings to his homeland, and would do it by force if necessary.'

'Many countries may have a problem with Scotland being given all that technology to itself.'

'The technology would only be given on the premises that people from of all Earth's nations would be welcome to join the project. Also, he would insist that the building of such ships would be kept to one place and that a command structure built from all nations would command the project.'

'Does he really think that would work?'

'The United Nations has worked for years sir, and if anyone really wants this technology then they better learn to work together. The dangers that face us out there will affect the entire planet not just one nation upon its surface.'

He nodded, 'you make a good point Miss Kaizu, but many will see this as a form of blackmail.'

'That's too bad sir. When we come home we would like to find it as we left it and not desolate from every nation fighting over what we left behind.'

'Tell me whom will you take your orders from Miss Kaizu?'

'I will take my orders from Mr. Gordon sir.'

'And he?'

'From the people of Earth. As everyone knows he has set up a website. On it there is a number of questioners. From it he will determine what it is the common people of the world would like him to do. There is also a section for scientists and heads of governments; it is free to be used by anyone.'

'I suppose in the absence of any form of structure it's the next best thing, but once there is structure will he conform to orders from a civil space governing body?'

'I don't know sir you would have to ask him that yourself.'

'I will given the chance. Do you know where he is?'

She smiled and sent out a silent order.

Ico rushed over the surface of the Moon and came to rest over a number of people out on the surface of the Moon not far from the other ship.

The prime minister was wide-eyed, 'what are they doing?'

'They are out for a walk sir.'

He burst out laughing, 'of course it was a stupid question.'

She smiled, 'Steven rescued his father from an American prison this morning. He wanted to go on a moonwalk and gather some samples of Moon rock, would you like to join them?'

The prime minister's jaw dropped, 'I would love to.'

CHAPTER 46

Steven was aware of the Japanese Prime Minister's arrival and of the conversations that had taken place since their first meeting. Babe had been feeding him live information as the meeting had progressed, and even though he had wanted to intervene at times he had let Komoru tell her own version of the story.

The ships had docked and the party had crossed to Steven's ship. The new members of their crews had been taken to the doctor, the others to get space suits. Even the children had managed to struggle into them although some of his people had tied up all the spare material with string.

It was quite a sight and lot of laughter bounced across the barren landscape. Steven couldn't help his own laughter. His father joined him and nodded towards the procession. 'Just think Steven, those are the first children in space and on the Moon.'

'I wonder if they realise that?'

'They will when they get home. Hero's they'll be one and all.'

'You too Dad and you've got a bag of souvenirs to prove it.'

'How much do you want to bet those kids will nick half of it?'

Steven laughed, 'no takers here.'

There was a lot of awkward bowing and laughing when the two parties met. Eventually Brian took most of the party away souvenir hunting, leaving the prime minister and Steven alone with Komoru and the news crew.

The prime minister bent down and picked up a handful of Moon dust and let it slowly trickle through his fingers. It floated gently back to the surface. There was a tear in his eyes, 'as a young boy I used to dream of becoming an astronaut but there never ever was a Japanese space program. I have now realised my last ambition thanks to all of you, and I promise I will endeavour to do everything I possibly can to help you.'

Every one of the visitors came away with their own piece of Moon rock to take home with them. By the time they re-boarded the ships the doctor had given all the new people their implants and Steven gave them their welcoming speech in private.

Returning to the bridge, he headed for Scotland and Komoru for Japan. It was a tearful reunion for Brian and Mary, but she laughed when he showed her his souvenirs.

The news began to spread around the globe fast. Parts of the meeting were already being shown on every channel. Pictures of the Japanese Prime Minister's children laughing and bouncing across the Moon's surface were a favourite of all the channels.

Steven and some of the scientists installed the transponder. A host of nanobots were left to reconfigure the transponder to accept commands from Earth's systems.

When they were finished Steven retreated to the Moon. Buzz found him pacing in his room.

'What's the matter buddy?'

Steven shrugged, 'what the hell do we do now?'

'There's plenty to do man.'

'I know, I know, it's just a case of where to start.'

'At the beginning.'

'We're already past that point.'

'So what point are we at?'

'We're at the part where we need to do too many things at the same time.'

'Like what?'

'Well we need personnel for a start, and there's thousands of applications for both ships that have to be sorted out, and of course the collecting of those people is a hazardous occupation at best. We need to appeal to the people on Earth for support to overthrow the president's policy on us.

Then there's the finishing of our base, it would be a brilliant place to select candidates, but of course we would have to be able to collect them first.'

'You were going to appeal on TV weren't you?'

'Yeah but the Japanese Prime Minister is up and fighting in our corner at the moment and the footage that crew took is going to be doing us a lot of good as well. I don't want to swamp people and detract from the good those broadcasts might do us.'

'So its round and round and round.'

'Yep.'

'OK, so why don't we get this base up and running first. Then in a couple of days when attention is beginning to flag a little we go in there with guns blazing. In the meantime we can sort through some of those candidates and maybe pick up a few.'

'It's not a few we need to pick up it's about a hundred at a time. The longer we're in close proximity to Earth, the more chance the president has of tracking us and firing more nukes.'

'I thought you had a few ideas about how to deal with them?'

'I do, but I also don't want to start an international incident. If we go screaming in there and start neutralising his nuclear capability there's no telling how he might react.'

'You think?'

'Yeah I do. Come on, you're a yank, how would you feel if someone came along and yanked away your nuclear comforter?'

Buzz thought the matter over seriously, 'you have a point I suppose. As long as we have a nuclear deterrent we feel safe and have done for near a hundred years.'

'Exactly, how is the man on the street going to react? It's his blanket too.'

'I know exactly how he'll think. He'll think we've left them open to attack from every other country with a grudge to bare and a nuclear arsenal of their own. Christ they could wipe out half the United States in the blink of an eye and we wouldn't be able to do anything about it.'

A slow smile spread across Steven's face, 'exactly the point I was trying to make my friend.'

'So how do we get around it?'

'I don't know yet.'

Buzz grinned, 'you'll work it out Buddy. Hey why don't you get everyone to make their way to Scotland or Japan? We can pick them up there.'

'Yeah and how nice a target would that make for the president. Something that big we couldn't keep secret for long.'

Buzz sighed, 'I think I'm gonna get a headache.'

'You can have mine if you want?'

Buzz grinned and stood, 'no thanks I can get my own. Listen, do you think the completion of our new base will put us in a better bargaining position. I mean we could offer up a contract to protect it, highest bidder wins.'

'I can see what you're getting at Buzz. Of course the States would win the contract and put up the man power to protect it, but how would we stop them taking over the whole thing and launching an assault on the ships at the same time once they were entrenched.'

'We could say no weapons.'

'We could but as soon as we're gone what's to stop them sending up a shuttle full? They have the capability.'

Buzz slumped, 'you're right, bad idea.'

Steven shook his head, 'no it wasn't a bad idea. It was a good idea, just unrealistic to our situation. I will take one piece of advice from you Buddy. I'm going to wait until this base is complete before I make our next move. It will improve our bargaining position tenfold.'

CHAPTER 47

The two silver ships slid slowly into their bays on either side of the structure. Steven shook his head in wonder. Both ships were over three hundred metres long but the massive building dwarfed them. They slipped into recesses on either side of the top of the building and Steven fancied it somewhat resembled the bridge of an old freighter he had seen in a picture once.

It stretched out behind them for over a mile. He decided thousands of people could live and work here and probably would. A slight tremor went through the ship as they came to rest and he detected a slight sense of satisfaction from Babe. From now on she would always refer to this place as home.

Steven wasn't sure if he or Komoru was the first to set foot in it, but it was a close thing. In an instant the crew seemed to vanish as they went on a tour of exploration.

Buzz rocked back on his heels and looked down at his friend, 'well Bud where to first?'

Steven shrugged, 'well I have a good idea where my quarters are and what they look like, I'm curious to see the command centre.'

'No shit?'

Steven frowned, 'is there something wrong with that?'

Buzz raised his eye brows, 'Stevie, there's a bar.'

Steven looked around him looking a little perplexed, 'yeah, but it ain't stocked Buzz.'

'Hey I hear it's got a great line in space water.'

Steven patted his friend on the arm in a gentle understanding manner, 'why don't you just go knock yourself out Buddy.'

Buzz grabbed him by the collar and began to march him towards the bar, 'oh no you don't. You've been working your butt off for days and you need a break. The first thing we're going to do is visit the new bar and have a drink. Then we're going to do a little exploring.'

'Buzz this place is over a mile square,' Steven sounded exasperated.

'Yeah well, we both need the exercise.'

The so-called bar was in the central complex. They weren't the first to reach it and the sound of laughter carried easily to them. Steven and Buzz swapped puzzled looks, but all was soon revealed.

They found Cookie and Lewis jumping off one of the balconies laughing as they leapt. They rushed to the rails but as they reached them something strange happened. They seemed to slow down and a large step bounced them over the rails.

Buzz just managed to catch a foot in the rail and grab Steven as he fell, but he wasn't falling in a normal fashion. With his heart hammering in his chest he managed to grab a rail and hold on. The sound of laughter reached up to them and they looked down to find Cookie and Lewis still in free fall.

They burst out laughing to as they realised there was no artificial gravity in the central plaza. Buzz suddenly reversed his grip on Steven and pushed. The look of surprise on his face made Buzz roar with laughter, 'now we really know we're on the Moon, eh Stevie?'

'I'll get you for that you shit,' Steven shouted back up.

'Yeah, you're making me sweat,' Buzz shouted back as he leapt over the rail and joined in the fun.

The bar was as big as everything else. Still feeling the effects of euphoria, Steven and Buzz poured themselves a glass of water from a strange looking dispenser. Buzz winced as he sat down at a table, 'we're going to have to get some decent furnishings. This Moon rock's pretty but it's hell to sit on.'

Steven laughed, 'you know we could probably swap one table and chair from here for a couple of dozen back on Earth.'

'Yeah the new 'in' thing, we could sell them for a couple of thousand bucks a pop.'

Steven shook his head grinning, 'and what would we spend it on or rather where would we spend it?'

Buzz's smile turned grim, 'the president has really turned the screws on huh?'

Steven sighed, 'yep, he sure has.'

'Can't we just waste him?'

'It's always an option.'

The two men slumped into silence to contemplate ways around the latest presidential manoeuvre. He had threatened any nation that gave aid to the two ships, with military action. That both ships would be attacked on sight by his nations armed forces and any base giving aid.

Japan and Scotland had both rejected the president's warning but within twenty-four hours, Navel Task

Forces had set out from their bases to prowl close to Japan and Scotland's national waters.

Buzz shook his head, 'there must be a way round it. What about giving shield technology to the bases that re-supply us?'

'I've thought about that, but what's to stop him hitting the rest of the country as punishment. It doesn't take much to disrupt a modern country Buzz, just a few well aimed bombs.'

'Yeah I know. Any help from our allies in congress?'

'No they seemed to have removed their support since my mother set up base in Scotland and Komoru took possession of the second ship.'

'So it all comes down to profit in the end. They're not making so they don't give a damn.'

'Oh come on Buzz, that's the way it's always worked. It's how we were brought up wasn't it?'

'Not me Dude and not you either, it went on all around us yeah but we never caught the bug.'

'I might have done if I never had the accident.'

A look of scorn lit up Buzz's eyes, 'yeah right.'

It forced Steven to smile, 'well thanks for the vote of confidence.'

Buzz smiled back, 'hey no probs, but it still brings us back to the same problem. We're up to our ears in cash and jewellery but have nowhere to spend it.'

'Yep and sitting here drinking water isn't going to solve the problem.'

Buzz took a deep draught, 'why the hell not. I'll bet half the world's problems have been solved in a bar.'

'Yeah and half its wars started as well.'

'We could declare war on the States, we would win easy.'

'Oh yeah we could reduce the richest nation on Earth to a pile of smouldering rubble, but then civilisation as we know it would probably crumble back into the dark ages.'

'He's really got us by the balls hasn't he?'

'Yep.'

Buzz sat forward, 'we really don't need to land, I mean that's what he said wasn't it. We can just beam everything aboard.'

'Agreed, but how long until he finds out and bombs those supplies before we can reach them?'

'Then there's the retaliation he will take.'

'Yeah.'

'Did you try Switzerland, they've always been neutral and they like gold?'

The corner of Steven's mouth pulled up, 'I tried but the man just looked at me as though I was mad and switched off, didn't even bother to talk to me.'

'The shit! What about stealing the supplies?'

Steven frowned, 'don't even go there.'

'Hey we could leave gold as payment.'

'Haven't you heard?'

'What?'

'He's trying to ban our gold from the market.'

'Can he do that?'

'Looks like it, and he's getting a lot of support from the gold producing countries.'

Buzz smiled grimly, 'I knew it wouldn't take them long to throw a wobbly.'

Steven laughed, 'yeah but the Scottish Prime Minister has already found a way around that.'

'Has he what's he doing?'

'He's minting them into collector's coins and selling them for ten times their market value.'

Buzz's head came up, 'Christ, of course he can't stop individuals buying souvenirs.'

'That's right and the interest is what's going to keep us in supplies.'

Buzz let out a great sigh, 'yeah but then we can't go and collect them, which brings us right back to the beginning again. What the hell are we going to do, we'll starve.'

A strange twinkle appeared in Steven's eyes, 'no we won't.'

Buzz was instantly alert, 'why what are we going to do?'

A smile slowly spread across his face, 'we're going to use a good old fashioned capitalist hammer to smash that bugger into the ground.'

Steven slammed his fist onto the table forgetting it was stone and cried out with pain.

Buzz doubled up in laughter, 'why, what are you going to do?'

Steven rubbed the side of his hand, 'what does this place remind you of Buzz.'

Buzz thought it over, 'a great big bloody mall.'

'Exactly! We're not allowed to go to Earth to pick up supplies but what if they come to us. We can lease out space to any company that will take it.'

Buzz shrugged, 'yeah that's a great idea but how do we get them up here in the first place? We can't go and get them.'

'No we can't but what if we build a couple of transport haulers and lease them out to someone else.

That and maybe a passenger liner of some kind to bring people up.'

'You mean tourists?'

'Of course.'

Buzz leaned back, 'that's brilliant Stevie. There's no way he could stop people coming. That would infringe on their civil rights.'

'That's right and all the big bucks would want a piece of the pie, and that's the people that pay for his campaign.'

'I think we might just be able to bring it off.'

'Yep but we're going to need the consensus of everyone else.'

Buzz stood, 'let's go try and round them up.'

Steven grinned and pulled him back down, 'I can get Babe to get them all, but first I want to bounce a few more ideas off you.'

CHAPTER 48

After their evening meal everyone gathered in the bar and Steven presented his proposals to break the deadlock. For a few seconds afterwards there was a stunned silence then Komoru stood up and began to clap. The applause was unanimous.

Steven laughed and he and Buzz shook hands. The plan called for a number of haulers and passenger liners and a string of hotels dotted around the moon's surface including one on the dark side. Proposals were put forward to supply bases purely for scientific research to be loaned out to interested governments.

Everyone came to a quick agreement and tasks were allotted to all personnel. The operations room became a hot bed of activity as plans were swung into action. Babe and Ico were as keen and together they set up factories within the asteroid belt to begin building ships and extracting the necessary building materials. They had a month until all their supplies were gone so they set to with a will.

One of the first things to be constructed were tagged Moon skippers by the crews. With them individuals could quickly cross the Moon's surface to deploy small armies of construction bots. Just in case someone came along at a later date and claimed the land they were using, a small team dedicated themselves to searching the companies who were already selling plots of land on the Moon to potential future prospectors, and at home Mary and Brian under the strictest secrecy bought off any plots of land they could.

If anyone was unhappy about the whole thing it was the soldiers. Their main concern was security. They were worried that teams of soldiers could take over a passenger liner and use it to gain access to the Moon base.

So sever security measures were brought into play on every vessel built. Everyone had sensors capable of detecting any form of Earth weapon, including disassembled weapon parts, to stop a slow infiltration. There was also another built in the docking area for good measure.

None of the ships built were anywhere as near as fast as the two mother ships. The liners would take two hours to reach the Moon and the freighters three. That allowed for a thorough search from the bases own sensors.

Slowly the day approached when Steven was to make the announcement. He chose the day when the American President was to make his address on the State of the Union. Everyone was gathered in the bar for the announcement except for Steven, Komoru, Buzz and Colonel Howe.

They stood on the bridge of Steven's ship. The president finished his address with a reference to the ships; every one of them listened intently.

The president turned over a sheaf of papers and took a drink of water, 'as you all know, I have taken strict measures against the pirates that stole the two alien ships from American soil and American possession. Latest intelligence reports suggests that these bandits will soon run out of food and have to surrender those ships back to their rightful owners.'

The round of applause he expected didn't come and he went a little red in the neck. It was enough for Steven to pounce. He nodded to Howe who pressed a button.

'Good afternoon Mr President.' Steven smiled as the president jumped in surprise. The president's eyes fixed on to a large TV screen that he had been admiring himself on.'

His face went bright red, 'who the hell are you?'

'I'm one of those pirates you've been talking about, as a matter of fact I'm the head pirate or so you've been saying anyway.'

'Cut that fool off.'

'Oh yes Mr President, you can switch off your TV if you want, that's the prerogative of every free man. But what you can't stop me doing is broadcasting to every nation on the face of the Earth. So if you do cut me off, you and the whole of the American congress will be the only ones left in the dark about our intentions.'

The president waved a negative signal to one of his aids and turned his attention back to Steven.

Steven smiled and walked towards the screen, 'you must be a very good chess player Mr president.'

'I'm a damn fine chess player actually.'

'I believe that, but do you actually believe you can starve us out up here?'

'I do and I will until you return those ships to us.'

'I can guarantee you will never see these ships again Mr. President and that's a promise. However many others might.'

The president ruffled, 'if you land those ships anywhere on the face of this Earth I will destroy them and anyone helping you.'

'That's check I believe.'

'Damn right it is Buddy.'

'Oh I'm not your buddy Mr President. As a matter of fact I'm going to make you a promise right here and now. The next time you fire so much as a potato gun at us I'm going to do this.' Steven nodded and Howe pressed another button.

The president stood back in shock as something materialised out of thin air right in front of his face. It fell at his feet with a thump. He scrambled back in fear falling over and into a heap.

Steven's smile was grim, 'don't worry Mr President it isn't a bomb only an ashtray. However the next time you fire a nuke or a missile of any description at us I am going to beam it straight into the Oval Office in Washington.'

The president struggled to his feet amidst some nervous chuckles, 'you wouldn't dare!'

'Oh doubt me not, and not only will I put them into the Oval Office but I will drop them in to your living room at home or anywhere else I may think you are at the time. Since the end of the Second World War you're the only man who has ever ordered the firing of a nuclear weapon in anger, and it just so happens those weapons were fired at me, my friends and members of my own family.

To me that makes you one of the most evil men in history and I will not hesitate to kill you if provoked again, do you understand?'

'Your dare threaten the United States of America?'

'Oh no, not the United States, just you. As far as I'm concerned this is personal. You ever try to hurt anyone I care for again and I will beam you out into deepest space and leave you to rot, deep freeze style.'

A hint of fear appeared in his eyes for the first time, 'don't you dare threaten me.'

Steven was satisfied, knowing he had hit home, 'oh it isn't a threat Mr President it's a promise. However, I am willing to go for a compromise.'

'Never,' the word was coated with hatred.

'Now, now, you won't be considered a good politician if you don't even listen to me. You have ordered that we should be fired upon if we ever enter Earth's atmosphere again, correct?'

The president was shaking with rage, 'yes.'

'OK, then in the interest of world peace I will accept your decision on this matter and never take our ships back into Earth's atmosphere while that law still stands or you are still president.'

A gasp went round the assembled members and a look of triumph crossed the president's face, 'good, I hope you all starve.'

'Oh we won't starve Mr President, you have outlawed us from visiting Earth but you never said anything about people from Earth visiting us. You see in the last month we have been very busy. Now I know the satellite we have orbiting the Moon has been blanking out all of your surveillance equipment, so I'll tell you what we've been doing and show you at the same time.'

He sent a silent message to Babe and the picture on the big screen changed; Steven was reduced to one small corner.

'What you're seeing now is a picture of the new base we have constructed on the Moon. It is over a mile square and capable of housing thousands of people. Of course you must be asking yourself how on earth would people get here?'

The picture changed. 'These are the transport craft we have constructed. As you can see there are three freighters and three passenger liners. We will lease these out to anyone who wishes to have them. The terms of that lease will be very strict. For example, any attempt at investigating the technology used to build them will result in an immediate loss of contract. The ships have a built in safety mechanism which will detect tampering. That will result in the craft taking off and heading straight for the Sun with whoever is on board, so be warned.'

Steven paced a little to let his words sink in, 'ten years from now we are going to release technical details of these ships which will enable those countries with the resources to build their own, so until then I suggest you behave yourselves.

The space station has its own automated defence system, as do all the ships. They can detect weapons or even weapons parts so don't try that either, the results will be fatal.

Now for the Moon base itself. Any company on Earth who wishes to lease out space up here, will be quite welcome to do so. Not only do we have this base but we have also constructed a couple of dozen others, which would make excellent hotels or research stations. Of course all of this space will be leased at reasonable prices. I can guarantee all of you now that we will consider applications from every country, with no bias.

Again there will be strict rules governing the operation of all business and controlling the conduct of visitors. There will be only one punishment, immediate banishment from the Moon, but of course all of this will be made clearer in time.

For now, I would like to give you a tour on what we have to offer. First I would like to introduce you to Captain Komoru Kaizu of the starship Ico, who will begin the tour.'

Steven sat down and Komoru took his place. She took them on a journey over the lunar landscape, visiting all of the new complexes they had built with detailed footage of the interiors. Steven smiled; they had researched this project well, basing many of the designs on some of the world's most famous hotels. Some even had working fountains.

When she finished Buzz took over and described the type of vehicles that they would be using to cross the lunar landscape and the type of activities that would be available to visitors.

When he sat down Colonel Howe took over. He gave details of the type of people wanted to run the operational side of the main complex and gave an over view of some of the security measures that would be in use.

At last they were finished and Steven stood forward once more.

'As you can see we have much to offer the people of Earth and we are here to ensure that no single company or government shall ever monopolise this valuable resource. The Moon will be open to all comers and we will set the price of travel to and from the Moon so it should be affordable to anyone who wants to come and visit us, even if it's only for a day.

Of course we will have little control over the prices retailers will charge for their products but I can assure you we will keep a close eye on them and if we believe they are overcharging anyone then we will retain the right to take action against those companies.

Now, you may be able to prevent us from coming to Earth Mr President, but you won't be able to stop the individual rights of your own countrymen from coming to visit us, and you certainly don't have the right to prevent any other person from wherever in the world they hail from to come visit us either.

However, just in case you're tempted to try, I would like to give you one more demonstration of our resolve in this matter.'

There appeared on screen an asteroid of gigantic proportions. 'This footage was filmed from Ico earlier in the week. What you're looking at is an asteroid of over fifty square miles in diameter.'

The ship went round the whole of the asteroid and then pulled back out of range. Then suddenly Babe streaked in. Green fire lanced out towards the asteroid and it disappeared in a fantastic explosion. When the dust settled there was nothing left of it but a large cloud of space dust.

Steven reappeared filling the screen, 'just a little demonstration of what we are capable of Mr President and a promise to you. If you ever step on my toes again I'm going to grind your face right into the ground.'

He began to turn away then swung back, 'I believe that's check mate.'

CHAPTER 49

It had almost been a full year since Steven's historical speech and they were finally ready to begin deep space exploration. Buzz found Komoru in Steven's quarters. She was standing by the window that stretched right across this whole level of the building, giving an unparalleled view of the lunar landscape. She smiled as he joined her at the window.

They were all a lot wiser than they had been at the beginning of their adventure. Both ships were now fully manned and the crews trained to a high standard.

The American President had unwisely tried to introduce legislation to prevent anyone from Earth from taking up on Stevens offer, but the great capitalist steamroller had left him flattened in its wake. Impeachment had followed and now he was a retired broken figure that campaigned endlessly on the fringes of government. His cause was a lost one and even the papers treated him as a figure of pity.

The passenger liners had been raised to six and the freighters seven to accommodate the large numbers of visitors each week. No one had ever tried to bring a weapon to the Moon and was considered a free port from all forms of terrorism.

Two months before, a new university had been built in one of the mountain ranges and within a few weeks its great halls were expected to be filled with Earth's brightest young scientists.

Not only was it the Moon that had benefited from the new technology. With the removal of the president the ships had visited some of the poorest countries and cities in the world. At each Steven had began a building program of schools, universities and hospitals, and money had been loaned to staff them.

The Moon was now the favourite place to be married and honeymoon and a huge business had sprung up around it. There were two distinct parts to life on the Moon. On one hand there were all the holidaymakers and the fun of exploration. While on the other there was the operational part that supported the ships and their crew.

The crew's quarters were strictly off limits to the tourists except by invitation. The operational staff were also quartered separately from the tourists, and were considered very much a part of the team, although that which had to remain a secret, remained so.

The crews' doctors had also been hard at work. Their results had been startling with the almost complete eradication of cancer and the dreaded AIDS virus. The profits from the drug companies ran many of their existing hospitals.

Komoru had that lost dreamy look in her eyes as she watched the figures below. Buzz smiled for it was a look he knew well, for it was reflected in the eyes of his friend every time he looked at the woman before him.

He hated to disturb her, 'sorry to bother you Komoru but have you seen Steven?'

She pointed to the figures below, 'you're not disturbing me Buzz, he's down there.'

Buzz burst out laughing at the sight, 'so that's where he went this morning.'

She laughed with him, 'yes, it was a surprise to me as well. I never thought he was serious.'

Buzz rocked back on his heels, 'well that's Stevie for you.' His manner became more serious for a moment. 'May I ask you a serious question Komoru?'

'Please ask me anything Buzz.'

'Are you in love with Stevie?'

She turned liquid eyes up towards him and Buzz felt the magic of them slam into his soul, 'yes.' She turned back to her vigil a hand coming up to gently touch the glass before her, 'how could I not fall in love with a man who even keeps a promise to a dog.'

Far below two figures attempted to race across the Moon's surface in pursuit of a brightly coloured ball. Steven roared with laughter as the similarly suited Rex crashed into the back of his legs causing both figures to disappear in a cloud of dust.

Rex broke free from the tangle first and raced off yipping with excitement after the ball, leaving a still laughing Steven far behind.

The End

its great halls were expected to be filled with Earth's brightest young scientists.

Not only was it the Moon that had benefited from the new technology. With the removal of the president the ships had visited some of the poorest countries and cities in the world. At each Steven had began a building program of schools, universities and hospitals, and money had been loaned to staff them.

The Moon was now the favourite place to be married and honeymoon and a huge business had sprung up around it. There were two distinct parts to life on the Moon. On one hand there were all the holidaymakers and the fun of exploration. While on the other there was the operational part that supported the ships and their crew.

The crew's quarters were strictly off limits to the tourists except by invitation. The operational staff were also quartered separately from the tourists, and were considered very much a part of the team, although that which had to remain a secret, remained so.

The crews' doctors had also been hard at work. Their results had been startling with the almost complete eradication of cancer and the dreaded AIDS virus. The profits from the drug companies ran many of their existing hospitals.

Komoru had that lost dreamy look in her eyes as she watched the figures below. Buzz smiled for it was a look he knew well, for it was reflected in the eyes of his friend every time he looked at the woman before him.

He hated to disturb her, 'sorry to bother you Komoru but have you seen Steven?'

She pointed to the figures below, 'you're not disturbing me Buzz, he's down there.'

Buzz burst out laughing at the sight, 'so that's where he went this morning.'

She laughed with him, 'yes, it was a surprise to me as well. I never thought he was serious.'

Buzz rocked back on his heels, 'well that's Stevie for you.' His manner became more serious for a moment. 'May I ask you a serious question Komoru?'

'Please ask me anything Buzz.'

'Are you in love with Stevie?'

She turned liquid eyes up towards him and Buzz felt the magic of them slam into his soul, 'yes.' She turned back to her vigil a hand coming up to gently touch the glass before her, 'how could I not fall in love with a man who even keeps a promise to a dog.'

Far below two figures attempted to race across the Moon's surface in pursuit of a brightly coloured ball. Steven roared with laughter as the similarly suited Rex crashed into the back of his legs causing both figures to disappear in a cloud of dust.

Rex broke free from the tangle first and raced off yipping with excitement after the ball, leaving a still laughing Steven far behind.

The End

Lightning Source UK Ltd.
Milton Keynes UK
UKOW03f2000110314

227952UK00001B/1/P